CO
INTE

SEDUCING THE DEFENDANT

"A slow burn that left me wanting more!"

—*Fresh Fiction*

BREACHING THE CONTRACT

"Fernando turns up the heat in the first of a new series that revolves around a company of legal eagles whose antics in and out of the courtroom are legendary. Engaging characters, witty dialogue, and a smoothly plotted story line made this a fast and enjoyable read."

—*RT Book Reviews*

Praise for the bestselling

WIND DRAGONS
MOTORCYCLE CLUB SERIES

DRAGON'S LAIR

"*Dragon's Lair* proves a badass chick can tame even the wildest of men. . . . Not to be missed."

—Angela Graham, *New York Times* and
USA Today bestselling author

"*Dragon's Lair* was witty and fast-paced. A delicious combination of badass biker men and laugh-out-loud humor."

—*Bookgossip*

ARROW'S HELL

"Redemption and forgiveness form the basis of the story, while laughter, tears, and some erotic sex scenes keep the reader engaged. Low-key violence blends well with the multiple plotlines and drama-drenched characters."

—*RT Book Reviews*

"Cheek-heating, gut-wrenching, and beautifully delivered! *Arrow's Hell* took me on the ride of my life!"

—Bella Jewel, *USA Today* bestselling author

TRACKER'S END

"Fernando's vivid characters burst onto the page . . . pulling readers into their world immediately and completely. This tightly told tale will leave readers eagerly waiting for the next installment."

—*Publishers Weekly*

"The physical chemistry between Lana and Tracker burns up the pages."

—*RT Book Reviews*

RAKE'S REDEMPTION

"You'll find yourself sitting on the edge of your seat in anticipation of how [*Rake's Redemption*] will unfold."

—*RT Book Reviews* (4½ stars, top pick)

"*Rake's Redemption* is a story about betrayal and loss, revenge and retribution, second chances and falling in love. The premise is emotional and entertaining; the characters are passionate and energetic; the romance is fated and hot."

—*The Reading Cafe*

WOLF'S MATE

"Chantal Fernando's latest romance delivers everything MC fans could ask for—incredibly sexy men and the women strong enough to keep them, passionate love scenes, thrilling adventure, and even a laugh or two along the way!"

—*Smut Book Junkie*

CROSSROADS

"*Crossroads* is an emotional journey of discovering what will lead to lasting happiness and the willingness to go for it."

—*Always Reviewing*

THE CONFLICT OF INTEREST SERIES

*Breaching the Contract**
Seducing the Defendant
*Approaching the Bench**

THE WIND DRAGONS MOTORCYCLE CLUB SERIES

Dragon's Lair
Arrow's Hell
Tracker's End
*Dirty Ride**
Rake's Redemption
*Wild Ride**
Wolf's Mate
*Last Ride**
Crossroads

*ebook only

LEADING
THE
WITNESS

The Conflict of Interest Series

CHANTAL FERNANDO

GALLERY BOOKS

New York   London   Toronto   Sydney   New Delhi

Gallery Books
An Imprint of Simon & Schuster, Inc.
1230 Avenue of the Americas
New York, NY 10020

First Gallery Books trade paperback edition April 2018

GALLERY BOOKS and colophon are registered trademarks of Simon & Schuster, Inc.

For information about special discounts for bulk purchases, please contact Simon & Schuster Special Sales at 1-866-506-1949 or business@simonandschuster.com.

The Simon & Schuster Speakers Bureau can bring authors to your live event. For more information or to book an event contact the Simon & Schuster Speakers Bureau at 1-866-248-3049 or visit our website at www.simonspeakers.com.

Manufactured in the United States of America

10 9 8 7 6 5 4 3 2 1

Library of Congress Cataloging-in-Publication Data

Names: Fernando, Chantal, author.
Title: Leading the witness / Chantal Fernando.
Description: First Gallery Books trade paperback edition. | New York : Gallery Books, 2018. | Series: The conflict of interest series ; 4 | Identifiers: LCCN 2017049739 (print) | LCCN 2017051721 (ebook) | ISBN 9781501172403 (ebook) | ISBN 9781501172397 (softcover)
Subjects: LCSH: Divorce—Fiction. | BISAC: FICTION / Romance / Contemporary. | FICTION / Romance / General. | FICTION / Action & Adventure. | GSAFD: Romantic suspense fiction. | Legal stories.
Classification: LCC PR9619.4.F465 (ebook) | LCC PR9619.4.F465 L43 2018 (print) | DDC 823/.92—dc23
LC record available at https://lccn.loc.gov/2017049739

ISBN 978-1-5011-7239-7
ISBN 978-1-5011-7240-3 (ebook)

Happy 30th birthday to the woman who came back into my life
just when I needed her.
Natalie, I love everything about you.

◇

Having a soul mate is not always about love.
You can find your soul mate in a friendship too.
—UNKNOWN

acknowledgments

A big thank you to my editor, Marla Daniels, and Gallery books. I love every second of working with you.

Kimberly Brower, I'm so lucky to have you as my agent! Thank you for everything you do—we make such a great team and you truly go above and beyond.

Natalie Ram—Thank you for being the most versatile best friend ever, from helping me proofread to making me swag, I appreciate everything that is you. I know I can always count on you to have my back, or help me when I need you. I kind of adore you, and I don't know how I survived before I had you by my side. You're my one woman army, and I love you heaps.

Rose Tawil—I really don't know what I'd do without you. I can't say thank you enough for all the work you put in to support my dreams, and you never ask for anything in return. You truly are one of the best people I've ever met. You also kick my ass whenever I need it. Love you infinity.

To my three sons, my biggest supporters, thank you for being so understanding, loving, and helpful. I'm so proud of the men you are all slowly becoming, and I love you all so very much.

Lust feels like love until it is time to make a sacrifice.

—UNKNOWN

RILEY

"WHAT CAN I GET for you?" I ask the two gentlemen who are looking a little out of place in my bar in their fancy suits. Since our opening two weeks ago, most of our customers have been of the blue-collar variety.

But I'm not complaining. One, because they are both ridiculously good-looking—especially the bearded man—and two, because I'm grateful to anyone who comes in here and gives my new business a chance. I've always wanted to run my own bar. I know this sounds like a ridiculous dream for a young girl, but growing up my aunt and uncle owned one, and I was there every day. I practically grew up in their bar with my cousin, Devon. Every day after school we'd help in the back, peeling potatoes for my aunt, or we'd order food and do our homework. Things that aren't really that common, but no one batted an eyelash about it back then. It was a real family vibe, and I have a lot of good memories there. I guess I wanted to re-create that in my adulthood. I've always wanted to be my own boss and not answer to anyone else. And now that I have it, I'll do anything to make it work.

"Hello there," the bearded man replies with a way too charming smile. "Knew I wanted to check this place out for a reason."

He caught my eye the minute he walked in; there's just something about him. He must have scores of women after him, with that dark scruff and those blue eyes. He's wearing black slacks and a light blue shirt, rolled up at the sleeves. It fits him perfectly, like the clothing was made just for his muscular build. He must go to the gym, because I doubt he'd get shoulders like that from whatever professional job he has.

"That reason had better be a beer and a meal," I instantly reply in a dry tone, my brow arched. "Because that's all that's on offer. For you, anyway."

I internally cringe. *Great job, Riley, already insulting new customers.* Sometimes though, I just can't help myself. My default mode is sassy, and the attitude just pours out of me.

The other man laughs at my comeback, and I find my own lip twitching. Maybe they don't mind my sass. His gray eyes are kind, and I find myself liking him already too. "Could I please order the steak?"

"Sure," I say, pulling my notepad from my pocket and jotting his order down. I don't show it, but I'm a little nervous right now. My chef hasn't made the steak for anyone yet. I know I'm being ridiculous, but every time someone orders something from the menu for the first time, it's like my anxiety kicks in, nerves and excitement hitting me as my menu comes together. I'm sure he will nail it. "How would you like it?"

"Medium rare, please, and with pepper mushroom sauce."

I can feel the bearded man's eyes on me, those blue fucking

weapons of his, but I pretend I can't feel his gaze on my face and instead continue to focus on the gray eyes. Safer eyes.

"Perfect. Fries or mashed potatoes?"

"Fries," he replies, then glances to his friend. "What do you want?"

Apparently he's doing my job for me now. Just who are these commanding, sexy, well-dressed men? I reluctantly bring my eyes to the blue ones.

"Just a beer, please, darlin'," he says to me, tone gentle and soft. And inviting.

He's the type of man songs are written about. Books are dedicated to. Movies are made, with fucking Jason Momoa playing him.

He's a fucking muse.

A heartbreaker.

Our eyes connect and hold, and a feeling I can't really explain comes over me. With a quick shake of my head, I push it away. "Gotcha." I all but rush to the back, pushing through the door that leads to the kitchen and staff room. Closing the door, I lean on it, breathing deeply.

"Fuck, she's hot," I hear the bearded one say. "She wants me."

I roll my eyes and push away from the door, not wanting to hear any more. Sure, he's attractive. I didn't miss those tats on his forearms, giving him the perfect mix of badass and professional. He's intriguing. He's the type of guy women should avoid. The exact type I *will* avoid. Determined to act like they were any other customers, I hand Cheffy the order. His real name is Trent, although no one ever calls him that. "Time to show off your skills."

His expression doesn't change. Then again, it rarely does. "I can cook a steak in my sleep."

"Good," I reply, grinning at him. "Let's impress the fancy men then."

He mutters something under his breath while I return to the bar to pour their drinks. I don't know why I was feeling a little nervous; Cheffy has it all under control.

As I open the door, my hand stills on the PUSH sign because I hear the bearded man say, "That motto isn't compulsory. Come on, it's a pretty sweet setup. It has a pool table, the menu looks good, and lots of alcoholic beverages to try." He grins. "And the waitress is a fucking babe."

I appreciate the pretty-sweet-setup comment and I pretend I don't hear the fucking-babe comment, although the way my heart starts to race tells me that my body has decided otherwise. I push the door open fully, revealing myself to them.

"Actually, I'm the owner," I say, then turn to Gray Eyes. "I'm Riley."

"Jaxon," he replies, offering me his hand. I accept it and give it a quick shake. The second I let go, my hand is gently clasped again, and soft lips are pressing onto my knuckles. "I'm Hunter." He raises his head. "We work down the road, at the Bentley and Channing law firm."

Hunter?

"Appropriate name." I roll my eyes and say out loud before I realize I'm insulting a customer. Again. I pull my hand away from his reach. *Get it together, Riley. You need this place to succeed.* I pour his beer, avoiding his gaze and ignoring the burning sensation his lips and fingers have left on my skin.

"Never seen a lawyer covered in tattoos before."

I don't know why I said that. Nothing else came to mind, and I felt like I needed to say something. I shouldn't have though, because now he knows I've been studying him. He doesn't need to know that. I might never have seen a lawyer with so many tattoos, but I've never seen one so fucking good-looking either.

I suppose I should be happy that I didn't blurt that out instead. It can always be worse.

"I'm one of a kind," Hunter replies, and I can hear the smirk in his tone. I slide the beer to him, then finally raise my eyes to his.

"Probably a good thing," I fire back, then disappear into the kitchen to check on Jaxon's meal. Or maybe to escape, I don't know. Why can't I control what I say around that man? I think I just need a little air.

A few moments later, I hear Preston. "Is the owner here? I'm late for work, and she's a she-devil."

I roll my eyes and shake my head in amusement. Preston is something else, but he's been growing on me. He's a huge pain in my ass, but he's also been such a help since Riley's opened. Preston's worked in many bars across the city, and he's truly good at what he does as a bartender. He comes up with delicious new, creative cocktails and mixed drinks. I was lucky that the bar he was working at closed and he needed a new job. With his talent comes his attitude though, which is usually amusing but can sometimes be exasperating. I can't exactly judge him for that—it's probably why we get along so well.

I walk back out, only to almost bump into him. "Preston, you're late."

"I know," he tells me. "It's a long story. One I'm sure you don't have time for, so I won't bother explaining."

I sigh deeply, exaggerating my annoyance with my hand on my hip. It's good to focus on him and not the bearded lawyer who gets under my skin. "How the fuck are you the best bartender in town?"

"I have skills," Preston says with a smirk on his face. "In the bar and in the bedroom. And I'm a mixologist, not a bartender. Don't make me sound average."

"Don't be late again, Preston. Fancy bar skills or not, I'll fire you without hesitation," I tell him, although we both know it's a lie.

"Noted," Preston mutters, but I don't miss his lip twitching. He loves me.

As soon as I head to the back again, I hear him say, "See? She-devil."

"I can hear you, asshole!" I yell, shaking my head.

I hear the men laughing.

Great, they're going to think this is the worst bar they've ever been to and they aren't going to come back. The owner mouths off to customers and the bartender is inappropriate.

Hunter's blue eyes flash in my mind.

Maybe it's a good thing if they never come back.

I can't afford to be attracted to some rich, arrogant, model-looking lawyer. A stranger who is now making me feel so weird in my own fucking bar that I'm hiding out so I don't have to face him again.

When did I become shy around the opposite sex?

Maybe I'm just out of practice.

"If you can hear back there, can you get me another beer?"

I can tell its Hunter calling out to me. This is just great. I already know his voice.

I grit my teeth. Luckily Preston is here now, so he can get him another beer and bring them their food. I don't need to go back out there again. Instead, I keep myself busy with inventory.

I'm married, I remind myself.

Not happily, but that's beside the point. My body shouldn't be reacting to any man like it just did to Hunter.

Shit.

What the hell.

I'll never see him again anyway.

chapter 1

RILEY

One Year Later

"WHO ARE YOU PUTTING on red lipstick for?" The question comes from behind me, making me jump. I turn from the small mirror hanging in our staff bathroom and scowl at Preston, pressing my lips together.

"What are you talking about?" My brow furrows. "I wear lipstick all the time."

He leans against the wall and studies me with his dark eyes, amusement written all over his smug face. "No, you don't."

I cross my arms over my chest, facing him. "What do you care if I'm wearing lipstick? I pay you to make drinks, not scrutinize my every move."

Preston may have started out as my pain-in-the-ass bartender—or mixologist, as he likes to correct me—but over the last year he's grown on me, like a fucking fungus. I don't have many friends, yet he somehow wormed his way into my heart. Don't ask me how, because he's completely inappropriate, can never take anything seriously, and is nosy as hell. But ever since I started going through my divorce, he's been there for me, and I really appreciate that.

"I don't care." He chuckles, running his finger over the gauge in his left ear. He has one on each side, and I think they suit him. "Just pointing out a fact." He glances down at his watch. "I'm sure it doesn't have anything to do with the fact that Hunter comes in around this time."

"Hunter who?" I sniff, lifting my chin. "I have no idea what you're talking about."

Instead of calling me out on my blatant lie, he just laughs.

I roll my eyes and head back to the bar, leaving his laughter behind me. Fiddling with the red bandanna I've tied around my neck, I ponder his words. So what if I want to look decent when Hunter comes in? Not that I'd ever admit it out loud to anyone, including myself, but there's nothing wrong with wanting to look your best. Hunter looks good every time he comes in for lunch, dressed in one of his expensive suits. So I can make sure I'm put together when he comes in. It's just good customer service.

With an audible sigh, I move behind the bar and stand next to Callie, my newest bartender. She's never worked in a bar before, but when she told me her story, I couldn't not hire her. She's having a life crisis and decided to take a break from her law career to find herself. When I asked her if she knew how to make cocktails, she told me she makes them at home all the time. For herself. I don't know if that counts as experience, but I hired her anyway, and she's been here about six months now. She's a cool chick, a fast learner, and makes a nice addition to the team. One of my regulars, Kat, also happens to be Callie's best friend. It's like a reunion every time Kat comes in, the two of them carrying on like they haven't seen each other in years.

"Is it just me, or does that guy keep staring at me?" she asks under her breath. I have no idea who she's talking about, so I scan the crowd, but none of the three male occupants are looking in our direction.

"Just you," I say, lip twitching in amusement.

She lifts her head, closing her eyes and wrinkling her nose, inhaling deeply. "You smell good." She then tilts her head and studies me. "And you look good too. What's the occasion?"

"There's no occasion. Do you want me to handle those tables, or are you good?" I ask, hopefully changing the subject.

She glances down at her watch and nods, then casually adds, "Oh, it's almost time for Hunter to come in. You worry about him. I'll make sure the rest of the customers are sorted."

I grit my teeth and throw my hands in the air. "What is wrong with all of you? One, I look nice every day." The threatening look I give her dares her to say otherwise. "And two, he doesn't even come in every day."

"Who doesn't come in every day?" Hunter asks, making my head snap toward him so fast I'm surprised I don't get whiplash. As always when I look into those blue eyes, it's hard for me to look away. I manage to give him a quick once-over though, taking in his gray suit, with, just my luck . . . a white shirt. Maybe I should turn up the heat in here so his jacket will come off. I love when he wears white shirts; I don't know why. Especially when he has the sleeves rolled up so I can sneak a peek of his tattoos. Is there anything sexier than a smart, successful man in a suit? Yes, there is. One who has tattoos hidden underneath, hinting at a bad side I'd like to explore but will never let myself.

Of course he had to walk in during this very conversation.

How much of it did he hear? I'm hoping just the last line, but I know I'm not that lucky.

"No one," I say, forcing a smile. I glance around but don't see any of the other people from the firm with him today. "Here without the squad?"

"They'll be here soon," he says as he sits down at the bar, bracing his hands on the wood and leaning toward me. I tighten my hands so I don't reach out and touch his beard, something I've always wanted to do. "I couldn't wait for them. I'm hungry."

Hunter manages to make normal things sound dirty. It's a talent of his. Or maybe it's just me with the dirty mind.

"No food loyalty today?"

"I guess not. When I'm hungry for something, nothing can stop me."

His eyes flash with something I pretend not to notice, instead focusing on his straight white teeth he shows off with his grin.

"Why, what big teeth you have," I joke, trying to lighten the tension between us.

"You calling me the big, bad wolf?" he asks, running his teeth over his lower lip. "Because I really would like to eat you."

I roll my eyes. Hunter likes to say inappropriate things, but he never crosses the line with me. He never tries to touch me, and he never gets in my space. He knows I'm unavailable. I personally think he just likes to get a reaction out of me, so I try my best not to give him one.

"Well, that's a sexual harassment suit looking to happen," Kat says in a dry tone as she walks up toward the bar, shaking her head at Hunter, her long dark hair bouncing with the motion. She then pins me with her brown eyes. "I'll be your lawyer if you choose to go ahead with it." How is it that I'm surrounded by lawyers every day? It'd annoy me if I didn't actually like them all. I know it's wrong to judge someone by their career, but lawyers have a stigma about them. They're right up there with real estate agents and car salesmen—and the butt of many jokes. One of my favorites is:

How does a lawyer sleep?

First he lies on one side, and then he lies on the other.

They are also compared to leeches and mosquitoes, or any bloodsucking kind of creature a fair bit, but all of these guys prove the stereotype wrong.

We all seem to get along great, even though we are on different levels in education and income. I guess alcohol brings together everyone. "I second that offer," Jaxon Bentley says, pulling out a barstool and taking a seat. His gray eyes are gentle as they look at me. "How are you doing, Riley?"

"Not bad, Jaxon, and yourself?" I ask, smiling at him. He's a nice man, a gentleman, and has always been kind to me. He is a renowned criminal lawyer, and in the year that I've known him, I've learned he's kind of a big deal. He always looks the part, dressed today in a navy suit.

He removes his reading glasses. "I'm good. Busy, but good. Looks like we managed to get here before the rush."

I hand him and Kat a menu, even though by now they probably already know it like the backs of their hands. Ever since Hunter and Jaxon wandered in here from their firm down the street when we'd just opened, they've been coming here a few times a week, bringing the rest of their colleagues with them.

It's been over a year since I opened the pub, and we've all gotten to know one another pretty well in that time. Customers can become friends pretty fast, and that's what happened here. Small talk turned into deep conversations; my being polite and professional turned into us laughing and joking. Although I don't think I was ever polite or professional with Hunter, which was my bad. The rest of them though. I love it when any of them decide to drop in for lunch, a drink, or just a chat.

Riley's is my baby, a business that is all mine, and one I'm desperate to keep, regardless of what else I have to give up in the divorce.

"Where's mine?" Hunter asks, bringing me out of my thoughts. His hair's different, shorter than before, no longer falling onto his forehead in a soft curl. He orders the same thing every time he comes here, so I know he's just asking for a menu to irritate me. Or maybe he just doesn't like being left out. You never know with him.

I slide a menu across the bar without looking at him, then start making the coffee I know he's about to order.

"I'll have a coffee, please," I hear him say. I place the coffee in front of him and arch my brow with a smug look on my face. Feeling my gaze, he looks up at me before glancing at the mug next to him, eyes narrowing.

"You're predictable." I shrug. "It's either a beer or a coffee."

"And how did you know it was a coffee and not a beer this time?" he asks, bringing the mug to his perfectly shaped lips. "And I'm not predictable. I'm just a man who knows what he wants. If it ain't broke . . ."

I roll my eyes and move down to Kat and Jaxon, ignoring their amused faces.

"Because you're wearing your fancy suit, which means you're going to court," I tell him. "If you came in looking more casual, I know that you don't have court, which is when you usually order a beer."

I need to stop letting him know how much I study him. I feel agitated every time I'm around him. I try to hide it, and I hope I do it well enough, because I don't want him to know the effect he has on me. Maybe it's just the fact that I haven't been touched by a man in over a year, and he's good-looking. No, that's probably too tame for what he is. He's sexy. Smoking. Intense.

Until he opens that mouth of his.

He may be a lawyer—and good at what he does, from what I've heard—but some of the things he says . . . Is there such a thing as playful arrogance? Because that's the only way I can think to describe him.

I clearly have terrible taste in men.

Although no one can be as bad as my soon-to-be-ex-husband, Jeremy. I shudder at the mere thought of him, then turn my attention back to Jaxon and Kat. "Ready to order?"

I write down their orders, feeling Hunter's eyes on me, but I pretend he's not there. This is what we do. It's our dance, and I guess from the outside it's an amusing show we put on. And part of me wishes it was an act. But each time he comes in, I seem to get more attracted to him, if that's even possible. So I mask those feelings with irritation and attitude. I don't know if it's working, but it helps me stay centered.

He's just *too* good-looking.

And, yes, that's a thing.

He knows it, and I don't like men with big egos.

My soon-to-be ex developed one during our relationship as he became more successful professionally, and it didn't look good on him. I think I'm more suited to a down-to-earth, easygoing, simple man.

"So, steak, chips, and a salad," I repeat the order to Jaxon. "And the creamy chicken breast for you, Kat."

They both nod, and Kat flashes me a smile, which I return. I quickly get them their drinks, also nonalcoholic, and then turn to him, unable to ignore him anymore. "Would you like to order something to eat? Or are you on a liquid diet?"

"I'll have the burger and fries," he tells me, rubbing his flat stomach. "I'm starving. Actually, maybe add some onion rings too."

I pretend to write down his predictable order with a tight nod and then disappear into the back.

Preston and Callie suddenly appear with knowing looks on their faces. Apparently no one does any work around here. I should fire them all. I hand Callie the order to give to Cheffy and then cross my arms and have a stare down with Preston.

"I don't like Hunt—"

"You like him." He cuts me off.

"No, I don't."

"Riley—"

"Preston, I don't," I say, daring him to argue once more.

"Okay," he says, surrendering, hands in the air in front of him. "But for the record, it's okay if you do."

"But—" I instantly object.

"But you don't; I know," he says in a dry tone, shaking his head. "You are one stubborn woman, you know that?"

That's probably why I'm getting divorced before the age of thirty. Not something to brag about, but being divorced isn't nearly as bad as being in a loveless marriage I never should have been in in the first place.

I take a deep breath, lift my chin, and return to my customers.

"HOW WAS EVERYTHING?" I ask, happy that they devoured the meal. I know they're regulars, but I take pride in my work. I want my food to be the best, my service to be the greatest, and, more than anything, I want my pub to be successful.

Over the last year, I've managed to get Riley's to a good place, finally getting out of the red and doing a little better than breaking even, but profits could always improve. I've put my blood, sweat, and tears into this place, using my inheritance from when my grandmother passed away to finance it. I didn't use a cent of my ex-husband's money, and I'm damn proud of that fact. And thank God I didn't, otherwise I'd be in danger of losing my baby.

"Amazing as always," Kat says with a smile. She glances at her watch, her face dropping. "Unfortunately for me, I need to get back to work. Thanks, Riley."

"No problem," I say, handing them their bill.

"I'm paying this time," Kat tells the two men, who simply ignore her.

"I've got it," Hunter says, taking out his wallet and placing a wad of cash on the bar. "Thank you, Riley. Food was delicious."

"You're welcome," I say, feeling the heat rise to my cheeks. Jaxon also thanks me, and then the three of them leave. I take the money to put in the cash register, my eyes widening at the size of the tip Hunter left me. He always leaves big tips, so do Jaxon and Tristan, another lawyer at their firm, but this time Hunter left me over a hundred dollars extra. I don't know whether to chase him down and tell him he's being ridiculous, or be thankful because this money will really help the rest of the staff. We put all tips in a jar and divide them equally at the end of each day.

I still have the money in my hand when Preston walks up and eyes it. "What's that for?"

"Hunter left it as a tip," I tell him, tucking it into the jar below the cash register on the bottom shelf.

"That's generous of him," he muses, grabbing a martini glass and inspecting it. Preston has an issue with glassware, they all have to be perfectly clean and clear; he doesn't like it if there's any dust or smudges on there. Another reason why he's an asset to Riley's—he's precise and particular, in a good way.

The "Despacito" remix by Justin Bieber and Daddy Yankee plays on our radio, filling the pub, and Preston starts to sing along, getting all the Spanish words completely wrong.

"What am I going to do with you?" I mutter under my breath, shaking my head as he busts out some salsa-like dance movements.

He offers me his hand, and I smile and take it. He spins me around, my laughter spilling out of me. Callie comes out to the front, probably to see what all the commotion is about, smiling as she watches the two of us dancing for anyone who walks in to see. Callie helps me with the business side of Riley's—the food orders, scheduling, and the bills and receipts—in addition to my training her behind the bar. She's such an intelligent woman, and to be honest, she is way too qualified to be working here.

"See? This shit wouldn't happen in a law firm," she announces, tucking her notepad for orders into her jeans pocket and joining in with her own sexy little moves. The pub is empty—the lunch rush gone after finishing their meals—but I know it won't last long, with the after-work crowd about to be upon us.

I'm trying to teach Callie how to twerk when Hunter walks back in, stopping in his tracks, a big-ass grin on his face.

"So this is what goes on here when no one is around. Can you do that move again, Riley? I didn't take you for the twerking type," he says, sounding pleasantly surprised. Of course he is; the man is such a pervert.

I straighten, cringing, wishing I could disappear, but when I turn around to face him, I look him right in the eye, my chin up.

Men can sense weakness like predators. And Hunter? Well, let's just say he lives up to his name.

"I forgot my wallet," he says, smiling widely, looking thrilled that he just saw what he did.

I hear Callie murmur, "I'll grab it." And a few moments later, she hands me the beat-up old wallet that is so very Hunter, and I pass it to him. As he takes it from my hand, I move mine away quickly as my fingers brush his. His fingers are rough, like I'd expect from someone who works with his hands, not from someone who works in an office. I don't know why that appeals to me, but it does.

I purposely ignore the spark I feel at our touch and the attraction between us. There's no use for it.

"Thanks," he murmurs, hesitating for a moment, before turning and leaving once more.

I watch him walk away.

And for a fleeting moment, I wish that things were different.

chapter 2

HUNTER

"**Y**OUR NEXT APPOINTMENT IS in thirty minutes," Yvonne, the receptionist at Bentley & Channing Law, says to me.

"Thanks, Yvonne," I call out to her as she already starts to disappear. I use the free time to check my emails, but I'm interrupted when Jaxon Bentley walks in. Before opening his own firm, Jaxon was a prosecutor, and he's gotten himself in and out of a few sticky situations over the years. Not only is he a great lawyer, one I'm proud to say I work with, he's a good man, and one of the best to have by your side. That's why he's not only my boss but also one of my very closest friends.

"You busy?" he asks, taking a seat opposite me. I swear my colleagues are in here more than any client ever is, although I can't complain, because whenever I have a spare moment I head over to their offices to annoy them, too. Got to get my kicks somehow. Being a smaller firm, it's allowed us to become friends and adopt an almost-family-like office culture. We aren't competitive with one another like in other firms. Not only is the firm known for its reputation as having the best lawyers, it's also such a great environment to work in. We support one another and help whenever we can. I never dread coming to work, because I love what I do, and I also get to see these guys every day. It's a win-win.

"Nope," I say, moving my laptop aside. "I'm just catching up on emails. Everything okay?"

My next client is a domestic violence case, one I'm working on pro bono. I always get a little worried about clients like this, because you never know what can happen in between court dates. Ever since I met Jaxon's girlfriend, Scarlett, who was a victim of domestic violence herself—and was actually accused of murdering her ex-husband, a local police officer— I've started volunteering my time to help more women who find themselves in similar situations, trying to do my part to put such abusive men behind bars and away from the ones they've been hurting. When Scarlett was arrested, all the evidence was against her, and there was no proof of her claim that he abused her. I don't think anyone believed she was innocent, except Jaxon, but she was, and he was able to prove it to the world. The two of them met and fell in love, and the rest is history.

It can be frustrating though, because I've seen a lot of the women go back to these men or retract their statements, which isn't a good feeling, but I can't help anyone who doesn't want to be helped.

"Yeah, everything is fine," he says, leaning back in the chair, getting comfortable. His eyes are impassive. I never know what he's thinking, unless he wants me to; it's probably what makes him a great lawyer. "I have an hour free and thought I'd come see what you're doing."

"Assumed I'd be doing nothing?" I joke, pulling out some carrot and celery sticks and dip I stole from Kat this morning. I place it on the desk between us. "Morning tea."

"Nailed it," he replies, grabbing a carrot and dipping it into the eggplant dip. Not my favorite, but it's better than nothing. "My schedule is hectic this week, so I really need to enjoy any quiet moments I can get."

"How's Scarlett?" I ask.

"She's good," he says, chewing thoughtfully as he grabs a celery stick. "To be honest, I don't remember a time that I've been happier."

"Good." I nod, slowly smiling. "Says something when a woman makes you happier than your career, right?" I tease.

We all work long hours, and work usually trumps all. I applaud Jaxon for being able to maintain a balance between home and work life. I only hope when I find the woman I'm meant to be with, I can manage to do the same. But until I meet her, I'm happy with being a workaholic who likes the company of different women.

Riley's face flashes in my mind, but I push it aside. She's married; it's never going to happen. I'd never do anything with another man's woman; I do have some morals, no matter what others might think.

Jaxon chuckles. "You're right. Work was my life until Scar came into it." He glances up and studies me. "You'll meet someone who will do the same to you."

"I'm not so sure," I tell him.

Or maybe I have, but I can't have her. I don't say that out loud.

I chose to pursue family law for a reason. When I was growing up, my parents would foster kids all the time. I still keep in contact with a few of them. I remember hearing some of the things they'd been through, or seeing the aftermath of it with my own eyes, and wishing I could do something to help. What most people don't know is that while I have a high-profile career representing celebrities and the filthy rich when they're going through a divorce or custody battles, I also do a lot of pro bono work, helping out families who need me and children who otherwise wouldn't have a voice. I love my work, and not just because I'm well paid for it.

"I don't know," Jaxon continues. "The men in this place are falling, one by one, and I'll place a bet you're next."

"What about the women? Can't Yvonne be next?" I groan, throwing her under the bus.

Jaxon starts to laugh. Hard. "Does Yvonne even date? Trust me, she's going to be single until the end of time."

He has a point. "Well, whatever this contagious disease is, I want no part of it."

"You say that now," he says enigmatically, standing up and wiping his hands together. "I'm going to go and grab a coffee. Do you want one?"

I shake my head. "No, but thanks. My client is due any minute."

"See you at lunch," he says, exiting my office.

I finish the last of the carrots and celery, pondering the conversation we just had.

Maybe I'm not as opposed to finding "the one" as I pretend to be.

My client, Laurie Karen, arrives, and we go through her case, and I write down her statement about her husband, who turned abusive and started threatening their three children. It's hard to listen to, but this is the reality of the world we live in. Pretending things like this aren't happening won't fix anything. There's bad in the world, but it's up to us to stand against it.

This is why I became a lawyer.

Everyone sees the status, money, and all that, but this right here is why I chose family law.

If there's anything I can do to help, I'm going to do it.

"LET ME GUESS, YOU want the usual?" Riley asks, fiddling with the red bandanna she always wears. "And a coffee?"

I nod, even though I really wish I could drink a beer right now, which I do order for lunch on occasion when the day has been stressful. "Yes, please. Pretty busy in here today." I glance around, taking in all the people. I'm glad it was her who came to serve me, even if I had to wait a few minutes. "Guess everyone is finding out about our secret spot."

She flashes me a lopsided grin. It's fucking cute. "I sure hope so. I really need the place to pick up a bit. How's your morning been?"

Why does she have to be married? And who is her husband? I don't know much about him, not even his name. Is he good to her? Does she love him? She must. Riley isn't the kind of woman to marry someone she doesn't love. She never mentions him though. But that doesn't surprise me. As friendly as Riley is with me and my coworkers, she always has a guard up. She never lets conversations about her ever get too personal, instead preferring to keep it professional yet friendly. She intrigues me.

Not that it makes a difference. As much as I like to have fun, and have been known to not have too high of a standard

LEADING THE WITNESS   ◊   23

for the women I date, I do have lines I won't cross. I deal with
people who get divorced, cheat, and play dirty every day, and
I see the destruction it brings to families. I'd never willingly
be the cause of that, regardless of how I felt about a woman.
Besides, I'd never want a woman who would cheat anyway.
But despite all that, I still find myself wanting to be around
Riley, to talk to her, even though I know that nothing can ever
happen.

Pretty fucked-up.

I need to meet more women. I haven't been putting myself
out there like I normally do.

Forget about Riley.

And I will, just not yet.

"Not too bad," I tell her as she slides me my coffee. "Had a
little free time, which was rare, but the rest of the day is going to
be busy. I have to go to court again."

"Your life is so much more interesting than mine," she
says, placing the coffee in front of me and leaning forward on
her elbows. "The best thing that happened here today was that
a girl Preston went on a date with last week walked in. They'd
met online and it was apparently the worst date ever, and she
had no idea he worked here. You should have seen both of their
faces."

I laugh at her story, at the way her face gets all animated,
like she's so excited to be telling it. I could listen to her talk for
hours; I don't care what she has to say. I'm hopeless; I know.

"So what happened?" I inquire, wanting to hear more.

"Well, Preston was the only one available to serve her, so he
had no choice. She hesitated for a bit, I think she was considering walking out, but in the end she awkwardly walked up to the
bar and ordered a mocktail," she says, softly laughing to herself.
"They both pretended the date never happened, that they didn't

know each other, but it was so painful to watch. Their body language . . . I almost felt sorry for Preston."

"He should have played it off, made a joke or something," I chuckle. "What was so bad about the date?"

"She spoke about her cat the entire time," Riley deadpans, shaking her head. "And asked Preston if he wanted to meet him. His name is Meowth, like the Pokémon, and when Preston said he didn't like cats, he's more of a dog person, she started crying."

I can't stop the laughter that spills out of me. Only Preston would find a chick like that.

"Bet you've got a few of those stories," she adds, her sassy attitude making an appearance. I'd never let her know it, but I like her attitude. She thinks I can't handle it, but she has no idea. And I guess she never will.

Right woman, wrong timing.

"I might," I reply, shrugging. Sometimes I play into who she thinks I am. It's safer that way. She thinks I'm a womanizer, and I have been in the past, but I'm not like that anymore. It's pretty hard to be when you only have eyes for one woman, whether she's yours or not. In my case, I'm a sucker for punishment. "But I'm not going to tell them. I think you'd enjoy that a little too much."

"I probably would," she agrees, our gazes holding. It's a little dangerous whenever we look into each other's eyes, because I can read her so easily. They give everything away. Big and hazel, all her emotions flutter through them. And when she smiles, she uses them too.

She's not as immune to me as she wishes to be, which is just another reason why this is so fucked-up. Yet here I am, getting my daily dose of her, even when I know this is all we'll ever be.

"Let me know if you want anything else," she says, heading to serve some other patrons who approach the bar.

I'm left there, watching her, waiting for my food to arrive, wondering what the fuck I'm doing with my life.

I'VE JUST GOTTEN BACK to my office when Yvonne sends a call through.

"Hello?" I say down the line, shuffling into my seat and turning on my computer.

"Hunter? It's Derick," my old friend from law school says. I haven't heard from him in months, so I have a feeling he's going to ask for a favor. That's the only time either of us call each other these days, and I should know, because the last time I called him I asked if he could call in a favor with one of his cop buddies.

We exchange pleasantries until he gets straight to the point. "I need a favor. Any chance you can take on another client last-minute? You're the best in family law, and this man is my real estate agent and he can pay your full rate. I kind of owe him one."

So everyone just owes everyone fucking favors now.

"What's the catch?" I ask him. Referrals and taking on a new client is no big deal, but there's usually more to it when someone calls and asks.

He's silent for a few seconds, then says, "Yeah, he has a mediation meeting with his ex tomorrow morning."

That would do it.

I check over my schedule. "What time?"

"Ten a.m."

"Why doesn't he have a lawyer already?" I ask, because this is leaving it a little fucking last-minute. I guess this is the catch. My schedule is pretty full, but I probably could fit this meeting in. Lucky for him.

"Well, I offered to help him out," he explains. "But he wants you. He called your firm, but your receptionist said you aren't taking on anyone new at this point because your workload is too full."

Shit.

I don't exactly have a good feeling about this, but I do owe Derick a favor, and if this man wants me, well, I guess I can give him that—for Derick, anyway.

"All right, send me over the details. And Derick—" I start.

"I owe you one. I know. I know."

Yes, yes, he does.

chapter 3

RILEY

"WHY ARE LAWYERS SO expensive?" I complain to my mom, covering my face with my hands. I really need Riley's to earn more money, because I have no idea how I'm going to cover all these fees. I need to do this on my own, especially since I don't want any of Jeremy's money in this divorce. The only person I can count on is me. "Why is divorce so expensive? I put all my money into the pub, and now I'm going to have to come up with more just to get out of this shitty marriage. Aren't I entitled to make a mistake or two without having to literally pay for it? They should put me in a class to teach me better decision-making skills instead."

To be fair, I was twenty-two when I married my soon-to-be ex and was not in a good place. Much too young to be making any type of rational decisions.

And this isn't even the worst mistake I've made, not by a

long shot. My fingers absently find the black bracelet on my left hand and hold on to it.

"Told you not to marry him," my dad calls out from the couch, where he's watching a basketball game.

"Thanks for the reminder, Dad," I say dryly, leaning back on the wooden dining room chair and studying my mother. We look nothing alike. She has short, light hair, while mine is long and dark, and her eyes are green to my hazel. "You liked Jeremy at the start, didn't you, Mom?"

She cringes and then shrugs. "He was okay, I guess. You loved him, so that's all that mattered to me, that you were happy."

My mom never once admitted to not liking Jeremy, but I could tell she wasn't over the moon about him either. I just assumed it was because she thought getting married so young wasn't a good idea, which it wasn't, but still. I was in love, and I was happy at the time, and I wasn't really thinking of the future.

When I met Jeremy at a bar, he was cute and kind of shy, and I liked that. He was a little on the geeky side, and not my usual type, but something about him drew me in, and we started dating. I wasn't in a good place, I was lost, and looking for escape from everything that was going on back then, and he helped bring me out of it. He had his shit together, and he was a good influence when I needed it. He was so different from the men I'd started hanging around, and the crowd that was slowly becoming my own worst nightmare. He occupied my time, away from the bad influences, and instead we got lost in our own bubble. Everything was a blur of I-love-yous and moving in together, followed by a quick proposal. I don't know why we rushed everything. It felt right at the time, I guess, and I couldn't have known how things would turn out.

I just need to take it as a lesson, learn from it, and move on.

"I was happy once, wasn't I?" I say more to myself than my

mom as I glance down at where my wedding ring used to be. The first few years were good. I remember being happy, and the two of us having a lot of good times together. We'd take long road trips, just enjoying being around each other, but as the years passed, things between us changed. I guess we both grew into different people.

I wanted to become more independent and follow my own dreams, and he just grew into a giant dick. He didn't want me to pursue my passions. He thought opening the pub was a bad idea. He told me I wouldn't make any money from it, and that it'd be a waste of my inheritance. He started making lots of money from his job as a real estate agent, selling high-priced homes, and the money became all he cared about. He grew up in a blue-collar family and always wanted the finer things in life. So as soon as he got a taste of what life on the other side was, he changed. Suddenly, I didn't fit into his new world—I wasn't flashy enough. I grew up in the country, and I'm not really into designer brands, nor did I know what he was talking about when he'd rave about them. I'm not materialistic, and I guess I just didn't understand him anymore, or vice versa. He never was abusive or mean; he just started to ignore me, like I wasn't even there. Our priorities changed, and so did our wants. We changed so much that we didn't seem to know each other anymore. We tried for a few years to make it work, but after I opened Riley's, I knew we couldn't go back to how it used to be.

I never thought things would turn out so ugly between us though. It was sort of amicable at the start. We knew we were both unhappy, and it was a mutual decision. However, things started to change when he started looking at our finances. I think he thought I wanted half of everything because he turned nasty, saying he'd make sure I wouldn't get a dime. The strange thing is that if he would've actually listened to me when I told him what I really wanted, we wouldn't have to be dealing with lawyers. We'd probably be divorced already. He let his new-found greed cloud his judgment.

I don't want any of his money. He can keep the big house he bought; it doesn't suit me anyway. I'm more than happy in my rental apartment. The only thing I do want is our dog, *my* dog, Bear. Jeremy knows this, and is refusing to give him to me out of spite. I love Bear, and just because Jeremy bought him for me for my birthday four years ago doesn't mean he belongs to him.

My lawyer, however, has other ideas, and thinks we should fight for a settlement amount. The independent woman in me disagrees. I want to leave the marriage as I came into it, with nothing but my determination.

"*Was* being the key word," my mom says, setting a mug of hot chocolate in front of me. "Now you need to concentrate on you, Riley. Find what makes you happy; maybe go do some traveling."

"The pub—"

"Will survive without you for a week or so." She cuts me off, pursing her lips.

"After paying for my lawyer, traveling is the *last* thing I'm going to be able to afford," I grumble. Riley's is making a little bit of profit, but not much at the moment. I need to get more regular customers, especially on the weekends. It's not at the place I want it to be just yet.

"You'll get there, Ri," she assures me, watching as I take a sip of the chocolaty goodness. "You'll be fine. You're always fine. And I told you, if you really need money we can help you out."

I love that they offered, but I know they can't afford it, and I'd never put them in that position.

"Thanks, Mom, but you know I can't accept that. I need to work this out on my own. I'm not asking for help, I'm just vent-ing about everything and feeling sorry for myself."

To two of the only people I'd allow myself to be honest and vulnerable with.

"Sympathy isn't going to help you," she replies with a frown on her face.

I sigh. "I know, but it might make me feel better."

"You're still young, sweetie," she says, tilting her head to the side and flashing me a smile. "There's no reason to be sad. Just start over. Your pub will thrive. And when you're ready, you'll meet someone new."

If only things were that simple.

chapter 4

Hunter

"I'M NOT GIVING HER a cent," the man tells me, chin high in the air. He's clearly a douche, and I'm already regretting taking him on as a client. No wonder Derick called in a favor, the man is an utter moron. I knew he was a douche when he showed up for our meeting ten minutes late without an apology. He was on his cell phone as he entered my office, paying me no mind, yelling at whoever was on the other end, calling them incompetent and being an arrogant asshole. I should've just walked away then, knowing he'd be a pain in my ass, but he signed the representation agreement yesterday and I already cleared my schedule for this.

And now I've spent the past twenty minutes explaining the process and what I expect to be the best-case scenario—making his ex an offer and hoping she accepts it. But he doesn't want to give her anything. He acts like the laws don't apply to him. Like he should be exempt for some kind of reason. I don't know why he feels so entitled, but it grates on my nerves. He married young and didn't have a prenuptial agreement—from what I know, he made most of his money after they were married. Because of that, she's entitled to half. He doesn't get to take everything just because he feels like it. It's no wonder he's getting a divorce. I can't imagine why any woman would marry this guy.

"Mr. Rodgers, it doesn't work like that," I tell him. "You were married for years without a prenup. As I've been explaining, you live in a community property state. The law dictates that you and your wife are to split all assets accumulated or received after you were married."

"What *I* accumulated, you mean," he grumbles, shifting in his seat. "Isn't there any way out of this? You're the best lawyer in the city, surely you can pull something from up your sleeve."

I study him for a few seconds while I gather my patience. I see men like this all the time, and normally it doesn't bother me. Whether I'm representing the husband or the wife, the rich and entitled are something I've come to expect. No morals or sense of fairness. If I turn into this, I really hope someone does the world a favor and takes me the fuck out. But this guy just will not listen.

"I *am* the best and I've saved people a lot of money. But I also can't change the law. The best-case scenario is that your wife accepts a reasonable amount that is significantly less than half. We want to settle this in mediation, Mr. Rodgers, because I have to be honest, if we take this in front of a judge, chances are he'll just give her half of everything."

"This is ridiculous. I don't know why I have to . . ." He goes off on a tirade that's full of the same shit he's been spouting since he came in here, and I have to take a deep breath. I put my pen down to rub my temples, cursing Derick for this batshit crazy client. He so fucking owes me.

"You don't have any children?" I interrupt, picking my pen back up to make a few notes.

"No," he replies, sounding thankful for the fact. Probably because otherwise he'd be paying child support out of his ass. "It's just us. And our dog, which I know she'll want."

"Is it her dog or yours?" I ask. Going by his tone, he doesn't really care for the animal.

"Hers. She can have the dog, I don't care. As long as she signs over everything else to me, and I get all the money. He's just shitting and digging holes all over my garden, anyway."

Charming.

"Okay, this is a start. If she wants the dog and we give her it, then she'll be willing to take less—"

"I just don't think it's fair that I lose any of my money when I made it all myself." He cuts me off.

I sigh as I look at my watch and see that it's time to go into mediation. "Mr. Rodgers. Look, let's not get ahead of ourselves. First we need to meet with her and her lawyer for this mediation session to see if we can solve this outside of court. We don't know what she's asking for yet, so why don't we see what that is and go from there?"

I know he doesn't like the fact that he's going to have to part with something, but too fucking bad. He shouldn't have gotten married then. Or he should've had a prenuptial agreement. I tell everyone to sign a prenup before they get married, but no one ever listens to me. It's all "we're in love" and shit, but then who do you think they come crawling to when things go wrong? I guess I shouldn't be so hard on them since they *are* the reason I have a job.

"Fine," he agrees, and we head to the big conference room. I hate attending these things, but it's an easier and more cost-effective option than running straight to court with accusations flying. It's also good for both parties to lay their cards on the table to see what each other is asking. If we can solve things out of court, everyone can save time.

When we arrive, my client enters first, and I step in behind him and casually glance around.

I have to do a double take, not believing my own eyes, when I see who is sitting on the opposite side of the table. Dark hair falling past her shoulders, knowing hazel eyes that I've looked into many times over the past year, now filled with surprise, framed in thick, dark lashes. The black blouse she's wearing fits her perfectly, buttoned up to the top, giving her a harder, professional-type vibe. She looks away, then back at me.

The two of us don't know what the fuck to do with ourselves right now.

Riley had better have become a fucking lawyer since I've last seen her, because otherwise that would mean that she is Jeremy's soon-to-be ex-wife. What. The. Fuck.

Now, I consider myself a good poker player, I can bluff and hide my expressions with the best of them, but I know that this time I can't conceal the surprise on my face.

Or the anger.

Oh, the fucking anger.

I honestly did not see this one coming, and I'm so pissed I can barely think. I look away from her and take a deep breath, knowing I need to get myself under control.

Be professional.

I think I've got it under wraps, but when my eyes land back on her impassive face, I feel my blood begin to boil all over again. I feel betrayed somehow, I don't know how else to explain it.

I didn't even *know* she was getting a divorce, or hell, having issues in her relationship.

She never said a word.

I'm a fucking divorce lawyer, and her friend, and she didn't even tell me. I would have saved her from all of this, I would have fucking *helped*.

And I sure as hell wouldn't have taken her husband as my client.

Fuming, I try to school my expression once more, especially when I see her glance down at her hands. She's probably feeling shitty right now, and she doesn't need me making this worse.

The woman is so stubborn she wouldn't ask for help. I can't believe her. Anyone who knew about this and didn't say anything is also on my shit list—my friends and hers.

The best course of action right now is for me to stay in lawyer mode and pretend this is just any other day at work.

Pretend that the woman sitting across from me isn't the one I've had a thing for ever since I laid eyes on her. She's tough on the outside, but oh so sweet inside, a heart of pure untouched gold. Why she married this idiot, I have no idea, but I'm glad she's getting rid of him.

Her lawyer and I make small talk, and I quickly learn that she's not very good at what she does. With the questions she asks, and what she gives away, the woman should not be practicing law.

Fuck.

She must have gotten her degree online.

When she hands me a piece of paper, I quickly read it once, and then twice, unable to believe the information I've just been given.

Fuck.

All Riley wants from this man is her dog.

Her *dog*.

He has more than a million in his bank account, several

properties, and a fucking yacht, and all she wants is their Alaskan malamute, Bear.

And Riley's.

I don't know whether to shake her for being so stupid, or kiss her for being so strong, so independent and unbreakable. What other woman would walk away from so much money? She's entitled to half of it, yet she doesn't want a cent from him.

Riley is one of a kind, and if I didn't know that before, I certainly do now.

I turn to Jeremy, who uncharacteristically has remained quiet this whole time, and slide him the document. He reads it and says out loud, "She isn't getting the dog."

Wait, *what*?

My head snaps to him. Fucking asshole.

I've never wanted to punch a man more in my life than I do right now. This dog obviously means a lot to Riley, and an animal is priceless. But Jeremy just wants to keep the dog to hurt her. He's not emotionally attached to him; he just wants the dog because he knows she does. I know I can talk him out of this, tell him it's either the dog or he pays up. Fuck, this is getting so complicated already. I have to have his best interests in mind, not Riley's, even though it's her I want to help more than anything.

Is it ethically wrong for me to advise him to give her the dog? It'd be a bargaining chip, one that would mean he could pay her less money. Giving her the dog *is* the best decision for him to make.

"Bear is *my* dog, Jeremy. He's my best friend, and you know it. He doesn't even listen to you because *I'm* the one who trained and raised him," Riley says, her expression giving nothing away. I'm so proud of her in this moment, even though I'm unable to give any indication of that.

"I left him with you and trusted you to take care of him until

I found a place to rent. You agreed to it. I was at my mother's for two weeks before I found my place, and when I came back to pick up Bear, you wouldn't let me take him."

My hands clench to fists under the table. How can he be so cruel? I just don't get it.

Or maybe he knows that he lost something he won't be able to replace, and now he's taking it out on her, trying to make her life hell. I've seen it all before.

"Considering my client isn't asking for alimony, or half of everything you own, Mr. Rodgers, surely giving her the dog is a compromise." Riley's attorney finally says something spot-on. She took the words right out of my mouth. Jeremy has to choose his battles, and if he isn't going to give her the dog, if I was her I'd go for what I can get from him anyway, because if he wants to be spiteful, two can play that dirty game.

"Give me a moment to confer with my client." I lean over to the asshole and whisper in his ear. "Let's give her the dog and the pub, and then call it even. You won't owe her any money." I internally cringe at what I'm doing, knowing Riley is entitled to so much more. But even turning her back on all the money, she's gaining more by getting rid of this asshole.

"So you want the dog and your stupid pub? That's it, and I don't have to pay you anything?" he says now, addressing Riley and her lawyer, the smug look on his face making my eye start to twitch.

"She's choosing not to take anything else," Riley's lawyer says, and going by her tone, she disagrees with Riley's decision. At least she learned something in law school. "If she wanted to, she would at least get a sum of money, and a property perhaps. If you didn't want to part with anything, you should have signed a prenuptial agreement."

Riley looks Jeremy in the eye then and holds his stare without flinching. I want to shield her, protect her, but this is her war, and she wouldn't let me protect her anyway. She must want to do this alone, and even though it's going against my instincts, I'm going to give her that.

"I wish it were so easy. Technically that pub is mine," Jeremy says, tone smug.

Riley loses her composure and jumps out of her chair. "*What?* I used my inheritance on Riley's. That is *mine*. Take your homes, your fancy yacht, take it all. Just give me what is *mine*." Her face is full of emotion, but I can tell she's doing her best to rein it in.

"Tsk-tsk," Jeremy muses. What an asshole. "Without me there won't be a Rileys' anyway."

"What do you mean?" Riley asks him, frowning.

"Who do you think owns the building?" he asks her, cackling to himself. "I'm your landlord. I own the company that you pay rent to. If I want to kick you out of that building, I can do it in an instant."

And there it is.

The trump card he was hiding up his sleeve and didn't even tell me, his own damn lawyer.

Now I can't just tell him to hand her the dog, because she needs to have her business too. She wanted both, and she will get both. I don't know how yet, but I will have to figure something out.

"Can he do that?" Riley asks her lawyer, voice cracking. He finally got to her, and I don't like it one bit.

Her lawyer looks concerned but doesn't reply, probably because she doesn't know. She will probably do a Google search when we leave.

The session ends without anyone agreeing to anything. In light of this new information, we all need to figure out the best strategy. But it pains me to admit that he has the upper hand here. He knows what she wants, and he's going to taunt her. I don't feel great with her having this lawyer of hers. There is no way this woman can go against me, even on my worst day. I want to help, but the independent woman in her will murder me with her bare hands if I try to intervene. As Jeremy's lawyer, I can't help her anyway. This is all too much. Today has taken a fucked-up turn, and I don't know how to fix it, or if I can.

I have to be smart with Riley. She doesn't like help; that much is crystal clear considering the position we're in this very moment.

We all exit the room, and I shake Jeremy's hand goodbye, even though all I want is to break it. As soon as he drives away, I stalk to Riley's car, open the passenger side, and get in before she can get away.

I'm so angry I almost don't even want to say anything, because I don't want to say something I'll regret. I don't want to upset her, but I just don't understand her train of thought or why she's done what she has. This all could have been so much easier for her, but she's decided to make it so hard, on everyone, just because she didn't want to come to me, or hell, one of the others at the firm.

I don't want Jeremy as my client, but I'm locked into representing him because we signed a representation agreement and I gave Derick my word. I can't bail now; it would turn into a really shit situation, especially if Jeremy found out about my friendship with Riley. I should be Riley's lawyer, fighting *for* her, not against her.

"What the fuck, Riley?" I grit out through clenched teeth, turning to her. "What were you thinking?"

She tightens her fingers on the steering wheel, her knuckles turning white. "That I wanted my business to be my own? This is my problem, Hunter, and I didn't want anyone else involved in it. You never even told me what kind of law you do, how was I meant to know you specialize in divorces?" she says defensively. It's true, we never really discussed my job, past basic details anyway, but that's not the issue here. She had to have known that one of us, *any* of us, would have helped her. This is what we do. She should have come to us for advice. I exhale deeply.

"I get that; I do. But am I your friend, or not? This is my territory, my domain, and if you'd asked anyone, they would've told you that. I'm the best in the city, Riley, and now your ex has hired me. I think you need to let that sink in, so you know just how fucked-up this situation is."

All I can keep thinking is that she doesn't trust me, even as her friend. And fuck if that doesn't hurt, not because I don't want to be *just* her friend but because she's not even giving me that. It's finally hitting me that Riley is now single . . . well, almost. I guess she will only be officially single once the divorce is finalized, but she's separated, which means she's free to do what she likes. This whole year I've been secretly pining over someone I knew I couldn't have. And now that she's free, I find out she doesn't trust me. Not even as a friend. And without a friendship, there's no point hoping for more, even down the line. Friendship is the foundation of a good relationship. Great, now I sound like a fucking episode of *Dr. Phil.*

"I wanted to face this on my own, and then forget about it," she admits, and the way her voice cracks a little lets me know that this is harder for her than she's letting on. "I just want my dog, and for Jeremy to get the fuck out of my life. I want my divorce finalized as soon as I can. And I thought I could handle it all by myself. He told me I could have Bear anyway, so I didn't think this would be that big of a deal."

Fuck, that doesn't surprise me after the hours I spent with

him this morning. That guy changes his mind at the drop of a hat. "I know you do," I say slowly, jaw tight. "You've just made this so much harder and complicated than it needed to be. I just really wish you had come to me, Riley. I don't want your ex as my fucking client and now I don't know how to get out of this. I should be in your corner, not his."

She lets her head fall back against the headrest and closes her eyes, exposing her slender neck. "I didn't want you to see me like this, Hunter," she admits in a whisper. "I don't want *anyone* to have to see me like this. I feel weak, vulnerable, and I'm only hanging on by a thread. I didn't want anyone to know the details of my marriage—do you know how embarrassing that is? These are my personal matters, and I don't like asking for help, okay? Especially when it's for something so . . . exposed for me."

"I'd never see you as weak, Riley," I tell her, reaching over and taking her cold hand in mine. "Everyone needs help sometimes. Everyone. Do not for one second think this makes you weak. You are one of the strongest people I know, but everyone has a breaking point. And during this time, it's okay to lean on the people around you who care about you. You are not invincible; no one is."

Her eyes open and she turns her face to me. "Why did he have to hire *you*?"

"I'm the best," I state without sounding smug. It's just a fact. "Which is why I should be yours."

In more ways than one.

She sighs, and I can see as her eyes soften that she finally lets her guard down a little, the reality of the situation hitting her. Without knowing it, she just put us on opposite sides of her divorce. "What am I going to do? I had no idea he was my landlord. Why would he do this? And behind my back? What is wrong with him? He knows how much I love my pub, and now he's using it against me."

"I don't know what we're going to do," I tell her in all honesty. "Let me think about it, okay? I'll try to come up with a solution."

Even though I know there are only two options here. One, I tell Jeremy I can't be his lawyer anymore, which is something I've never done before in my career. It's unprofessional, and something I wish I didn't have to do, but it's a conflict of interest. I can't give him my best when I'll be looking out for Riley's interests instead. Option two is that I keep him as my client, do my job, and try to minimize the effect on Riley. All she wants is the dog and her business, and if that's all Jeremy loses, he's still winning, and I'm still doing my job. Riley gets her dog and her pub, but Jeremy walks away with the rest of his assets. The biggest issue is that Jeremy owns the land. If I can find a way to give Riley that land, then he'd be out of her life for good. Since Riley isn't asking for much and he wouldn't be giving her much, it won't look like I'm being unreasonable by telling my client to give her what she wants.

The biggest detail, though, is that Riley isn't committed to anyone anymore.

This changes everything, yet with me as Jeremy's lawyer, it also changes nothing at all.

Fuck.

chapter 5

RILEY

I CLEARLY HAVE THE WORST luck in the world. The one person I didn't want knowing about this now knows and has somehow gotten dragged into it. Hunter is right; I should have just pushed my pride away and approached him for his advice before I went and got myself another lawyer. I can see why he's not happy with me. I know I can be stubborn. I wanted to try and handle it on my own. I would have handled it on my own.

I also didn't want Hunter knowing about my past, and the details of a marriage I just want to forget. But now nothing will be simple anymore. Hunter will find out things about me, things I don't want him to. There's no way Jeremy will stay quiet. The truth is, after my cousin died, I was not in a good place. I had a period where I turned to drugs to get me through, a period of weakness, and Jeremy is the one who got me out of it when I met him. Every time he got mad at me, or we fought, he'd throw it in my face. And when Hunter finds out, he'll never see me the same way.

And when Kat finds out I didn't even tell her, she's going to kill me. I told Callie, because when she broke down and let me in on her story, I gave her the same in return. We both keep what we say to each other private, and I know she didn't tell anyone, because she said it's my business, not hers. I inhale and exhale deeply, trying to regain my composure and push all these stressful thoughts aside.

"I need a drink," Hunter says from my passenger seat, where he's been patiently waiting for me to say something. "And if you just happen to need one too, and coincidentally end up in the same place as me, that won't be a problem. And we can talk." He pauses and adds, "Not about the case, but we can talk about other things."

Like my marriage?

I don't think I'm exactly ready to have that conversation with him. It all feels too raw right now, and I'm still reeling over the way Jeremy acted in mediation. I cannot fathom how I was so blinded to marry such a man.

"Can we have a drink, minus the talk?" I ask, flashing him a hopeful smile.

Something works behind his eyes before he replies. "That's probably for the best." He arches a brow. "We're just going to have to figure out a way to get through this. Everyone gets tested in life, right?"

"Ha. Is that what this is, a test?"

"What else would you call it?"

"Stupid decision making leading me to one giant moment of failure," I reply, adding a smile to try to lighten things up.

He simply shakes his head at me in frustration.

"This is going to be so awkward," I tell him, glancing straight ahead now. "You hearing details of my failed marriage? It's so personal, you know?"

And it's only going to get worse as the details emerge.

"I've been doing this for years, Riley. Trust me, there is nothing I haven't seen or heard. There's no judgment, that's not what I'm here to do. I'd especially never judge you. I know you. And you should know me better than that to think that I would."

I think I really needed to hear these words from him, because something in me relaxes.

"Okay," I tell him, nodding. "Thank you, Hunter."

"No need to thank me," he murmurs, and I can feel his eyes on my profile. "You should've trusted me and known that I would have been able to handle this, Riley."

Something in his voice makes me think that I actually hurt his feelings by not coming to him with this, but that can't be right. He has to understand *why* I wouldn't want him involved with this. I'm attracted to him. I might even like him. It has nothing to do with me not trusting him; it's just my stubborn pride making my decisions for me. I didn't want him knowing my secrets, it's that simple. Hell, I don't want any of them to know.

He scrubs a hand down his face, and I know that I've really fucked up when I see how torn he looks, frustration and pain etched on his expression. I wish I could fix this somehow. "I have no doubt you can handle anything, Hunter," I tell him, then decide it's a safe option to change the subject. "I guess I'd better head out, and maybe, I'll run into you very soon." Code: Meet you at the pub in ten.

He nods. "Sounds good." He opens the door and moves to slide out of my car, but before he does, he says one more thing to me. "Your ex is a fucking idiot."

As the car door closes and he walks back over to his car, I can't help but smirk.

He really fucking is.

"WHO CHOOSES THE PLAYLIST?" Hunter asks, nursing his Scotch.

"Why, don't you like it?" I ask, grinning at the pop tunes.

"No," he admits, making me burst out laughing.

"We take turns," I explain. "It's fair."

"So who's is this? Callie's?" he guesses, amusement dancing in his eyes. "I can see her listening to this shit."

"Actually, it's Preston's," I say, then watch as he starts laughing, blue eyes alight with humor, his smile deep.

I can't look away.

Hunter laughing just makes me feel warm inside, like I'm sure it does most women. There's something about being around him that calms me. It makes me feel good, at peace, and like nothing else matters. I don't know how else to explain it, except that when Hunter is around, the world isn't so bad.

"I shouldn't be surprised," he says, shaking his head. "He's a fucking character, isn't he?"

"Perfect way to describe him," I say as the man in question approaches us.

"Cheffy is in a mood," Preston tells me, eyes going wide. "I made a joke, and he just gave me an evil look and stormed away."

"Probably because you offended him," I remind him.

"I just told him he'd get more chicks if he got rid of the monobrow. How is that rude? I was trying to help out a fellow coworker."

"I've never even seen what your chef looks like," Hunter says, smirking at Preston. "But now I'm picturing it."

"What? Oscar the Grouch from *Sesame Street*? Because that's about right," Preston says, then pauses and adds, "Same temperament too."

"He's going to hear you and spit in your food," I tell Preston, keeping my expression neutral. "Cheffy is a nice guy; leave him alone."

"You call the chef 'Cheffy'?" Hunter asks, shaking his head. "You're all fucking nuts in here."

"Probably why you walked in and it felt like home," I fire back at him.

He studies me for a second and then says, "That's not why it feels like home."

My whole body stills, shutting down like it can't function anymore as it processes his meaning.

He thinks *I* feel like home?

Or maybe he meant something else.

I swallow hard as my eyes connect with his. He knows I'm in the middle of a divorce and it's messier than ever. There's something in his eyes that wasn't there before, although I can't pinpoint exactly what it is.

"Okay," Preston drawls, looking between Hunter and me. "You two need to just fuck already, because the sexual tension is so thick it's making *me* hard."

I turn and give him a look that says he needs to shut up *right now*, but he simply winks at me and goes to serve new customers who just walked in. I slowly drag my eyes back to Hunter's. He's already watching me, of course, those blue eyes always up to something. I shrug, not knowing what else to do, and his lip twitches in response.

"And on that note, I better be heading back," Hunter says, winking at me before he departs.

I close my eyes and throw back the rest of my gin and tonic, and then lay my head on the table.

"I don't know why you look so depressed when Hunter Brayze wants you. I'd be jumping over the moon," Callie says, sitting down next to me. "You look like you need another drink. Or some dick. Hunter dick. Why did he leave without you?"

"Because we're playing hide-and-seek," I tell her, sighing. "And he's it."

"Well, he should be running toward you, not away then," she huffs, grinning at me. "Looks like Hunter likes to play with his food."

I don't want to talk about Hunter playing with anything, because I have no idea how to feel. It's like my brain and heart are at war. I want him, but my mind keeps telling me to not be so fucking stupid, and to be realistic about the situation. Yes, I overthink.

That's probably my biggest issue.

That, and I haven't had Bear to vent to for some nonjudgmental dog therapy.

I lift my head and take a deep breath. "What am I doing with my life?"

"Not living it yet," she says, eyes softening on me. "But you will. Soon. As soon as he catches you."

"Whose side are you on, Callie?" I ask her.

"I'm on the side of your happiness," she replies, leaning against the bar. "I think you need to ask yourself why we aren't both on the same side."

"Hunter is Jeremy's lawyer," I blurt out.

"*What?*" she asks, sounding shocked. "Are you kidding me?"

I shake my head.

"You should have gone to him, like I told you to," she points out.

"I know," I groan. "But it's too late now, and Jeremy has Hunter, and I don't know what the hell is going to happen."

"Hunter will sort it out," she says, sounding nothing but confident. "It's a messed-up situation, but there's always a way out, Riley. Are you going to be okay?"

I nod. "I'll be fine."

"You relax; I'll take care of everything else in here," she says, sounding sympathetic.

She walks away, and I lay my head back down on the table.

Is she right? Am I the one stopping myself from being happy? Am I my own worst enemy?

Or am I just being smart?

Self-preservation.

If I try to close myself off, I won't get hurt.

And Hunter—oh, he's going to hurt.

chapter 6

HUNTER

"SO WHAT YOU'RE TELLING me is your new client, Jeremy Rodgers, is Riley's husband," Jaxon clarifies, as he sits across from me in my office. "And she didn't tell you that, nor did she tell you she was getting divorced in the first place? Oh, and the reason Jeremy is your client is because you're doing a favor for a friend from law school, so there's that added complication too."

"Pretty much," I reply, cringing. "How do I get myself into these situations?"

"I keep asking myself the same thing, although to your defense, how would you know that he was her husband?" Jaxon thrums his fingers on the table as he contemplates what I just told him. "So what are you going to do? Is it going to be an easy divorce, or a messy one?"

"She doesn't want anything besides her dog and her business," I tell him, unable to keep the pride from my tone. "But he wants to hurt her, so he's treating the dog like a child he wants to win custody over."

"So they're fighting over . . . a dog."

"Essentially," I tell him. "But really he's just being a douche. There's also Riley's drama thrown in there as well."

Jaxon raises his eyebrows in confusion. "Aren't we talking about Riley's drama?"

"No, Riley's the pub. So while the pub is hers—she started it with an inheritance she received—it came out during mediation that Jeremy owns the actual land. He's been her landlord all this time and she never knew."

"What. The. Fuck."

I nod in agreement. "My thoughts exactly. So there's another monkey wrench thrown into the mix."

"Sounds like one," Jaxon mutters, then looks me in the eye. "Riley has awful taste in men, doesn't she?"

"I think her luck is about to improve actually," I reply, ignoring his dig. "She's not ready now, I know that, but I can still be there for her. I'm a patient man."

Jaxon barks out a laugh. "Since when?"

"Since Riley."

"Hunter . . ." he starts, and I can tell he's about to say something I'm not going to like.

"What?"

"I just hope this isn't about the chase is all," he says, studying me. "Riley is a challenge right now, and I know you enjoy the game. Just make sure you're going to be ready to keep her when you catch her. Because I know she's a strong woman, but she's also a sensitive one. She can try to hide it as much as she wants, but that woman feels everything. She's thoughtful, caring, and kind. Yes, she has a mouth on her, and can be bossy as hell, but her bark is worse than her bite."

I don't like that Jaxon is talking to me like I don't already know all this, like I don't know her, when I do. I also don't like that he seems to think I'm some kind of player, or a man who doesn't know how to treat women, when that's not true either.

"Riley is different for me, Jaxon," I tell him. "This isn't a game, and I'm not just looking to fuck her, if that's what you think."

He puts his hands up in retreat. "I'm just saying, don't get angry. I know you're a good man, I do, but I also know you tend to treat everything as a game. This isn't allowed to be one of those times."

"It isn't," I assure him. "I have no intention of hurting her, Jaxon."

He continues to talk as if I didn't just say anything. "On top of that, with the situation here, now isn't the best time, don't you think? Have you thought about those repercussions? He's your client. Dropping him would tarnish your reputation and possibly bring us a lawsuit."

"Of course I've considered all of this—I'm not going to drop him as my client. I am going to get Riley a better lawyer though. Someone who will actually challenge me."

"Okay," he says instantly, nodding. "So you're going to get her a better lawyer to go up against you? But you think you can still win?"

"Yes, I can still get Jeremy more than what he deserves and more than what the law requires," I admit, leaning back in my chair. "But this way, at least Riley has a fair chance. The lawyer she has now is useless. Some advice would be great right now."

"I don't think you have many other options," he murmurs. "I think you also need to stay away from Riley until all of this is over. A conflict of interest exists here, and if Jeremy finds that out, he can use it against you if he doesn't get everything he wants in the divorce."

He's right. I know he is.

But I don't fucking want to stay away from Riley. I only just found I actually have a chance with her, even if it's not right now, it could be, whereas before being with her was just a pipe dream. There's only one solution I can think of. I might not be able to represent her, but someone I trust can. I have a few other friends at different firms all over the city. I know I could get one of them to step in and take care of her, and I know just who to call.

I pick up the phone and ask for Arabella Jameson.

One of the only lawyers in the city who can give me a run for my money, and someone who happens to owe me a favor.

I KNOCK TWICE ON Kat's door, then enter, even though she doesn't tell me to come in. We should probably have more boundaries here, but I know she's not with a client.

"Hunter," she says in welcome, lifting her head from her laptop. "Is everything okay? You have that crease in your forehead you get when something's wrong."

I rub my forehead and scowl. "My sister told me I should get Botox to fix that."

Kat's eyes widen before she starts laughing. "You have a sister? And if you get Botox, I'll give you shit for the rest of your life."

"Didn't say I was going to," I grumble. "And yes, I have a younger sister, Cleo. You'll get to meet her at my birthday." I normally don't talk about my personal life, even though I consider the people I work with family. My sister has been through a lot, and her story isn't mine to tell. I decide to get straight to the point. "Okay, so I'm here for a reason."

"You are? Normally you're just here to talk shit with me and steal my snacks."

"I know," I tell her. "Did you know that Riley is getting a divorce?"

"What?" she asks, eyes going wide.

"Yep. She didn't want anyone to know, so she didn't tell any of us, and yes, I know, it's ridiculous. Anyway, I found her a better lawyer than her current one, and I know that makes no sense since I'll be going up against her, but shit. I couldn't do nothing." I pause, watching the shock play on her face, then add, "And I still want to steal some snacks, so what do you have?"

She pushes her chair back from her desk. "Riley is getting a divorce and didn't tell any of us?"

I nod.

"We're lawyers."

"I know."

"This is our thing," she mutters under her breath. "And she didn't even fucking mention it? She has some serious issues."

"I know," I repeat, rubbing the back of the neck. "And there's more."

"Tell me everything," she says, leaning forward, that determined gleam in her eye. When I first saw it, I knew she'd be a great lawyer. And she is. She's amazing. "And then I'm going to go and have words with a certain brunette pub owner."

I tell her everything from start to finish.

Jeremy.

Riley.

Bear.

The pub.

Everything.

"Fuck," she murmurs, tucking her hair back behind her ear. "You're not in a good position, Hunter."

"I know," I say, scrubbing my hand down my face. "But let's worry about me later. Right now, we need to get Riley through this."

"Okay," she nods, once, then twice. "We can do this."

I'm glad she's confident, because I have the feeling it's not going to be so simple.

But for Riley—I don't give a fuck.

chapter 7

RILEY

WHEN KAT STORMS INTO my bar, eyes narrowed and heels stomping, I know Hunter told her about my divorce, and she's taking it personally. I pour her a drink and slide it over to her as soon as she drops onto a barstool. She glances around to make sure no one can hear us before she speaks.

"I can't believe you—"

"I wanted to tell you, Kat."

"But you didn't," she whisper-yells. "You didn't tell your bunch of lawyer friends that you needed a lawyer. That's like me going to a different bar to get drunk. Wouldn't you take offense to that?"

I cringe a little, because I would. "It's not the same! You aren't bringing your problems to my bar, you're bringing business and company."

"I tell you about my problems all the time! We all do! You

might as well be our therapist! Should I go to another bartender to complain about my life instead? No, I come to you, because you're my friend, and because I trust you. Where's that trust in return?"

More valid points.

I sigh, letting my shoulders droop in defeat. "I'm sorry, okay. I should have opened up and told you I was in a shit marriage and finally trying to get out of it. And that I've been unhappy for years and made to feel like a shit, useless wife, and I haven't even had sex in over a year. Are you happy now?"

Her face falls, and I instantly regret my words.

"I'm sorry, I—"

"You haven't had sex in over a year?" she asks, eyes going wide. "No wonder you're so grumpy all the time. Damn, woman. How are you surviving? Doesn't every male look good to you right now?" She glances around the bar, as if looking for penises.

"That's all you heard from that whole rant?" I ask, arching a brow at her. "And I'm fine. My vibrator works perfectly well and doesn't snore afterward."

"It's not the same," she says, wrinkling her nose. "I don't know how you can even be in the same room as Hunter when you haven't had any action in so long."

I purse my lips. "I manage, Kat. And Hunter doesn't have anything to do with this."

"Okay, but I'm still angry about this, Riley," she says, scowling at me. "There's no excuse for you not to come to me with this. It feels like you don't trust me, and I'm allowed to take that personally."

"I do trust you," I tell her gently. "I didn't want to inconvenience—"

"Don't even give me that one, Riley," she groans, cutting me off.

I roll my eyes at her, but inside I do feel badly. I don't want them to feel like I don't appreciate them, or the fact that I knew they would help me in some way or another. I'm grateful to have such good friends, I am, and all because Hunter dragged Jaxon to my pub for lunch, making Riley's their regular hangout and me part of their close-knit group. But I couldn't involve them in this; I was too ashamed.

"Next time I'm getting a divorce, you'll be the first person I come to," I promise Kat, who sighs, like I'm the hardest person in the world to deal with, then puts some money on the bar for her drink.

I shake my head. "On the house."

"How are you going to make money if you keep trying to give us shit for free?" she asks me, sighing. "We can afford it, Riley. And we all want to pay, no one expects you to not charge us just because we're friends. You need to think about the business."

"Yet you guys keep offering me free legal advice, how is that different?" I ask her. I gesture to all the bottles of alcohol behind the bar. "This is all I have to offer. So if I want to give my friends some, they can take it without complaining."

"That's not the same at all," Kat squeals, shaking her head. "You have a business to run. If we help you, we don't lose any-thing, it's just us helping by giving our time. Which we want to do. So quit trying to compare the two."

"I just can't win today, can I?" I ask her, crossing my arms over my chest. "Anything else you want to throw in?"

"Just trying to help," Kat quickly inserts, lifting her chin. "Or at least I could have if you had come to me. Now I have to sit on the sidelines and hope for the best outcome. Do you know how much that pisses me off?"

"I can only imagine," I say, covering my face with my hands, not caring if it rubs off any of the light foundation and bronzer I put on this morning. "It's not ideal, but everything will be fine. I'm not asking for anything, so it's not like I can lose here."

"That's not the mentality I want to hear," Kat grumbles. "This is fucked. Luckily Hunter was able to do something though. At least in your new lawyer's hands we know you have a great chance of getting whatever you want from the divorce."

"Yes, about that. I don't need a new lawyer. The one I have now is fine," I tell her. "A lawyer is a lawyer, right?"

She shakes her head. "How good the lawyer is can make or break your case, Riley. Can you just trust us on this, please?" Kat begs.

I nod and hesitantly agree. I don't want to sound bratty, or ungrateful, and I know they're just trying to help, but I kind of feel out of control now, and I don't like it.

"I just read about a case where the couple had to share custody of the dog," I tell her, leaning over the bar top. "Is this a thing? Because I want full custody of Bear. Jeremy doesn't even care about him, he's just using him to hurt me."

"I think you'll get the dog," Kat says, sounding confident. "Hunter can't say anything to you about the case, given the circumstances, but I can give you my advice as a lawyer, unofficially, since I don't know anything about what Jeremy has said to Hunter. You're asking for so little that if he doesn't give you the dog, he'll have to pay you out, and he doesn't want to do that."

"Okay, good."

Her words about Hunter suddenly make what I did real. He can't even comment or be part of any conversation that has to do with my case.

This is worse than his knowing all my personal hell; this is him on Jeremy's side. We can't even speak freely anymore, which was what I wanted, or at least what I thought I wanted. Now I just want him on my side.

Kat nods once. "Don't worry about anything, Riley. It'll be fine. Besides, you have bigger problems now."

"Like what?" I ask, bracing myself. Am I forgetting something else I have to deal with?

She leans closer to me and looks me in the eye. "Now Hunter knows you're available."

My mind flashes to the man in question. I might have to agree with Kat.

I'm in trouble.

Hunter likes the chase, and I'm running from being hurt. I don't want to feel how Jeremy made me feel ever again; I don't want to be in that position, or ever give someone that power. But with Hunter as Jeremy's lawyer, I think it buys me some time to figure him out. There's no way anything can happen between us until this is all sorted.

"I'm not ready to date," I explain to Kat. "I still haven't gotten rid of my last mistake, not ready for a new one just yet."

"Not every man is a mistake, Riley. Now and again, one comes along and shows you why it doesn't work with anyone else," Kat says, smiling dreamily. "I never thought I'd meet anyone like Tristan. I didn't even like him when I first met him, but you just have to give things a chance sometimes and see where life takes you. I never forced anything with him, it kind of just happened, you know? And I'm sure it will for you when you're ready, but for now, let's just concentrate on getting you divorced. I'll talk to you tomorrow, okay? I better get back to work."

She smiles and gets up to leave, but I call out her name.

"Yes?"

"Thank you," I whisper, emotion coming through in my voice. "For not being angry."

Too angry, at least.

"Oh, I'm angry. But I'm always here for you, Riley, I just wish you knew that," she says, smiling sadly, placing some money down on the table, and heads back to work.

Guilt fills me, and I feel even worse than before.

I watch her leave and wonder how this is all going to end.

We'll all be okay, right?

Hunter and me?

I expel a deep breath and get back to work.

chapter 8

HUNTER

"I'M SORRY, MR. RODGERS, but I really think it's in your best interests to give her what she is asking for," I tell the idiotic man. I've been talking to him for the past hour, discussing the phone call I had with Riley's new attorney. After telling Jeremy that all they want is the dog, the pub, and the land the pub is on, he has just been ranting and raving like a lunatic. He somehow got it in his head that he is going to be able to keep everything: the money, the properties, the yacht, get her pub, and keep . . . the dog. I just don't understand where he is coming from. Even my most obnoxious clients have been more reasonable than this.

"You are the best divorce lawyer in the city," he tells me, shaking his head. "If anyone can pull this off, it's you."

While I'm flattered at his faith in me, even I can't go against the damn law and make my own rules to please him. Going to court will work against him.

"In the grand scheme of things, she is asking for such a small percentage of your net worth. If this goes to court, it's the judge who will decide your outcome, not me," I tell him, keeping my calm facade.

"I have dirt on her, if that's what you need," he says, shrugging. "Riley has a few skeletons in her closet. If we let the judge know that, slander her character, will the judge grant me what I want?"

I don't know how I can explain this to him any simpler. It doesn't matter what skeletons Riley has, they don't have any children, so no matter what it is, it doesn't affect anyone. Unless of course she abused animals or ran a dog-fighting ring.

When I don't say anything, he continues, "Do you know that she's a murderer? Maybe that should be brought up in court too."

Murderer? What is he talking about? This guy is certifiable.

I close the folder in my hands and tap the bottom of it on the desk. "I think that's a whole different case, Mr. Rodgers, and I'm not a criminal attorney. Can I ask you why giving her what she wants is such a big deal?"

For the first time since I've met him, Jeremy seems to contemplate what I'm saying. He's quiet for a bit before he speaks, another first. "When I met Riley she was an entirely different person. She needed me. She wanted me. I did so much for her and helped her through a lot of hard times. But when I started to need her when my career took off, she wasn't there for me."

As I listen to him show a smidge of vulnerability and hurt, I actually start to feel sorry for him. He loved her. He is hurt. He—

"She wouldn't go to the country club and entertain potential clients with me. She wouldn't learn to play tennis or golf. She dressed inappropriately. She was such a selfish bitch. So she should suffer. Do you know what this divorce does to my reputation?"

And any sympathy I may have started to have for him goes right out the window. Fucking prick.

"Okay, Mr. Rodgers. If you aren't willing to compromise, then I guess we are going to have this conversation again, except in front of a judge. I'll let you know when the court date is." I stand, hoping he takes the hint and does the same.

"I'd better get a win here, Brayze. I called in all my favors to get you as my attorney when I realized Riley was going to go through with this." He shakes my hand as he leaves my office.

I tidy up my desk and step into Kat's office.

"How did it go?" she asks, putting down her pen and giving me her full attention.

"He won't give in," I say, sitting opposite her. "He thinks some old dirt he has on Riley is going to persuade the judge to just give him everything."

"What a dumb-ass," Kat murmurs, shaking her head. "The judge might even give Riley a house for all we know."

"I tried to tell him that," I grumble. "And speaking of Riley, can you stop scaring her off me? We have enough going against us; I don't want her afraid to even try something when we finally have the opportunity. I'm going to bide my time and just grow on her."

She takes a sip from her bottle of water and almost chokes on it. "That's your plan? To 'grow' on her? What kind of plan is that? I thought you were a ladies' man."

"This isn't exactly an everyday situation for me," I tell her dryly. "I want her, Kat. As in I want to be with her. That changes everything. And although everyone seems to think I'm going to hurt her, it's my heart on the line too." I stop her before she speaks. "And yes, I do have a heart."

"Just checking," she teases, grinning at me. "Well, you can't go near her now anyway. So I guess you have no choice but to take it slow until you settle this case. And by slow, I mean just be friends. Get to know each other more. Don't push or pressure her. She's got a lot on her plate right now."

I know all of this. I've probably spent the most time with her out of everyone. And all the while I thought she was married, when she was already separated. Does everyone realize how much this changes things for me? Something I've wanted so badly, that was completely out of the realm of possibility before, is now within my grasp, so close I can almost taste her sweet lips.

I should stay away from her until the case is over, and I will. At least I'll try.

Yes, I need to be patient, but that doesn't mean the two of us can't spend time together, talk, and get to know each other without my thinking about how she's fucking married the whole time.

"I know this. I want to be there for her," I say, for what feels like the hundredth time. "I mean, I know I can't really do that until the case is over, but shit, I'm doing the best I can with what I've been given."

"I know you are," Kat says, smiling a little sadly. "It'll all work out in the end."

"I hope so," I say with a sigh, then stand up and walk to the door. "I've got to get to my next client."

I walk back to my office, feeling like shit.

This is not how I would have chosen for things to be.

But like I said, I'm doing my fucking best.

AFTER WORK I HIT the gym for an hour to do some boxing before I head home. When I get there, I decide to tinker in my garage with my car. If I hadn't become a lawyer, I think I would have become a mechanic. I love fixing cars and working on mine. It's kind of peaceful, and I like to use my hands after just using my mind all day long.

After a long shower, I throw on some gray sweatpants and walk into my kitchen. It's late, and I haven't had anything to eat yet, but the last thing I want to do is cook right now. Does Riley cook much at home? Why does my mind always wander to her? I don't know what's going to happen once this case is over, but I do know what I want. I know that under all that iciness is pure sweetness, I just have to get there. She has to let me in, so I can show her that I'm different. I will cook for her and spoil her as much as I can. My mom taught me how to cook when I was a boy, because she didn't want me to be like my dad, who can't even fry an egg. She raised an independent man, and for that I'm thankful. I don't need a woman to look after me, but that doesn't mean I wouldn't appreciate one who tried.

Especially if that one happened to be a fiery brunette with hazel eyes.

A knock at my door has me closing the fridge and forgetting my food search. I'm not expecting anyone, which means it can only be one person.

I open the door and my baby sister flashes me a smile and then gives me a warm hug. "I was in the neighborhood."

"You should have brought some food with you," I grumble, locking the door behind her.

"You should have told me and I would have."

"You didn't tell me you were coming over."

We enter the kitchen and she opens my fridge and scans its contents. Unlike me though, she apparently sees potential meal ideas. "Do you want me to make you a stir-fry? Or how about some pesto chicken pasta with sundried tomatoes?"

"Pasta, please," I tell her, grinning at the fact I was just thinking about how I didn't need a woman to look after me. Here walks in my baby sister though and does just that. "Did you have dinner?"

"Nope," she says as she pulls out ingredients and places them on the countertop. "I came here straight from work."

My sister works in aged care. She opted not to go to college and instead spent time traveling before she got her certification to care for the elderly. She hasn't always been a saint, and has gotten into her fair share of trouble over the years, but there's nothing I wouldn't do for her. She's always there when I need her, and I try to do the same for her.

"Is everything okay?" I ask her.

Yes, she comes over now and again, but it's usually not just to say hello. Her house is about a twenty-minute drive from here, and when we're catching up we usually make plans. Our parents live a few hours away, so we see them a lot less than we see each other.

"Yeah," she murmurs, but the way she draws out the word gives it away for her. "I kind of need a favor, Hunter."

"What is it?" I ask, watching her hands as she starts to chop up the chicken breast.

"I was wondering if you could loan me some money," she asks, glancing up at me. "You know I hate to ask, but I'm kind of falling behind on my expenses and bills, and—"

"How much do you need, Cleo?" I ask, cutting her off. I earn good money, and I have no problem giving her however much she needs. I would never expect her to pay it back either. I grab my phone from the table and open my banking app.

"A thousand or two?" she asks, flashing me a hopeful look. "If you can't, I totally understand, it's not your responsibly to look after me, and . . ."

"I'll put it in now," I tell her, and then transfer four thousand to her. I don't want her to have to worry about money, especially when I make more than enough to get her through when she's having a rough time.

"Thanks, Hunter," she whispers, stopping her movements. "I really appreciate it. And I'll pay you back."

"Don't worry about it, Cleo," I tell her. "And you know you're always welcome to move in here if you want to save money."

"I know," she says, cutting an onion now. "We'd probably kill each other though, and I'd never be able to bring any men home."

I cringe and shudder. "I'm going to pretend I didn't hear that. My baby sister would never do that, she respects herself too much."

"So none of the many women you bring home respect themselves?" she asks, arching her brow, challenging me. "Hypocrite much?"

"I'm not going to comment on my sex life with my younger sister," I tell her, then decide to change the subject. I love my sister, but sex is a topic I do not want to get into with her. If I'm being completely honest, there's a huge double standard when it comes to sex, and yeah, I might have slept around in the past, but the thought of her doing the same makes me want to strangle someone. Come to think of it, the thought of Riley being with another man makes me want to do the same, and I already have one of hers as my client. "So tell me what's new with you."

We spend the next few hours chatting and catching up.

Sometimes that's all you need.

chapter 9

HUNTER

A COUPLE OF DAYS LATER, I'm sitting in my office, replying to emails, when Arabella walks in, paperwork in her hands.

I stand, surprised, and offer her my hand. "You doing house calls now?"

She smiles, her blond hair framing her face in a new, shorter cut than I remember. "When you call in a favor, you don't fuck around, do you? Your client is a nightmare. How do you put up with him? I can't wait to rip him a new one in court."

"Ah, come on, I'm sure he has some charm hidden somewhere," I joke.

"I'm assuming he's not going to give her an inch?"

"He's not agreeing to her requests," I say. "Hence the court date later this week."

"The judge isn't going to go in favor of him," she says, pointing out the obvious.

"We will have to see how it goes," I say, even though I agree with her.

"I'm curious, Hunter. Why did you call me in for this? You could have saved the favor for something much more important than this. You did save my life, after all."

What feels like a lifetime ago, Arabella and I used to be a little more than friends, but less than lovers. To put it mildly, we were friends who fucked in between classes and exams, helping each other out with the stress. One night on campus, though, she was attacked by three men. Luckily I was returning to my dorm, and I was able to stop them before anything serious happened to her. I, on the other hand, got the crap beaten out of me.

"Riley is a friend, and I care about her, but my hands are tied," I explain, shrugging. "Needed someone I can trust. And Arabella, you're making quite a name for yourself."

She arches her brow, a smug look passing through her blue eyes. "Not as big of a name as your firm . . . yet, anyway."

I throw my head back and laugh. "You always were competitive."

"And you always gave me a challenge." She stands and studies me. "Riley seems nice, and she's beautiful too. You always had good taste, didn't you, Hunter?"

My lips kick up in the corners. "You making assumptions, Arabella?"

"I know you better than to make assumptions. Just be careful, Hunter. You're on a slippery slope," she says.

Why does everyone have to remind me of this? "I know." Silence follows.

"Well, I will see you in court. It's a shame you handed me an easy win on a silver platter," she says, offering me her hand.

I take it, glancing at my watch on my other wrist. "Speaking of court, I'm meant to be there soon. The stripper is officially divorcing the CEO today."

"Who says divorce law is boring?" she murmurs, a contemplative look on her face. "It's like you get to be petty all day and realize that your life isn't so bad after all. Don't you think?"

I laugh at that. "Is that what we do? Pretty sure there's more to it than that."

"You help your clients be petty and fight for whatever they want, usually things they've accumulated with people they once loved but now dislike. Come on, look at Jeremy. That's some petty shit right there," she replies, expression daring me to disagree.

I start laughing again. "Fine, Arabella, our job is to assist people with their pettiness. Let the pettiest lawyer win."

She grins at me and shakes her head, her hair flipping with the motion. "Nice seeing you, Hunter."

"You too," I tell her, watching as she moves to leave.

She stops and then adds, "And as Riley's attorney speaking to Jeremy's attorney—Riley will be getting her dog, her business, the property that business is on, and if I can help it, some money as well, and she's walking away with her head held high. Jeremy is going to lose. He's already lost by fucking things up with such a beautiful woman. And when I say beautiful, I'm not even touching on her looks."

"I know," I reply, a little surprised at how much she seems to have taken a liking to Riley. "Trust me, I know."

Riley is a teddy bear, she can deny it all she wants, but I know who she is, even when she thinks I don't. I know she gives free meals to the homeless. I know she drives drunk people home some nights when she doesn't have to, and even though it's unsafe for her, because she doesn't want anyone to crash. I know that she pays her staff more than she probably should, because she doesn't want them to struggle, and I also know that she feeds the stray dogs on the street behind her bar, where the trash cans are.

"See you in court."

I nod and watch her leave.

Arabella is going to give me a run for my money, and that's just what Riley needs.

I WALK INTO WORK on Monday morning, making two stops before I hit my office, one to chat with Yvonne, and the other to steal some snacks from Kat's office. Hands full, I sit down, placing my stolen goods on my desk, then turn on my laptop. When Yvonne sticks her head in my office not even an hour later, I can tell something is wrong from her expression.

"What is it?" I ask, standing up. "Is everything okay?"

She steps in and closes the door behind her. "Jeremy just rang and said to pass on a message to you."

"What's happened?" I ask her.

"He admitted that he doesn't know where Riley's dog is. He says Bear escaped his house."

Rage fills me. He lost Riley's dog? Did he even go looking for him? How the hell did he let this happen?

"How long has he been missing for? Do you think he did this on purpose?"

That fucking bastard. The only thing Riley wants is the dog, and now he's "lost" him. I bet he dropped him off somewhere, gave him away, or left him at the pound. The man truly is a total piece of shit. And he tells me this via a phone call with our receptionist? As Yvonne leaves, I call Kat into my office and give her a quick rundown on the situation.

"I can't fucking believe this," she growls, pacing up and down. "I can only guess, but I'm thinking this must have been his plan all along. He knew he was going to have to give her the dog in the end, and he probably didn't want to do that," she says, covering her face with her hands. "How the hell do we handle this? We can't tell Riley, because of client confidentiality. How do we get out of this one? That dog is the only thing getting her through everything right now. All she wants is him back."

I don't know. I'm supposed to be supporting Jeremy, and if this was any other client I'd remain adamant that this was indeed a mistake, and that there's no proof to say otherwise. But this is Riley's beloved pet that's lost, and instead of me finding excuses, I need to find the dog. Riley is not going to lose someone she loves, fur baby or not.

"I'll fix this," I whisper, jaw clenching. "I really want to beat the shit out of this asshole, but we all know I can't do that. We need to find Bear. Do we have a picture of him? Maybe I should go to the local pounds and have a look? This is going to stress her out if she finds out about this."

"I can get a picture of him from her social media," Kat says, pulling her phone out of her pocket. "How busy is your day? Can you clear it? Who knows how long this dog search will take."

I press the button on the phone that reaches Yvonne.

"Yes, Hunter?" she says into the line.

"I need you to clear my day," I tell her. "Can you reschedule my appointments?"

"Sure thing. Bear hunt?" she asks, worry in her tone.

Bear hunt? I'm assuming that pun was unintended.

"Yes," I tell her.

There's silence for a few seconds, and then she says, "Okay. If you need me. I'm there."

"Someone has to run this place, Yvonne."

"Fine," she sighs, hanging up on me.

I do a search for all the pounds in our area and write down all their numbers. "Let's get searching then," I say to Kat.

I figure if we call all of them up, it will save time. If none of them say they've found an Alaskan malamute, then I'm going to have to come up with a plan B. In an ideal situation, I'd have found him and brought him back to her before she even knows he's lost, but we all know that life doesn't always work like that.

As a matter of fact, it rarely does.

A FEW HOURS LATER, four to be precise, I find who I think is Bear in a shelter on the other side of the city. He looks like the picture Kat showed me, but what if it isn't him? I can't go up to Riley and say, "Hey, look who I found," only for him to be some doppelgänger dog.

"It has to be him," Kat says, eyeing the large animal. He doesn't have a collar on but appears to be in good health. He keeps looking between the two of us, probably wondering who the fuck we are. He even has his tongue lolling out the right side of his mouth. Can a dog look ditzy? Because that's the only word I could use to describe him.

He's clearly a friendly dog, who obviously doesn't know about stranger danger, because he jumped onto me without hesitation.

And he's huge.

I mean *enormous*.

No wonder she named him Bear.

Still, he doesn't have a threatening look about him. He looks like a big softy, a giant teddy bear, even. I don't think Riley could use him as a guard dog. Then again, maybe he just likes us because we saved him from impending doom.

"Bear," I call, testing to see if he responds to his name.

He licks me, then starts to sniff around my foot.

What does that mean in dog language?

"Ummm," I murmur, examining him. Why couldn't he just have one of those name collars on? Although I guess then he would have been able to find his way home, something Jeremy clearly didn't want. I glance up at Kat, silently asking for her opinion.

Kat glances down and studies him, and then calls out, "Rover?"

He licks her.

And then starts to sniff her.

We share a look.

If it's not him, we are all fucked, doppelgänger Bear included.

Is one of us going to have to adopt him if he's not Bear?

The three of us head to Riley's, and hope for the best.

chapter 10

RILEY

*H*UNTER WALKS IN UNEXPECTEDLY, when he wasn't here around his usual lunchtime I assumed he was busy and wasn't coming in.

"Hey," I say, surprised to see him.

"Hey," he says, shifting on his feet. "We kind of have a situation, and I'm not even supposed to be here right now."

"What is it?" I ask, brow furrowing. "Is everything okay?"

He glances around and then pulls me to the side. "Can you come outside for a second?"

He looks like he wants to say something but can't. I nod and start walking with him to the exit. Oh God, I hope everyone is okay. Did someone get hurt? Is Kat okay? And the others? We quicken our pace as we walk through the parking lot, and I see Kat standing there next to Hunter's car. When I glance down and see who is sitting at her feet though, I almost feel like crying.

"Bear?"

I know the minute he recognizes my voice, his ears perk, body going into alert mode. He starts to run toward me, almost pulling Kat to the ground in the process. She lets go of the leash, and we rush toward each other. I fall to my knees and wrap my arms around him, grabbing on to his fur as he licks my face and jumps all over me, so excited to see me, and the feeling is mutual.

"I've missed you so much, boy," I tell him, smiling to myself. "What are you doing here?"

I glance up at Kat, who walks over to me and starts to explain. "We didn't know what to do, but we were never here, Riley. We did *not* bring you this dog."

I hold Bear closer, my brow furrowing with worry. "Tell me what happened."

Kat glances behind me at Hunter. "You should go back to work."

He hesitates but then nods and gets into his car. We move aside and watch him drive away before she continues.

"We got a call today that indicated we should look for Bear. Don't ask me for any more information than that," Kat says, sighing. "We called up a few of the shelters and asked if they had any Alaskan malamutes come in, and luckily one did. We're going to need an explanation as to how you found the dog, and it can't have us in the story."

I pet Bear, feeling so grateful that they found him but also bad that they've been put in this position. "I'll come up with something, don't worry. This won't fall back on you guys."

I can't believe this has happened. Poor Bear, he must have been so scared!

"Thank you so much for finding him for me," I tell her. They didn't have to do this. They've gone above and beyond to make me happy.

"You're welcome," she says, softening. "I better get back to work. And you better take him home before someone sees."

I can't believe Jeremy. How the hell did Bear end up in a shelter? I don't even want to think what would've happened to him if they hadn't found him.

I knew he was an asshole, but this is next level, after his claiming to love and care about Bear so much.

The man is a vindictive, spiteful liar.

Little does he know, I got what I want, my dog with me, and I don't care what happens now.

I just never want to see Jeremy again.

MY COURT DATE FINALLY arrives, and I sit and listen as everyone speaks about me but not to me. It's quite a weird feeling, like I'm watching a movie about my life except I'm not playing me. Hunter is everything I thought he'd be in court, strong and imposing, eloquent with his words and confident. Arabella argues right back, keeping up with him though, and I can see why Hunter wanted her to be my lawyer. She's phenomenal.

"The dog in question was found in the pound, so I'm assuming Mr. Rodgers doesn't care much for his whereabouts," Arabella tells the judge.

"Your Honor, my client feels horrible that the dog got loose. Of course he cares about his dog and—"

"The dog belongs to my client, and she should be able to keep him instead of him being used as a pawn by Mr. Rodgers." Arabella cuts him off. I'd be annoyed if I cared.

"The dog can stay with Ms. McMahon," the judge rules, reading over the paperwork. "I understand Ms. McMahon doesn't want any money from the separation, but I believe she is entitled to something after being in this union for many years."

I open my mouth, then close it. I truly don't want any of his money. I don't want anything to do with him.

"Ms. McMahon can keep her business," the judge continues. "Mr. Rodgers can keep his properties, except for one piece of land. As settlement, he will give her the land her business is on. Ms. McMahon will also receive fifty thousand dollars."

Jeremy looks at Hunter and his face contorts in anger. "Your Honor, this is ridiculous. She shouldn't get anything. Do you know what kind of person she is? She—"

The sound of the judge's gavel interrupts his outburst. "That is enough, Mr. Rodgers. I've made my ruling. From what I can see, you had the opportunity to settle this out of court but instead you wasted everyone's time, including mine. You're lucky Ms. McMahon isn't asking for half of your assets. I'd be inclined to give them to her."

Jeremy's face drops.

After the judge finalizes everything, the divorce is granted, just like that.

We will both get certificates to prove as much.

Jeremy stands up, clearly unhappy with the outcome, and I don't know why, but I feel a little bad over the money thing. Maybe I could donate it, or something, I don't know. I'll worry about that later.

"You were supposed to prevent her from getting anything," I hear Jeremy sneer to Hunter as I walk past them with Arabella. "You're meant to be the best, and we just lost."

"You didn't lose," Hunter replies, keeping his expression and tone impassive. "You had the opportunity to settle this out of court and you didn't want to. This is the consequence. You've kept all of your properties, assets, and much more than half of your money. In a divorce, Mr. Rodgers, that's considered a win."

Jeremy mutters something under his breath, but Arabella pulls me aside, and out of earshot from their conversation.

"How do you feel, Riley?" she asks me, smiling. "I know you didn't want the money, but I'm happy you got something." She puts up her hand. "Save me your arguments. This is how divorce works. Think of it as a payout for putting up with his shit for so long." She winks.

Jeremy storms past us, banging the courthouse door like a baby. I can't help the small laugh that leaves my lips. "I don't feel good about it, but I'm done stressing over all this. It's over with; I'm free. My dog is mine. And I couldn't be happier about it."

Hunter walks past us, and Arabella reaches her arm out to touch his shoulder. "I'm calling it even."

She gets a tight nod from him, and my own eyes narrow.

"Thank you," he says.

"You're welcome," she tells him, then says goodbye to the both of us.

Hunter and I share a look, but I know we can't discuss anything here. Why am I wondering if he's ever slept with Arabella instead of enjoying my moment of freedom?

We walk to our separate cars and both get in. I head to Riley's, knowing he's going there as well. I beat him there due to traffic, and by the time he walks inside I'm already sitting down, nursing a drink. After calling Callie to update her on my way over, she arranged an impromptu "Riley is divorced" happy hour, and everyone starts coming to the pub.

"How are you feeling?" he asks when he finally arrives, sitting beside me.

"Wonderful," I tell him, smiling. "Bear is mine, I'm free,

and now I get a fresh start. There's nothing to describe how I'm feeling right now."

We all have a drink, toasting to my freedom—Kat, Callie, Preston, Cheffy, Jaxon, and Tristan joining us. I probably see Tristan, Kat's husband and another lawyer at the firm, the least in the pub, but his blue eyes, brown hair, and dry comments are always welcome with me.

"Thank you all so much," I say, my hand on my heart. "Especially Kat and Hunter. I can't thank you both enough."

"For the record, neither of us, nor anyone at the firm, did anything to help you. But off the record," Kat says, lifting her beer up, "you deserve this moment, Riley."

I feel like I'm about to cry. I never let my guard down, but if I learned anything from this mess it's that these people are my family. I can let them in. Hunter pulls me against him and whispers into my ear, "Are you okay?"

I nod, overwhelmed. "More than okay."

"Good," he replies, kissing the top of my head.

He's never done that before.

What does this mean?

Does this mean he's done playing the waiting game?

Is it open season on my heart?

Did I really just think that?

I'm just going to savor this moment.

chapter 11

HUNTER

SHE SNUGGLES AGAINST MY chest, in front of everyone, and I can't help but enjoy the moment. I know it doesn't mean anything—she's just giddy—but I can only hope that we have more moments like this.

We're finally free of Jeremy and ethics and attorney-client privilege. Riley is finally single. There is nothing stopping us now. There is just so much going on, my mind cannot catch up.

Kat settles next to me, a smug look on her face. "Arabella is good at what she does."

"I know," I tell her, smiling gently at her. "And you could have done the same. I know how great of a lawyer you are, Kat. You prove yourself over and over again. Just because you're the youngest and newest on the team doesn't mean you can't stand with the rest of us."

"Oh, I know that," she murmurs, smirking at me. "Just wanted to make sure you did."

"I do now," I reply, laughing when she elbows me in the stomach, then turns to Riley and whispers, "I think his abs just broke my elbow."

Riley reaches out and touches my stomach through my shirt. "They are pretty hard, aren't they?"

Kat glances between us and fans herself. "Okay, well, I'm just going to leave the two of you alone."

I chuckle, and Riley steps away from me, cheeks flushed. "Another drink?"

I nod. "Yes, please."

How could I not, with so much to celebrate?

"SO THERE'S SOMETHING I wanted to ask you," I say as I pull up outside of Riley's apartment. She had way too much to drink, while I stopped at two beers before I started on the water. I made sure I wasn't over the limit before I left to take her home, but she sure as hell is.

"What is it?" she asks, her rosy cheeks just asking to be kissed.

"It's my birthday next weekend, and I'm having a get-together. I want you to come. Everyone is invited, so bring Callie and Preston, and whoever else you want."

She turns to me and grins. "You trying to steal my thunder, Hunter? Tonight is my night."

I laugh and reach out to tuck her hair behind her ear. "Never. Why do you think I waited until the end of the night?"

"So I'd be drunk and say yes to coming even though it's a terrible idea?"

"Why is it a terrible idea?" I ask, learning that drunk Riley is a very honest Riley. I could get used to this Riley, the one who doesn't hide and keep everything to herself. Maybe one day she'll be open with me all the time.

"Because I'm officially divorced now." She turns to me and adds, "I'll bet you're happy this case is over."

"You have no idea," I chuckle. I'm surprised myself that everything worked out in the end. "And yes, you're officially divorced now, but everything comes down to one question, Riley. What is it that *you* want?"

"What do I want?" she asks herself, then clicks her fingers. "I want to know if you've slept with Arabella before, how about that?"

Well, fuck.

I should have seen this one coming, because I saw the look she gave me outside the courtroom.

"A long time ago, yes. Now we are just friends," I say, giving her nothing but honesty.

"I see," she murmurs, glancing out the window. "So you got a woman you've slept with to be my lawyer."

"She's the best aside from me, and she owed me a favor," I say in a gentle voice. "And like I said, we're just friends now, Riley. You don't have anything to worry about."

Her head snaps to me. "I have plenty to worry about, Hunter."

I don't really know what that means, but having this conversation with drunk Riley isn't the best idea. She opens the passenger car door and I quickly get out, wanting to walk her to her door and make sure she gets inside safely. We walk to the staircase together, and then I offer her my hand to help her walk up, and she takes it. I take the steps slower than I would alone, allowing her little legs to catch up to me. When we reach her door, I wait for her to unlock it and step inside.

"Good night, Riley," I say to her.

"Good night, Hunter," she replies, reaching her arms out to pull me into a warm hug. "And thank you for everything you've done for me."

I squeeze her tighter, and kiss the top of her head. "I didn't do anything, remember?"

She laughs. "Yes, yes. Then thank you for not doing anything for me."

I smile. "Drink some water."

"I'm trying to thank you, and you're being bossy," she grumbles, stepping inside. I wait until I hear the door lock before I return to my car.

It's not just a fresh start for Riley; it's one for me, too.

IT'S ONLY BEEN A week since her divorce was finalized and I haven't had a chance to see her much since. My caseload was intense this week, but I'm glad she decided to come to my birthday party at my house.

No matter where I move to, or who I'm speaking with, I can sense her. I know where she is, even if it's just out of the corner of my eye. I know who she's talking to. I can hear her when she laughs, the sound hitting me straight in my gut. I want to be the one making her laugh.

What is it about her?

"You're staring at her again," Callum, a guy who used to work at our firm as an intern, points out, tapping me on the back in sympathy. "You going to ask her out, or what? Make that shit official. Lock her down."

Great, I'm getting sympathy from someone younger than me, not what I need right now. And how the hell did he get his woman when he clearly has no game. *Lock her down?* Jesus.

"Where's Medusa?" I ask, trying to change the subject. Callum somehow managed to fall in love with a woman all lawyers in the city know by that name. A judge known for her cutthroat ways and no-bullshit personality. Apparently one look into her eyes and his dick turned to stone, and hasn't softened since.

"You ever going to stop calling her that?" he grumbles, crossing his arms over his chest. "And don't try to change the subject."

"I have no idea what you're talking about," I lie, taking a draw from my beer and trying to pull my thoughts away from Riley.

"I'll bet," Callum murmurs, amusement in his tone. The bastard has always been too cocky and confident for his own good, and giving me shit right now showcases that. I'm about to take him down a notch when Yvonne approaches me and wraps me in a warm hug.

"Happy birthday, Hunter," she says, smiling up at me. Even with her extremely high heels, she doesn't even reach my chest.

"Thanks, Yvonne," I tell her, making sure not to spill my drink. I glance around to find her here alone. "No date?"

"You should know me better than that," she says, not sounding put out about it, just stating a fact.

"What about the guy you were chatting to online?" I ask, brow furrowing.

I know there's been some office talk about us sleeping together, but that actually isn't true. Yvonne and I are close, yes, but she's just a friend and always has been.

"I got bored before we even met. Welcome to dating in 2017," she replies with a smirk on her hot-pink lips. "Everyone is temporary, and everyone is replaceable. Too many options."

I don't think anyone would ever call me a romantic, but for some reason her words make me feel a little sad.

"I can't even remember the last time I properly dated," I admit, cringing when the truth hits me. I've fucked, sure. I've had fun. I've been so immersed in my work, in my career, that after I ended things with my ex about three years ago, I never bothered to try to pursue anything meaningful again.

Fuck.

Maybe I just haven't met the right woman yet.

I glance toward Riley once more to find her chatting with Preston, their heads together. I know they are close, and Riley is his boss, but I still find myself wanting to punch him in the face.

"You're having fun," Yvonne says, shrugging. "Nothing wrong with that. You'll meet someone eventually, and that will all change. I'm going to go say hi to everyone."

"Okay," I say, pondering her words. She gives me a quick kiss on the cheek and then heads over to Kat and the group. When I see Preston leaving his seat and heading inside, I quickly walk over and steal it, smiling at Riley.

"Can I get you another drink?" I ask when I see that hers is long gone.

"Preston went to get me one," she says, looking to where he disappeared to. "But thank you. Are you having a good night?"

It could be better.

"I am," I tell her, nodding. "Are you?"

"Yeah, I am. It's nice to actually be out of the house besides for work," she replies, tugging on her black dress, bringing the slinky material back over her knees. She was born to wear this dress. It fits her perfectly, hugging her like a second skin, showing off every enticing curve. She has such a feminine, hourglass-shaped body, one I'd love nothing more than to explore with my tongue. "Thank you for inviting me, even if I did have to get Cheffy to close for me."

"You deserve a night off," I tell her, words I've said to her many times before. "Especially after the month you've had."

"I've drunk more this week in celebration than I have so far all year," she tells me, tilting her head to the side and grinning. "Hanging out with lawyers is turning me into a lush."

"Don't blame us—you own the pub," I tease, leaning closer so only she can hear what I have to say next. "Do you know how beautiful you look tonight?"

She glances down, blushing. "I clean up pretty well, don't I?"

I chuckle at her surprising response. "Yes, you do. I'm glad that you came."

"Me too," she replies. We share a smile, our eyes connecting and holding. Preston returns, bending to hand Riley her drink.

"Thanks, Preston," she says to him, immediately taking a sip.

"No problem," he tells her, then turns to me. "Dude, I didn't even know women this good-looking existed in our city."

He works with one every day, but I decide not to point that out. In fact, I prefer that he doesn't notice.

"Which ones? Want an introduction? Most are friends from law school, or my baby sister's friends"—I pause, looking around—"who is somewhere around here."

"I'd love an introduction or two," Preston says, waggling his brows.

I cross my arms over my chest and study him. "You might not want to do that in front of them though."

His brows cease their movement and settle into their normal arch.

Riley starts laughing and shakes her head. "He's going to need a little more help, I think, Hunter. Maybe you should give him an opening line or something."

"Can't do all the work for him," I grumble, standing up and patting him on the back. "Come on, let's go do this."

So I can sit back down with Riley and continue my conversation with her. On second thought, I glance down at her and ask, "Care to join us?"

She laughs and shakes her head again. "No, I think the two of you will do better on your own."

Two of us?

I need to clear this up straightaway. "We all know who I want, and I'm looking at her."

Her eyes widen and she swallows. I press a kiss to the top of her head, smiling against her hair. "Let me know if you need anything," I tell her, pulling back, my gaze dropping to her pouty lips. Those lips should be illegal. "A drink, or something to eat, whatever."

"I can manage, but thank you," she replies, amusement flittering through her hazel eyes. Callie grabs her arm and pulls her attention away. I turn to Preston, who points at the woman he wants to meet.

I've already slept with her.

Fuck.

Here we go.

chapter 12

RILEY

"YOU GOT ME A present?" Hunter asks as I approach him in his kitchen, gift in my hands. When I walked in, he was surrounded by a lot of his friends, so I waited to give it to him when he was alone.

"I did," I tell him, glancing down at the marbled wrapping paper.

"You didn't have to get me anything," he murmurs, accepting the package from my hands. He shakes it a little and offers me an excited, boyish smile, one that makes the long day of shopping, looking for something just right for him, all worth it. "Do you want me to open it now?"

The two of us are in the kitchen, surrounded by muted noise, bottles of alcohol, and a platter of food. I pick up an olive and pop it into my mouth.

"Up to you. You have a lot of friends, don't you?"

He watches me and simply grins. "Wouldn't call all of them friends."

"Then why are they here?" I ask, arching my brow and leaning against the countertop. "Is today your actual birthday?"

"It's tomorrow," he says, glancing at his watch. "Few hours to go. And they're here because I like them and have a good time with them, but that doesn't mean I trust everyone here."

"Acquaintances, not friends, then," I surmise, glancing around the house once more. "Your house is beautiful."

"Not as beautiful as you," he returns, not hiding the heated look he gives me. It looks like he's not hiding anything anymore. He's not toning himself down, or censoring me from his thoughts. He's not exactly pushing me, either, though. He hasn't touched me inappropriately, although we have gotten more affectionate with hugging, and he kisses the top of my head, or my temple.

Never my lips though.

At least not yet.

I decide to change the subject. "Who is into the gangster rap?" I ask, smirking at the music selection.

"That would be me," he chuckles. He shrugs. "I like hip-hop and R and B."

"And it's your party, so tonight we all have to like it?" I tease him. I actually don't mind the music; I just didn't think it would be his genre of choice.

He sends a wink in my direction. "Everyone else, yes. But you can ask the DJ for anything you like. Tell him I said so."

"Free music rein? How did I get so special?" I flirt. Or at least I think this is flirting. It's been a while since I've had to do so.

"I don't know," he says softly, eyes dropping to my lips. "I wish I knew. You just are."

I clear my throat, and turn to the crowd, away from those

eyes of his. "OMG" by Camila Cabello starts to play and I nod my head toward the door. "Callie is probably looking for me."

We walk through the double doors together, side by side. His hand casually brushes mine, and I pretend I didn't feel it. Someone calls him over, and he leans down and says to me, "I'll be right back."

"I'll be sitting with Callie," I tell him, and head in her direction. As soon as I sit down, she's on me.

"Hunter, Hunter, Hunter," she murmurs. "You are one lucky woman."

I turn to watch him standing, facing away from us, speaking to a group of men, and can't help but drag my gaze down to his ass. His is the best I've ever seen: round, tight, and completely bitable.

I wonder what he looks like naked. The picture I imagine has me shifting on my seat and squeezing my thighs together. I clear my throat and swallow a mouthful of the gin and tonic. "I need to go to the bathroom."

"I'll come with you," she offers, standing up. I've never really had a lot of close female friends before, and I've definitely never had one who wouldn't let me go to the bathroom alone, so Callie's offer has me feeling oddly content. She links her arm through mine and we walk back into Hunter's house, passing a lot of unfamiliar faces on the way.

I finish my drink and place the cup on the kitchen table as we walk past it. "Any idea where the bathroom is?"

"Nope," she says cheerfully, glancing around. The house is huge, and there're a few different doors we could try. There's a staircase that leads upstairs, but also a hallway with several doors. "Let's see what's behind door number one."

She opens the door, only to reveal an impressive theater room.

"What about there?" I ask, pointing to a door down the hall. Callie knocks on the door to see if it's vacant, but a deep voice replies with "Someone's in here." We both back away from the door.

Awkward.

"There's probably another one upstairs," I whisper, leading her toward the staircase. I'm busting to go at this point, and need to make it quick.

"Time to break the seal," Callie comments, snickering to herself.

"Just how many drinks have you had?" I ask her, noting her rosy cheeks and extra-happy expression.

"Just two," she says, with a silly smile on her face, then adds, "And a few shots."

"You did shots without me?" I tease, pretending to be outraged.

"You were inside, talking with Hunter," she says with a defensive tone. "You flirt, you lose."

"I was not flirting." I quicken my steps.

"You weren't *not* flirting," she replies, teasing me. "Just admit it. You are so into him, and now you have no excuses to hide behind anymore. I for one can't wait until the two of you finally fuck. I'm team Riler. Or does Huntley sound better?"

"Please, Callie, never say that again," I advise her in a dry tone. "And yes, of course I like Hunter. I mean, what's not to like? But my divorce just went through last week. Last week. It's not smart to jump into something."

"I know," she agrees, but then adds, "You know I'm just teasing you. Yes, I think Hunter would make you happy, but I see where you're coming from. You should do what's right for you, because you know what?"

"What?" I ask.

"I may go on about how hot Hunter is, but he's the lucky

one to have you, not the other way around," she says, reaching out and squeezing my shoulder. "Although, for the record, imagine how hot the birthday sex would be. Especially after over a year of no sex."

Birthday sex sounds fucking fantastic, but I don't think I'm ready for that. I'm in no rush right now, and I hope that Hunter is okay with that, because Callie is right, I do want him.

We find the second bathroom, but that one is taken too.

"Dammit," I groan, just as the door opens and a dark-haired beauty walks out, bumping straight into me.

"Shit, sorry," she says, blue eyes flaring. "I keep bumping into people everywhere I go tonight." She wipes her hands on her tight white jeans.

"Hey, if that's the worst you do tonight, I'd say you're doing well," I point out, shrugging it off.

She laughs, rubbing her nose with the back of her hand. "You make a good point."

I watch her movements, and it hits me exactly what she was probably doing in that bathroom.

"I have my moments," I reply, glancing to Callie. "Do you want to go first?"

Callie nods and disappears into the bathroom, closing the door behind her.

"Are you okay?" I ask the woman. I wonder if this is what I looked like when I was stupid enough to take cocaine back in the day. I remember the rush, the loss of reality, and the addictive yet temporary feeling of euphoria that the high would give me, but I also remember the rest of it. The way I hurt everyone around me, the way I lost control of my own life and who I am. I feel sorry for the beautiful girl, and I hope she's just taking something as a party drug, and that's it. I wouldn't wish a drug addiction on my worst enemy.

"Yeah," she replies, offering me a smile. "I'm good. I'm go-ing to head downstairs. Was nice meeting you."

"You too," I say, and watch her leave.

Does Hunter know people are taking drugs in his house? I wonder how he knows this chick. Should I say something? Or is this none of my business? I don't exactly have any proof, and I can't tell him how I do know about it, considering my previous drug use never came out in court. I still don't know whether Jer-emy told Hunter any of that, but he hasn't said anything to me. Callie comes out, and I quickly use the bathroom, then we head back downstairs and make our way to the kitchen.

Callie tucks her hair back behind her ear and glances up at me, her brown eyes filled with mischief. "So, do you want to catch up on those shots, or no?"

I study her. Blond. Petite. Unassuming. Maybe even sweet-looking. But the chick's middle name should be Trouble. "Are you trying to be a bad influence on your boss?"

"Maybe," she replies, grabbing a clear shot glass and start-ing to pour. "Or maybe I'm just looking out for you, because it's a party and you never let loose. You're always working, stressing, or overthinking. How about you just let your hair down and enjoy yourself for once?" I can't be sure, but I think I hear her mutter something about Hunter under her breath afterward.

"Fine." I catch the shot she slides my way.

"You doing a shot without the birthday boy, Riley?" Hunter asks me as he walks into the kitchen, coming up to stand right next to me. He smells good. I want to lean closer to him but re-frain. Callie pours Hunter a shot and we all clink them together in a toast to Hunter.

"Happy birthday, Hunter," I say, before we down the ice-cold liquid. I make a face as the taste hits me, but the other two don't even flinch. Hunter picks up my present that he'd left on the table and smiles to himself.

"I should open this now," he says, ripping open one side. Callie steps back and mouths "Kiss him," before disappearing outside, leaving Hunter and me alone once more. I watch, a little nervously, as Hunter rips the rest of the paper and opens the box where there are two items—hand wraps to wear when he's boxing, and a wallet monogrammed with his initials, *HB*.

I saw his hands in the pub one day, and he told me he'd been boxing at the gym bare because he lost his wraps and kept forgetting to pick up some new ones. I figured I'd save him a trip. I would always see his worn wallet, and when I finally asked him why he didn't just get a new one, he told me that his mom once told him it's bad luck to buy yourself a wallet. She told him that it's good luck for someone to gift it to you instead, with money inside, no matter how much the amount. So inside the wallet is a twenty-dollar bill.

"You are so thoughtful, Riley," he says, voice low. "I love them both, thank you."

He pulls me into a hug, and I rest my cheek on his warm chest. I'm glad he likes them, really glad. I close my eyes for a second and allow myself to block everything else out except being in his arms. "You didn't have to get me anything," he rumbles. "But those are the best gifts I've ever received. I guess the even better gift is knowing that you actually listen when I ramble on."

I laugh at that, lifting my head and smiling up at him. "I'm happy you like them. I had no idea what to get a man who has everything."

"Not everything," he murmurs, hand tightening on my lower back. I press my hands against his chest, but then he pushes his body away, putting some space between us. I take the hint and drop my hands completely, the two of us just silently watching each other.

Behind the lust, and the want, his eyes look right into my soul. He sees me. I don't know how it happened, or why, but this man in front of me really sees *me*. It makes me feel uncomfortable and vulnerable, but also accepted and not alone. It's why my guard was always up around him. Why I was so standoffish. It's why I didn't like being around him, yet craved it at the same time.

Sometimes you just don't understand what you have with another person. Maybe there's a draw, or a tether between the two of you, one that sometimes doesn't make sense, and I have to wonder why it's there in the first place. I believe that you make your own fate, and if you want something bad enough you need to fight for it, because nothing worth it comes easily, but why do I have this soft spot for the man standing in front of me? It makes no sense. Maybe connections hold no logic, no explanation, and maybe it's just up to you what you do with them.

Up to me.

Preston walks in, interrupting us, and saving me. "Okay, who has a condom on them? It's kind of an emergency. Some lube would be great too."

Nothing or no one can ruin a moment like Preston.

chapter 13

HUNTER

*I*F IT WOULDN'T HAVE upset Riley, I'd have punched Preston right in his face. After being his wingman and hooking him up with the girl he wanted, he comes and ruins my moment with Riley, and is now asking me if I have fucking condoms in front of her.

I sigh, gritting my teeth as I reply. "Go into my bathroom, in the cabinet on the top shelf."

Riley flashes me a look of amusement mixed with suspicion.

Does she think I've slept around a lot in my life? Because I kind of have. That doesn't mean I'm not a good man though, or that I can't be loyal to one woman. I would be to her.

"Thanks," Preston remarks cheerfully, disappearing upstairs.

Wait, where exactly is he planning on fucking this chick? I suddenly feel a migraine coming on.

"He's your friend," is all I can think of to say to Riley, noticing the judgment in her hazel eyes I know she's trying to hide but is failing miserably.

"Is he?" she asks, lips kicking up at the corners. "Because he seems pretty comfortable with you. And you did invite him."

"Only because I knew you wouldn't come without your squad," I admit, which is only half true. I do like all the staff at Riley's, and Preston has grown on me. Callie is hilarious too, and she's also friends with Kat, which makes her a friend of mine, but I don't really care who came tonight except for Riley, and there's no way she would have come alone.

"My squad?" she asks, laughing. "If anyone has a squad here, it's you, Hunter."

Feeling like we're navigating into dangerous territory, I decide to change the subject. "Let's get something to eat. I'm feeling a little hungry."

"Nice change of subject," she murmurs, amusement obvious.

Taking her off guard, I cup her face in my hands and look her square in the eye. "Don't know what rumors you've been listening to, but how am I meant to have a squad of women when wanting you seems to be a full-time fucking job?"

"No one asked you to apply for said job," she fires back, eyes narrowing to dangerous slits.

My temper spiking slightly, and without thinking, I kiss her. Not even a gentle kiss, no, nor a long one, just a quick, punishing, sensual kiss that has her lifting on her tiptoes and wrapping her arms around my neck. She tastes better than I'd ever imagined, her soft lips and taste making me hard as a rock. When I pull away, I look her in the eyes and say, "No one had to ask me to apply for the job, but I know I'm more than qualified for it."

She lets go of my nape, eyes wide, and takes a deep breath. I kiss her forehead, then walk to the dining table to grab a tray of food, needing a little space from her, then place it on the kitchen counter in front of her. The tension between us builds, neither of us knowing what to say or do next. I decide to leave the ball in her court, but she pretends like the kiss never happened. I wait until she picks up a sandwich first, before I dig in and grab one too.

"Did you have all of this catered?" she asks, licking a little bit of mayonnaise off her lips.

Fuck.

That kind of looked like . . .

Never mind.

I allow the change of subject, even though she called me out on mine.

"Yeah, I did. It's not bad, right?" I ask her, grabbing another sandwich.

"Cheffy would have done a better job," she says, lifting her chin. The twinkle in her eyes lets me know she's just messing around.

"I didn't even think of asking you if you catered," I reply, chewing.

"It's okay," she replies, picking up a piece of chicken and avocado sushi and dipping it in the soy sauce. "I should add sushi onto my menu."

"If you're taking requests, can you add some oysters onto there too?" I ask, flashing her a charming smile. "I love oysters."

"Consider your request noted," she tells me, just as Cleo walks into the kitchen, looking extremely drunk, and wraps her arm around me, bringing her face close to mine.

"Your lawyer friends aren't so bad, Hunter. And they managed to tell me a few good stories about you that I can bring up at dinner next time," Cleo says, looking pretty happy with herself. "But as for right now, I think it's time to make my exit."

I turn to Riley and watch as an odd expression plays over her features, and it hits me what this might look like. If a random man came up to Riley and hugged her and spoke with such familiarity, I'd probably be wondering what the fuck too.

"Cleo, this is Riley. Riley, this is my sister, Cleo." I introduce the two of them.

Riley looks surprised, and something else. Sad? Regretful? It confuses me.

"Nice to meet you," my sister says to Riley. "Although we already met in the bathroom."

"You did?" I ask, glancing between the two of them.

"Not officially," Riley says, masking her expression, and smiles back at Cleo. "I didn't even know Hunter had a sister."

"I'm embarrassed by her," I lie to Riley, getting an elbow in the stomach from Cleo. "She's my only sibling and a general pain in my ass."

"It's the other way around," Cleo tells Riley. "Can you imagine having a brother who looks like this? All through school I had every bitch in heat trying to get me to hook them up with him." She narrows her eyes into an evil glance. "And nothing has changed."

I shrug, claiming innocence. "I don't believe any of that is my fault, baby sister."

Cleo turns back to Riley. "He doesn't think anything is his fault."

"I can see that." Riley nods with a contemplative expression on her beautiful face. "Or he just charms his way out of it by making a joke or saying something so inappropriate that no one knows what to say or how to react to it."

"Nailed it," Cleo replies, shaking her head at me. "Finally, a woman who sees through your bullshit."

"You both going to gang up on me on my birthday?" I

ask, looking back and forth between the two. "Pretty sure today is the day you tell me about all my amazing feats and qualities, not have a group discussion about my supposed flaws."

"See, 'supposed,'" Riley murmurs to Cleo, who nods, repeats the word with finger quotation marks.

"He doesn't actually believe he has any flaws," my sister continues. "I could tell you some stories."

"I'd rather you didn't," I insert in a dry tone. I glance down at my watch. "Didn't you say you were leaving?"

She laughs and reaches up on her tiptoes to kiss me on the cheek. "See you at family dinner tomorrow."

Fuck.

I forgot about that.

"I'll be there."

Cleo says 'bye to Riley, and then the two of us watch her head to the front door.

Preston returns with a black box of condoms and an exasperated look on his face. "You have two upstairs bathrooms. Two. And they are huge. Seriously, how many do you need?"

Riley covers her smile with her hand, but the amusement doesn't leave her eyes. "Where are you going now?"

"To find the chick and take her somewhere. My house is too far. The car works," he says, pushing out his lips in thought. "Or the bush outside this house, perhaps."

He leaves and we both watch him. Riley openmouthed, and me just plain old fucking confused.

"He's . . . weird," I conclude.

"I only hire weird," she replies, turning to me and resting her hands on my chest. "I've never seen him hooking up before, this is a new experience for me."

"The bush outside my house?" I say, cringing. "Jesus Christ."

"What?" she teases, bracing her elbows on the black marble counter. "Never had sex in the bushes?"

"Not in my own bushes."

She laughs and pours us both a shot.

"Why? Have you?" I ask, watching as she licks a drop of vodka off her finger. I've never wanted to be a liquid more in my entire life.

"No," she says, tilting her head and studying me. "I have not. Is it a rite of passage?"

"Maybe," I reply, accepting the shot, lifting my chin and downing it. Jaxon and Scarlett walk in, hand in hand, and I don't miss the look Jaxon gives me. He likes Riley, I know he does, and he also knows her situation. She's un-fucking-available, and he thinks I should keep my ass away from her.

I'm trying.

"You two leaving?" I ask them, as Scarlett comes to my side, smiling up at me.

"We are. It's getting late and I have work in the morning," she tells me. Scarlett works in a library, and I know she loves her job. Sometimes on her days off she will drop by the office with cupcakes and baked goods for everyone, for no apparent reason other than that she had some free time and thought of us. "Thank you for inviting us, I had a great time." She steps over to Riley and pulls her into a hug. "I'll drop in for lunch sometime this week."

"Sounds good," Riley says, a gentle look on her face. "Get home safely."

She loves Scarlett—I think everyone does.

Jaxon rests his hand on my shoulder and says, "There will be a present on your desk on Monday."

Then leaves.

I call after him. "What present?" but I'm ignored.

"What the hell is he up to?" I say to myself. "I hope it's doughnuts and not something else."

Riley laughs under her breath. "I'm sure it can't be anything too bad. What trouble could Jaxon get up to?"

"You'd be surprised," I mutter under my breath.

Callie walks inside, an odd look on her face. "Preston just left with some woman, after making out with her in front of everyone."

"Be glad that's all you saw," Riley says sarcastically, shaking her head.

Callie laughs and then drags both of our hands to lead us back outside. "It's a party, people. Let's dance."

And so the moment my birthday hits at midnight, I spend it dancing between two beautiful women.

One, a new friend, and the other, something completely different.

chapter 14

RILEY

CALLIE AND I TAKE a cab home, which is how we got here because we knew we'd be drinking. Hunter walks us to the cab, opens the door for both of us, and then pays the driver our fare. He also says something I don't hear clearly, but it sounded like he told him that we better arrive home safely.

Who said chivalry was dead?

We wave at Hunter through the window, then turn to each other as the vehicle heads to my apartment, where Callie is staying overnight.

"I had a really good time tonight," she says, laying her head back and closing her eyes. "And after seeing Hunter's house, I think that was all the motivation I needed to get back into my law career."

I rest my head against her shoulder, hoping the slight buzzing will stop. "You should follow your dreams. I'd miss you though."

My phone beeps with a message.

It's from Hunter.

Message me when you get home safely.

Another message comes through.

And thank you for the presents. You are something else, Riley.

I smile to myself, eyes still closed.

"YOU'RE A MURDERER."

I lift my head, my eyes slamming open, the words that haunt me still lingering in my head. I cover my forehead with my hands and let my thumbs rub my temples, hoping to ease the pain. If only it were so easy. When there's pain inside of you, nothing can heal it but yourself, your thoughts, your own conscience. And mine will never let me be at ease, ever. I don't think that I deserve to be happy. I don't know how to get past it, maybe I'm never meant to.

"You need to go grocery shopping," Callie says as she barges into my bedroom. She's wearing nothing but a loose T-shirt I gave her to sleep in last night and her underwear. She doesn't have a shy bone in her body and, from what I've seen, is pretty much comfortable in any situation.

I yawn and move over as she slides onto my bed. "What do you want to eat? There's cereal and toast. And coffee. What more can a girl want?"

"I feel like pancakes, or ham-and-cheese croissants."

"There's ingredients to make pancakes," I tell her, rubbing my eyes.

She pauses, then says, "Who makes pancakes from scratch? It's modern times, Riley. I don't need to be doing that old house-wife shit."

I laugh into my pillow. "I'll make you some." I pause. "Only if you do the dishes."

"Deal," she says instantly, stretching her arms up in the air and making a sound like a mewling kitten. "Does your head hurt? I feel like hangovers are getting the one up on me these days."

"Happens as you get older," I advise her. I reach over to my bedside table and pop out two ibuprofen for her. "Here, take these."

"Thanks," she says, closing her fingers around them. "I feel a two-day hangover coming on. Last night was worth it though. Have you heard from Preston? We didn't even message or call to see if he got home safe."

"I'll send him a text now," I tell her, picking up my phone. When my phone beeps I assume it's a message from him, but it's from Hunter instead.

Good morning. How are you feeling?

Confused, that's how I'm feeling.

I know I shouldn't be looking at getting involved with anyone romantically, casual hookups or more. But Hunter is different.

I just *know* he is.

When I'm around him, I feel safe, I feel beautiful, and I'm always laughing. There's something there.

I'm distracted right now, not blinded.

I know what I can feel, but it's just so soon. On the other hand I need to think about how I would feel if he gave up on me, stopped being patient, and decided to pursue someone else. I'm not really being fair on him. I'm giving him nothing, yet he's still waiting for me.

"There's no rush with these things," I mutter to myself, sliding off the bed. "The pancakes, however, aren't going to make themselves."

I head toward the kitchen. She sits on the counter, dangling her feet off while I make her pancakes.

And then she does the dishes.

Why can't other relationships be this simple?

"I HOPE THIS BEARD trend never goes away," Callie murmurs the next morning, fanning herself with her hand. "I mean, seriously. Love me a good beard."

"Hunter has the best beard," I say without thinking. "No man can beat that."

I've always wondered how he got away with the whole beard-and-tattoos thing, but it's easy to see that at the firm, they're a family. There's no judgment, and I don't think that they care how many tattoos Hunter has.

I do find myself wondering though. Just how far down his body do they go? Maybe I should ask him. Or wait to find out.

Callie's eyes dart to me, and the smile she gives me is all mischief. "Really? I hadn't noticed."

"Liar," I tease, stepping to the side to grab a tea towel to wipe the wet glasses.

"Okay, I'm lying," she admits, puffing a breath. "But he's yours, so I need to keep my eyes and hands off him. Warning you that I can't control my mind though."

I laugh and shake my head at her. Callie can joke all she wants, but she's a good friend. "Duly noted. Can I ask you something?"

"Sure," she replies cheerfully, turning to face me, giving me her full attention.

"I know you joke about it, but do you think you'll ever actually go back to law?" When I first hired Callie, she told me her story. Law graduate, dropped out of her associate's position after a fling gone wrong with a coworker and the passing of her mother.

"I've somehow gotten lost," she'd said.

I know the feeling.

In completely different ways, two completely different people in different places in their lives became kindred spirits.

When I got lost though, I was weak and turned to drugs to take my mind off things. Callie just pulled away from her career goals and decided to work in a pub until she figured her life out.

I wish I could have taken her route.

She nods. "I do think I will. I just need this break for now, maybe for a year, then I will get back on track. It was always a dream of mine to be a lawyer, and I'm not ready to completely let that go just yet." She tilts her head to the side and adds, "Plus, who are you going to find to replace me? No one else will be this good, this attractive, make as much in tips . . . and don't get me started on my witty personality. I'm the backbone of the establishment."

"Don't forget humble," I insert, rolling my eyes. "And I'm pretty sure I'm the backbone, dear."

"Po-tay-to, po-tah-to," she grumbles, but her following smile lets me know she's just playing. "Do you know who is also pretty hot? Preston's friend Parker. Don't you agree?"

I shrug, not wanting to be mean, but he's not really my type. "I guess so." Parker comes in every week for a drink and a chat with Preston. Their bromance is kind of hilarious, and it's never a dull moment when he's around. "Are you going to harass the poor man?"

"Maybe." She shrugs, closing her eyes and smiling to herself. "You never know with me."

"You're a bit of a wild card, aren't you?" I say, studying her. "When's the last time you had a boyfriend?"

"I don't have boyfriends," she says in all seriousness. "Boyfriends are for high school."

I blink slowly, once.

"Don't even try to understand her," Kat says as she sits down in front of us. "She's got an ethereal angelic appearance about her but the mentality of a male." She pauses, and then adds, "A male whore."

"Hey," Callie growls, no heat in her tone. "I didn't think you were coming in today."

She reaches her arms out to hug her best friend over the bar.

"Me either, but I had a long-ass morning, and I needed a break."

"Wine?" Callie offers, but Kat shakes her head.

"I'd love to but I have to get straight to work soon. I was hoping for a chocolate sundae though," she says to me, smiling. "Please. I've been having a craving for ice cream all day."

"Are you pregnant?" Callie gasps, eyes going wide. "If you are, can I have your job?"

"No," Kat replies instantly, while I go and ask Cheffy to make a chocolate sundae for my friend. When I return Preston is also leaning over the counter chatting to Kat—and Hunter, who has now joined them.

"Hello, beautiful," he says to me, smile on his face.

"Hunter," I say in response. I look like I usually do for work, in all black, red bandanna tied around my hair like a headband, my dark hair up and out of my face. Callie tells me I have a pinup girl look to me, which I guess is the kind of style I like. I'm not wearing much makeup today because I was running late, just some mascara and lip gloss. "Having a good day?"

"Much better now," he murmurs, eyeing Kat's sundae that

arrives moments later. "I want one of those. Why haven't I tried one of these before? Can I have one?"

My lip twitches. "Just the dessert? Or do you want lunch too?"

I don't bother to pull out my notepad, or pretend to write down his order, because we all know he orders the same damn thing, even Cheffy knows his order by heart, but at least trying a different dessert is something new.

"Lunch too, please, but can I get the ice cream first?" he asks, a boyish grin playing on his lips.

"'Course you can," I tell him, amused. He can be such a contradiction sometimes, an overbearing Neanderthal some days, and others sweet and charming. "Do you want anything else, Kat?"

"I'm good, hun," she says, smiling around a spoonful of ice cream. "This is just what the doctor ordered."

I hand in Hunter's order and then return to them. Callie moves to serve some other customers who walk in, but I stay and chat a little with the two of them.

"So Arabella never sent me a bill for her services," I tell Hunter, leaning against the table. "And when I called up to tell her so, she said it had been covered and I didn't owe her a cent. Care to explain?"

"She owed me a favor," Hunter explains. "You don't have to pay anything. I thought you knew that."

"I don't feel right not paying," I tell him, glancing to Kat. "Are favors the currency of the lawyer world?"

"Something like that," she murmurs, lip twitching.

"How do you think I got your ex as a client?" Hunter says with his eyebrow raised.

I never thought of that. Huh. "Well, thank you. But you know I'd never expect you to do something like that for me. I don't expect anything for free."

"I know," Hunter replies in a dry tone. "We know exactly what you're like, Riley. It's not really a big deal. She owed me a favor, and I called it in. And trust me, she got off easy."

I blink slowly. Did he just use the words *got off* in regards to a woman he's slept with?

Yeah, I'm not touching that one.

"I seriously don't know how to thank you guys," I say, looking between them. "Other than giving you free shit when you're here, so don't even bother trying to pay today."

"Why do we have the same argument every time we're here?" Kat asks, scraping the bottom of her bowl with a spoon. "First, stop thanking us. We didn't do anything, got that? No one is keeping tabs here, you don't owe us anything, and we're not leaving here without paying."

"What she said," Hunter murmurs, taking off his suit jacket. He's in a light blue shirt today, and it looks good against his smooth tan skin. When he starts to absently roll his sleeves up, one by one, exposing his tattoos and muscular forearms, I can't seem to drag my eyes away from him.

"Did you hear what I said, Riley?" he asks, breaking me out of my Hunter-induced trance.

"What? No, what did you say?" I ask, licking my suddenly dry lips. I can almost forget what sex is except when he's around, and then all of a sudden it's all I can think about, flashes of him on top of me, behind me, and inside of me running through my mind.

"I asked if you're feeling okay. You look a little flushed . . . Do you want me to get you some water?" he asks, brow furrowing in concern. At first I think he's teasing me and calling me out on my perving on him, but I soon realize that he's serious, he thinks I'm not feeling well, when really I'm just flushed from looking at him.

Oh God.

"Oh, she's flushed all right." Callie smirks as she rejoins us. "But water isn't going to help. Only thing that will is some d—"

I cover her mouth with my hand, cutting her off. "Don't you have any work to do, Callie? Because if not, I can totally give you some."

I remove my hand and dare her to finish saying the word *dick*. Yes, it may be true, but she doesn't need to be saying it in front of the man who owns said dick that I'm curious about.

"Ahh, come on, we all want to know what she was going to say," Hunter teases, amusement written all over his face. He braces himself on the bar and leans forward. "What will help her, Callie? I'd be happy to provide whatever it is for her."

"I'll bet," Callie and Kat mutter at the exact same time.

"Jinx!" Callie calls out, and the two of them share a grin.

"Why are you guys even my friends?" I wonder out loud. I bring Hunter his dessert and place it in front of him.

"Thank you," he says, our hands touching as he takes the spoon from me. "Do you want a bite?"

"I'm okay, thanks," I tell him.

I'm working, and he wants to feed me over the counter with a spoon?

The thought amuses me.

When he finishes, I bring him his meal.

"You never mentioned what surprise Jaxon had on your desk for you on Monday morning," I say as he picks up a fry and takes a bite.

"I was right, it was doughnuts, but there was also a voucher sitting next to them," he explains, shaking his head in amusement.

"Voucher for what?"

"For a lap dance at Toxic," he says, referring to the local strip club.

"Oh yeah? Are you a regular there?"

He chews slowly, lips kicked up at the corners. "No. I have been there before though. Have you?"

I shake my head.

"Maybe you should use the voucher then," he teases, offering me a fry.

I shake my head again. "No, thank you, to both."

He licks the salt from his lips before saying, "I don't need it. Maybe I'll give it to Preston; I'm sure he'd enjoy it."

"Why don't you need it?" I ask, tilting my head to the side, eyes narrowing. What single man would say no to a free lap dance?

"I just don't," he murmurs, eyes raking over me. "Things change, Riley. You just have to keep up."

I clear my throat and glance away from him, his blue eyes too intense for me right now.

"How's Bear?" he asks, and I'm so thankful for the change of subject that I sigh in relief.

"He's great. I'm so happy to have him home. Coming home to him is everything."

"Good," he says, nodding once.

We chat a little more about how the pub is doing, and some promotion ideas I was thinking about. He tells me some funny stories about Yvonne, who he seems to be pretty close to, and his other colleagues. He eats slowly, as if wanting a reason to stay longer, and I pretend that I don't notice.

And when he leaves, there's money with a large tip on the table left behind.

chapter 15

RILEY

"LOOK AT THAT SLAPPERASAURUS rex," Callie growls, watching as the woman openly flirts with Hunter, batting her eyelashes and reaching out her bloodred nails to stroke his arm. It's a busy Friday night, and Hunter and Yvonne have come out for a few after-work drinks. Still in his business attire, Hunter is getting all the women's attention in his white shirt and black slacks. I haven't seen him touching anyone, or anything like that, but he has been smiling and conversing with a few of them. Not that there's anything wrong with that. He's single after all, right? I mean, technically. Yes, he's made his interest in me apparent, but we aren't together, and that's because of me. Then why the hell do I feel this stab of jealously every time one of them makes him laugh? What the hell are they saying that's so damn funny?

When did all the female occupants of my pub become fucking comedians?

Should I hold an open mic night or something?

"It's fine," I tell Callie, forcing a smile. He's not mine. "Can you clean a few of the tables for me, please? I'll get everyone served."

"Sure," she replies, her eyes still on Hunter though. "You're hotter than all of them anyway."

I hide my grin at her petty, yet oddly satisfying comment and continue to attend to all the customers until there are none left standing at the bar.

"I think tonight is the busiest night we've had," Preston says to me, shaking a cocktail mixer. "It has to be my one-of-a-kind drinks. The 'mother puncher' one I created has been a big hit tonight."

"I've noticed," I reply, giving credit when it's due. "Good work, Preston. I knew there was a reason I hired you, and I'm only realizing what that reason is now. Almost worth all the other shit you put me through. Almost."

He sticks his tongue out at me. "I'm the backbone of this place."

I roll my eyes. "Why does everyone here keep saying that to me?"

"When I grow up, I want to be Hunter," he murmurs, and I follow his gaze to where Hunter is talking to a beautiful blonde. "Chicks love him. Maybe I need to grow a beard."

I'm about to reply but a few more customers arrive, wanting drinks and food. With the live music playing and people dancing, the place has just the atmosphere I wanted it to, and I can't help taking a moment to enjoy watching my dream become a reality.

When Callie approaches me, I can tell something is wrong by the look on her face, her lips tight and her brow furrowed.

"What's wrong?"

"That guy wants more alcohol but he's pretty drunk. I think

he drove here too," she explains, nodding her head to a young gentleman stumbling on his feet.

"I'll handle it," I tell her, walking over to the gentleman. I notice he's spilled alcohol all down his white T-shirt and onto his blue jeans. I speak to him for a few moments and realize he is indeed extremely inebriated, and he admits that he drove here. His dark eyes are all red and glassy, and he slurs his words a little. I never let people drink and drive. I'd never have that on my already heavy conscience. One mistake can ruin and impact the rest of your life, and I wouldn't wish that on anyone. "I'm sorry, sir, but you need to have some water. We have a responsible service here, and I'm going to have to cut you off. Would you like me to call you a taxi so you can make it home safely?" I offer.

"I'm not even drunk," he lies. "I've only had a few beers. This is fucked; you can't cut me off."

I gesture to the Breathalyzer I had installed near the entrance. "You can go and check for yourself. It will tell you all you need to know, just blow into it with one of the disposable plastic tubes."

The Breathalyzer was my idea, and I think a good one. Instead of guessing whether someone has had too much, it gives us the proof.

The man starts to yell, and I notice Hunter coming over quickly, at the same time our bouncer/security guard does the same.

"Do we have a problem here?" Hunter asks the man in a calm manner. He gives me a once-over, as if making sure I'm okay.

"I want a fuckin' drink," the man says, eyes unfocused. "And she's cutting me off."

I slide a glass of water over the bar to him, but he slaps it off so it hits the floor.

"All right, that's enough," Hunter seethes, his teeth clenched.

The air around him turns tense, dangerous. This is not the playful Hunter I'm used to. This is him on alert, almost like he's gone into protection mode. Hunter is not a small man, he's both tall and muscular, and I can imagine he can be quite the imposing figure if he wants to be.

"I don't want fuckin' water! Give me a drink, you stupid bitch!" the man sneers at me, taking me aback. Sure, we've had angry customers before—that happens when you're serving alcohol—but nothing to this extent. A fight has never broken out at Riley's before, but it looks like tonight might be the night for it. I'm glad Hunter is here.

He tries to calm the man down, but the man takes a swing at him. Luckily, Hunter is able to move out of the way before the man's fist connects with his face. Bobby, our security, then grabs the man from behind and puts him in a headlock to subdue him. He and Hunter then escort him outside, all while he struggles and curses at them.

"Should I call the cops?" I ask Yvonne, who comes and sits in front of me.

"Yeah, probably a good idea, just in case," she replies, looking concerned.

For Hunter?

Have the two of them ever been more than friends?

The thought has entered my mind more than once, but I've never said anything or asked anyone, for several reasons. One, I don't think I want to know the answer; two, I really like Yvonne; and three, it's none of my fucking business. Why does everything have to be so complicated?

"I'll call them," Preston says, grabbing the pub wireless phone and pressing buttons. I decide to head outside and see what's happening, but when I open the door Hunter rushes toward me and tells me to stay inside.

"What's going on?" I ask, as he closes the door with both of us inside.

"He's just starting shit, being belligerent," he explains, glancing back outside. "Not safe for you to be out there."

"Preston called the cops."

"Good," he murmurs, hands on each of my shoulders. "Are you all right?"

I nod.

"I don't like the idea of you having to deal with shit like this. Can't you up your security on weekends?" he asks, scanning the crowd. "If a big fight broke out here, your one dude isn't going to be able to do shit."

"Yeah, I can do that," I tell him. "Thank you for handling that, Hunter."

"Wasn't going to let him talk to you like that," he whispers, then places a sweet kiss on my forehead. "Stay inside. I'll wait outside until the cops come."

"Okay," I tell him, and watch as he disappears outside again. My forehead tingles where he kissed me. I return to behind the bar, put on a smile, and continue to serve everyone their drinks. Hunter's right: I need more than one man here just in case something goes wrong. I make a mental note to contact the security company tomorrow. Riley's is slowly expanding, and I need to keep up.

"How hot was Hunter just now?" Callie whispers to me. "Every woman in this place wants him, and you're the only one he has eyes for. Don't take that shit for granted."

"I agree," Yvonne says, sticking her head in. Fucking hell, I forgot she was sitting there. "Hunter turned down more women tonight than men hit on me." She grins before adding, "And in case you didn't know, that was a hell of a lot."

"Shit, you weren't meant to hear any of that," Callie groans, cringing. She turns to me and mouths "Sorry" before beelining out of here.

I dare to look at Yvonne, who simply smirks at me. "I'm not going to say anything to him, don't worry. I'm with Callie on this one. I don't know what the hell the holdup is with you two."

"I just got divorced."

"Yes, but haven't the two of you being pretending not to like each other for the last year?" she fires back, eyebrows raised. "He liked you. He thought you were married but still liked you. Don't get me wrong, he'd never act on it, but that doesn't change the facts. Meanwhile, you knew he liked you, you must have, and you pretended you were still happily married to buy yourself some time, and then he found out the truth, when he was Jeremy's lawyer, which meant he had to wait some more. But now, all the drama is over."

Well.

I don't owe her any explanations, but she's right. Still, what comes out of my mouth is, "Yes, all the drama is over, and in a perfect world, I'd be ready right away to start something with him. I don't want to hurt him. But this is between me and him, Yvonne. I don't want to rush into any kind of commitment."

"Who says he does? Why are you thinking so hard into it?" she says. "Come on, Riley, give me the truth. What is the real reason you don't want to give him a chance? Because if you truly don't, maybe you should let him know that he doesn't stand a chance so he can stop wasting his time, and then you won't have to worry about it anymore."

And there it is. She's fucking right, but it's not her place to confront me. It's none of her business.

I'm being called out on all my shit, by a woman who is closer to Hunter than she is to me, so she clearly doesn't care too much about walking around the subject like everyone else around here.

"I'm fucking scared, okay?" I admit, and I don't like how small my voice comes out. "Yes, I'm intrigued by him, but look at him, Yvonne. I hear you all talking about him. I see what he's like with women. My life is in shambles, and I need to sort myself out, so excuse fucking me if I don't know what I want right now. I just don't want to make any more mistakes. And if he's the right man for me, he will understand where I'm coming from."

Hunter walks back in, and I stand up straight, squaring my shoulders. I don't have anything else to say to Yvonne, although I'm not angry, I know she was just looking out for him. I get it; I do. No one wants anyone to get hurt here; however, staying away is the best thing for me to do to make sure that doesn't happen. The thought of me letting him go though, or telling him to leave me alone and find someone else, really hit me, because I guess deep down inside I'm hoping that maybe at some point we would be together. I guess timing waits for no one though.

I run my hand down the back of my neck as Hunter stands in front of me, scanning my face. "He's gone; the cops took him. Is everything okay?"

I force a smile. "Yeah, it is. Thanks, Hunter. You didn't have to deal with all that, but thank you."

He studies me for a second, then comes around the bar and gently takes my hand, leading me back to the staff room. He sits me down, and lowers himself in front of me, and gently brushes his thumb along my cheekbone.

My guard is down, and we shouldn't be alone right now.

Especially when he's looking at me like that.

chapter 16

HUNTER

I DON'T KNOW WHAT SHE'S thinking right now, but the look I saw on her face earlier has me worried.

"What's wrong?" I ask, glancing up at her, her beauty up close hitting me like a truck. Did that guy scare her? Maybe she realized the shit she has to deal with when running a bar? "Are you okay?"

She nods, licking her lips and exhaling deeply, like she'd been holding in her breath this entire time. "I guess tonight has been a bit much."

I cup her face with my hand, and she leans into it, closing her eyes. "What are we doing, Hunter?"

"Nothing, yet," I whisper.

All night I couldn't take my eyes off her. It didn't matter who I was talking to, or who was trying to get my attention, I could always sense where she was. I've never been more drawn to a woman in my life.

"I don't want either of us to get hurt," she finally says to me. "I know there's something here between us, Hunter, I don't know what it is, but there's something. I don't want to lead you on though." She takes a deep breath before she continues. "And I know that sounds like I'm assuming you like me when you haven't even said anything other than innuendos and jokes and—"

I kiss her.

Words don't work with her; hints don't work; I'm going to give her actions.

She can't question whether I want her now, because I show her, with my lips, my tongue, and the feeling I put into the kiss. She doesn't kiss me back at first, but then slowly, tentatively, she moves her lips against mine.

She tastes sweet, her lips as soft as I remember as I fall into everything that is her. I break the kiss and rest my forehead against hers, while her fingers tangle in my beard, tugging gently. I open my eyes and look at her, detecting freckles on her nose that I've never noticed before. I can't help but pepper kisses over them. She opens her eyes and pulls back, trying to hide her emotions from me. When she touches her lips with her fingers though, I know she felt what I did, the tingling still on my lips.

"So . . . you like me then," she whispers, letting go of my beard and sitting back.

"Something like that," I murmur, lips kicking up at the corners. "I've wanted to kiss you from the first second I saw you, Riley. And ever since my birthday, all I've wanted is another taste."

She opens her mouth, and then closes it, like she's not sure what to say back to that.

"I need to get back to work, Hunter," she decides on. "Can we talk about this later?"

"Tomorrow?" I suggest, not wanting to give her any time

to overthink and change her mind. I'd never ask from her more than she's willing to give, but I want to spend more time with her. I want to kiss her again, and I want to get to know everything about her.

I just want her to let me in.

"I'm working tomorrow."

"Sometime this week then?" I push.

"Okay," she replies, standing up, while I do the same. Before she walks back out, I grab her hand and bring her to a stop, raising her fingers to my lips and placing a kiss on them.

"I'll hold you to that," I announce, flashing her a grin and opening the door for her. She steps in front of me, and I can tell she wants to argue, but she manages a nod, giving in—the first time she's ever done so. I walk back around the bar and sit down next to Yvonne, ignoring the surprised and curious glances from everyone who knows us. Callie can't stop smiling, Yvonne looks smug, and Preston looks shocked.

I don't care what any one of them thinks, the only person whose opinion matters has hazel eyes and is currently avoiding looking in my direction.

Still, tonight is a win.

It couldn't have gone better.

I wait until close, and then walk Riley to her car afterward.

"You don't need to look after me," she tells me as I open her door. "Preston is here. He makes sure we all get into our cars safely, and then we all message one another when we make it home."

"I know I don't need to," I say, stepping closer as she brushes past me. "I was here, and I wanted to make sure you're safe. Is that so bad?"

"I guess not," she replies, shifting on her feet. Is she nervous? If only I knew what she was thinking right now. "I'm just used to being independent and doing everything on my own. Even when I was married, I pretty much was used to doing my own thing."

"Making sure you get to your car safely is not taking away your independence, Riley," I point out, trying to see where she's coming from. "It's me caring about you, being a gentleman, and trying to show you that I'm not all bad; I do know how to treat a woman."

Contrary to popular belief.

She turns her body more toward me, hand resting on the top of the door. "And if I was yours? Then what? You'd be here every night, watching my every move like a caveman?"

"No," I tell her, then shrug. "Well, maybe, but not how you're explaining it. It's not to watch your every move. I trust you, Riley. I've watched you curb every man who tries to hit on you, and you're not even taken. It's more me just wanting you to be safe, you saw how it was tonight."

"And I've seen you flirt, so maybe it should be *me* keeping an eye on *you*," she fires back with sass, even cocking her hip a little, hand resting on it.

"If I was flirting, Riley," I say, lowering my face to hers. "You'd know about it."

She narrows her eyes and lifts her stubborn chin. "You spoke to pretty much every woman tonight."

"No." I shake my head. Is she jealous? I don't know why, but I kind of like the thought of her being so. It means she cares, and maybe considers me hers even if she won't admit it to herself just yet. "They spoke to me, and I was friendly in return. That's who I am. Not once did I let them think I was interested, or ever going to be interested. In fact, I told a few of the pushier ones I was taken, and we both know that's not exactly true, don't we?"

She looks down before giving me her eyes again. "I don't like the fact that I care who you're talking to. I shouldn't; I know. It's completely fucked-up."

"I like the fact that you care," I tell her with a grin, cupping the back of her neck and lowering my lips to hers.

"I love it, actually," I murmur against her lips, kissing her deeply and giving her a taste of what could be if she let it.

If she wasn't so damn stubborn and complicated.

If she put just a little bit of faith in men, in me.

It's me who pulls away, sucking on her lower lip, and even though her kiss left me a little breathless, I'd never admit that out loud.

I need to leave her feeling the same way she leaves me.

Although going by the dizzy look in her eyes, the feeling is more than mutual.

"Message me when you get home safely," I tell her, kissing her one more time, my hand trailing down the small of her back and up to her waist.

She nods, then gets into her car.

I watch her drive away, wishing I could be going home with her.

But I need to be patient.

More than ever, I know that Riley is meant to be mine.

Now I just need to show her that.

chapter 17

RILEY

"THE DAY YOU WENT Away" by Wendy Matthews plays on the radio, and I sing along to it while I wipe down all the tables. We haven't opened yet, but sometimes I like to come early and make sure everything is spotless. It's my moment of peace, before all the hustle and bustle of the day begins. I vacuum and mop the wooden floors and then make sure all the glasses and plates are sparkling, and that we are all stocked up with everything we're going to need for the day.

Callie comes in thirty minutes early, and we both sit down at one of the booths and have some breakfast together. I don't know how this became our morning routine, but I really enjoy it. On the menu today is smashed avocado, toast, and poached eggs. It's not as good as Cheffy's, because we made it ourselves, but it still tastes pretty good. I don't mind cooking. I'm pretty decent in the kitchen, although I don't have the time to cook every day like I used to.

"Whose playlist is it today?" she asks me, eating a bite of toast. "I really hope it's not Preston's."

"I think it's Cheffy's," I reply, smirking. "Love songs all the way today then."

"Why can't the men here have cooler taste in music?" she asks, sighing. "I like working to upbeat stuff, and not just Preston's pop music, it makes the day go faster, and I can dance when no one is looking."

"As if you care if anyone *is* looking," I point out.

Actually, I'm pretty sure she likes it.

"True," she says, chewing slowly and swallowing. "I really don't care. I like to think I'm a good dancer."

"For a pole, maybe," I tease, laughing when she looks outraged but then eventually nods, agrees, and murmurs, "Who am I kidding?"

Without so much as a pause, she asks, "So are you ever going to talk about what happened with Hunter the other night? I'm over making hints and hoping that you will tell me of your own accord."

I laugh, because she's been hinting so obviously but hasn't straight-out asked until now, so I kind of avoided the subject. "Well, we kissed. And chatted a little, and that's about it."

"About fucking time. How was the kiss? Months of pent-up sexual tension exploding into a clash of lips and tongue?"

The shit she comes up with.

"The kiss was . . ."

How do I explain the kiss? I've never been kissed like that in my life. He's so good with his mouth, with his tongue, and the way he was looking at me . . . It was the emotion behind the kiss that really hit me. I'm so drawn to the man, and I've been fighting it; just after that kiss I have to ask myself: Why? Yes, it's a risk, and yes, I could get hurt, but . . .

That. Fucking. Kiss.

It was worth it, and it's worth what will or won't happen.

No one has looked at me like that before either.

I see lust in men's eyes all the time.

But what I saw in his, it was something else.

"Perfect," I finish with. "It was perfect. He clearly knows what he's doing, and . . . shit, Callie. This is what I wanted to avoid, you know? How am I going to see him now, to be around him without wanting more?"

"It's okay to want more of him," Callie tells me. "And he wants you back, Riley, so you can do what you want. Kiss him when you want. Don't question or think, just feel."

"Easier said than done," I grumble.

Cheffy arrives, and love songs from the eighties start to fill the room.

"I feel like I need to tease my hair and wear blue eye shadow for this music," Callie groans, standing up. "I'm going to open the doors. Another day, another dollar."

I stand up and go and say good morning to Cheffy, then stand behind the bar and wait for people to start filing in. We don't get too busy in the mornings, but I like to be prepared, just in case. Callie comes and stands next to me and smiles.

"I bet you fuck him by the end of the week," she says, bouncing on her feet in excitement. "And I bet it's going to be epic. What a way to end your yearlong dick drought."

I sigh and shake my head. "That's not going to happen. You know how skeptical I am; rushing into things isn't going to help."

"Yeah, I know, but sometimes your vagina makes decisions, not your head, and I think this is going to be one of those times," she says with a straight face. "Trust me, I know a thing or two about that. I'm the queen of bad decisions, and welcome to my world."

I study her, blinking furiously, considering her words.

"I am not joining your world just yet, Callie," I say to her.

But fuck, it's tempting.

I'M RELAXING IN THE bath, surrounded by bubbles, candles lit and music in the background, when I hear a knock on my door and Bear's bark. I take a sip of the glass of red wine in my hand and wonder if I ignore it, will they go away? I only just slid into the warm water, and I don't want to get out any time soon. When the knocking continues, I get out of the bath with an audible groan, bubbles clinging to my soapy body. I grab a fluffy white towel to my left and wrap it around me, rushing to the front door. When I glance through the peephole and see Hunter standing there, panic fills me. He knocks again, making me jump and almost lose my towel. I decide to open the door a little, sticking my head out.

"Hunter, what are you doing here?" I ask him.

He gives me a once-over, a slow-spreading smile transforming his face. "Came to say hello. Perfect timing, by the looks of things."

"I just got into my bath, and I've been looking forward to it all day," I groan, opening the door a little more. "Can you come back another time?"

"I can wait until you finish your bath," he says, lifting his hands and showing the bag he's brought with him. "I got you food."

"What is it?" I ask, eyeing his hands.

"Mexican."

"I love Mexican," I tell him.

"I know," he replies with a wide grin, a picture of the emoji I use with the cheeky side smile.

My stomach rumbles.

I open the door and let him in, food winning out over my shyness of my being in a towel, my hair slightly damp in some areas. Bear smells him, then retreats back to his bed, I guess assessing him as unthreatening. Who am I kidding, Bear likes everyone. "The food smells good."

"You smell good," he rumbles, glancing over me once again. "I've never seen you with—"

"So little clothes on?" I insert, looking down at myself. "Let me get dressed."

"Take your time," he croons, eyes alight with humor. "No need to put on any clothes on my behalf."

I roll my eyes and show him where my living room is, waiting until he's sitting, before disappearing into my bathroom, where I blow out the candles and then put on panties, a bra, and my white robe. I'll refill the bath and try to have another one when he leaves. When I come out again, I've found he's already made himself at home, putting on the TV.

"That's your idea of clothes?" he teases as I sit down next to him. He slides over the food. "There's nachos, two tacos, and a burrito."

My eyes go wide. "That's a lot of food. Then again, you could probably eat it all, couldn't you?"

"I could," he says, resting his arm behind my head, running it along the couch. "So choose what you want and hold on to it for dear life."

I grin and take out the nachos, then slide the rest over to him. "Better be jalapeños on there."

He makes a scoffing sound. "Of course, who do you think I am, Riley? I know you like it spicy."

My lip twitches as I open the white Styrofoam container, grabbing a plastic fork and taking a bite of the cheesy goodness. "Thanks for bringing me dinner."

"You're welcome," he says, watching me. "I knew it's what would get me through the door."

I swallow my bite, suddenly feeling a little self-conscious. "You don't need to bring me food to hang out with me. You could just let me know when you're coming so I expect you."

"But then I won't see you wet, in a towel, cheeks flushed," he replies, and I can feel myself blushing.

"You just say whatever you feel like saying, don't you?" I ask him, realizing that he likes putting me on the spot. "No filter whatsoever."

"How do you get to really know someone if they're not being honest about their thoughts? There's no point sugarcoating who I am, and yes, I like to joke around and tease. I'm honest. And I like it when you blush. Not many women do anymore."

"You'd know," I mutter under my breath, eyes on the food instead of him now.

"Would I now? Been listening to gossip, Riley?" he asks, and I don't miss the amusement in his tone.

"No. I don't listen to gossip. I believe what I see with my own eyes," I tell him, bringing my eyes back to him. "Don't forget that you've been coming to my pub ever since it opened, Hunter."

"How could I forget, when you're the reason I keep coming back there?" the charmer fires back at me. "I remember the first day I saw you."

"I remember too," I tell him. He and Jaxon together are quite the view, how could I forget? Hunter is the one who caught my eye though; the first thing that went through my mind when I saw him was *This one is trouble*. I stick to my first impression.

I stare at the TV, which is hard because I can feel him watching me. I like it though. He likes watching me. It makes me feel—I don't know—special, I guess, as stupid as that sounds. I'm not used to having someone pay so much attention to me, be so focused on me. It's like he can't look away, even if he wanted to. Like just being near me is enough. With Jeremy, after the first few years, I kind of faded into the background. He didn't look at me like Hunter does, and the fucked-up thing is, I don't think he ever did, but I didn't have anything to compare it to, so I didn't know any better.

Maybe I still don't know any better.

chapter 18

HUNTER

I'M AT HER APARTMENT, and she's in her robe. Dreams really can come true. We finish eating, and then I slowly slide my arm around her. She's tense and stiff at the start, but her body soon relaxes into me. I don't want to freak her out; I know she's a flight risk, so I need to play this very carefully.

"Your hair smells good," I tell her, breathing in her scent.

"Your beard smells good," she replies, flashing me a cheeky smile. "I have to admit, I've been wanting to touch it ever since I first laid my eyes on it."

I take her hand and bring it to my beard. "All you had to do was ask. I just rubbed some oil on it this morning."

"You rub oil on it?" she asks, blinking slowly. "Pampering the beard?"

"Something like that." I grin.

She tugs on it gently, and I stop myself from groaning. "I wonder what else you tug like that."

Her fingers stop working, and she stills for a second, before throwing her head back and laughing. All I can do is watch and admire her with a smile on my face. When she laughs, she's as beautiful as I've ever seen her. "You're a fucking creep, you know that?"

Now it's my turn to laugh. "I've been called many things, Riley, but a creep has never been one of them."

"First time for everything. You like to stare at me and you smell my hair. What other conclusion am I meant to come to?" she says, lifting her chin. I can see the humor in her eyes though, and honestly she can call me what she wants, because I'm that infatuated with her.

"That I like you, perhaps," I suggest, tucking an errant lock of her hair behind her ear. "That I think you're gorgeous. Stunning. Sweet." I kiss her softly. "Sexy."

She glances down, her long eyelashes fanning on her cheek. "And what about the rest of it?"

"What do you mean?"

"You see what you want to see. Everyone has a bad side, Hunter. Everyone," she explains, closing her eyes as she speaks, as if she doesn't want to face me. Jeremy's comments about Riley's skeletons run through my mind. He never explained what he meant, but I know she's got some demons. Maybe one day she will trust me enough to let them out.

"I'd love to get to know *all* of you, Riley, not just the good parts," I say softly. "If you just give me the chance."

She opens her mouth but then closes it, clearly deciding to say nothing on the subject. We both turn our attention to the movie, *Wonder Woman*, for a few moments before she speaks.

"How long have you been single for?" she asks.

"About three years," I tell her. "I dated my ex for about two years, but it didn't work out."

"Why not?" she asks, no judgment on her expression.

"We went on vacation together, and I kind of realized that I didn't imagine myself marrying this girl. They say when you travel with someone, only then do you see their true colors, and it must be true, because I learned a lot about her on that trip to England."

"I've always wanted to go to England," she replies, her face lighting up. "Where else have you been?"

I rattle off the countries I've visited while she hangs on my every word. Her ex had money, yet he didn't take her anywhere? I want to show her the world and watch her face light up when she talks about it for the rest of our lives. I want to see everything through her eyes for the first time, and feel her happiness and excitement.

"Whoa, you've been all over," she beams, smiling. "I've only left the country once. There's so many places I'd love to see before I die."

"You've got plenty of time," I say, reaching out and taking her hand.

She glances down at it, unsure, but then gives mine a little squeeze. "You'll have to show me pictures from all your travels one day."

"Deal," I tell her, but really, I want to show her in person.

We spend the next few hours talking about everything and anything. Laughing. Learning. And when it's time for me to go home I leave knowing one thing.

My gut instinct was right.

This is where I'm meant to be.

◇

"ARE YOU . . . WHISTLING?" TRISTAN asks me, eyes narrowing. "What have you done, Hunter?"

"Or *who* has he done?" Jaxon inserts, entering my office and standing there, studying me, his hands full of paperwork.

"I haven't done anything," I tell them, my chirpy tone only making them more suspicious. "Or anyone."

"Seriously, I could hear you whistling from the hallway," Tristan remarks, sitting down opposite me and waiting for me to spill. "What's going on?"

"Can't a man be happy?" I ask.

Jaxon glances at his watch. "At nine a.m.?"

"You're not even a morning person," Tristan points out, which is the truth—I'm really not. But still, after spending the evening with Riley yesterday, I'm probably going to be in a good mood all week. She's letting me in. Slowly, but it's happening. I can feel it.

"I hung out with Riley last night," I tell them, smiling widely. "So I'm happy today. Sue me."

Not something I should probably say to two lawyers, but anyway . . .

"Did the two of you . . ." Jaxon clears his throat, trailing off. "You know?"

"Did we what?" I ask, my expression a picture of innocence.

"Fuck," comes out of Tristan's mouth.

"No, we just watched movies, had dinner, and hung out," I tell them. "Now you're both ruining my good mood. . . . Don't you have work to do?"

Jaxon studies me, then smirks and asks, "Is this the first time where you haven't gotten laid on the first date?"

I don't know if I'd call last night our first date. I want to take her out somewhere and put a lot more thought and effort into our first official date, but Jaxon is right.

I've always fucked on the first night.

I don't know what that says about me, or about the women I date in general, but I'd rather not get into that.

"Wasn't a first date. Just two friends getting to know each other a little," I reply, ignoring the rest of his question. "And while you're both here, did you hear about the work party Yvonne is organizing? I can't imagine the two of you dressing up."

"What's the theme?" Tristan asks, not looking too happy about the idea.

"Heroes and villains," Jaxon tells him, shrugging. "Yvonne wanted to do it, and it's something different from our usual dinners."

"I like our dinners," Tristan replies grumpily, crossing his arms over his chest. "Kat's going to be all over this, isn't she?"

"At least you won't have to organize your own costume. I'm sure she'll pick out something great for you," I tease, smirking at him.

"Who are you going to go as?" he asks me.

"I don't know yet," I reply, but to be honest I'll probably go as Iron Man because he's my favorite superhero. I wonder if Riley will come as my date. I could just picture her in a Wonder Woman costume . . .

Holy fuck.

"Did you see that look on his face?" Jaxon asks Tristan, like I'm not even here.

"Yep. He's a goner," Tristan replies, flashing me a look of sympathy. "Don't worry, Hunter, it happens to the best of us."

"Or the worst of us," Jaxon snickers, the asshole.

The two of them leave with that parting comment. With Riley on my mind, I decide to send her a quick message.

How's work? I'll be there for lunch. Feel free to save my seat for me.

She doesn't reply for an hour, probably because she's actually working.

Your seat is saved. Not too bad. We have some new things we're trying on the menu. Feeling adventurous?

Cheffy expanding his horizon?

I reply, still amused that no one calls her chef by his real name, whatever that may be.

Yes. And we need a guinea pig.

I know she's giving me shit because I always order the same thing, but I do like a challenge. I finish up at work and head over there, R & B music hitting me as I open the doors. Must be Riley's playlist today. The pub is about half-full, but my spot near the bar is free. I sit down and wait for her to see me; her smile when she does is everything.

She hands me a menu and leans over the countertop. "Finally, some eye candy around here."

"Are you objectifying me?" I ask, acting affronted. "I could sue you for sexual harassment. I'm just a hungry businessman looking to eat some meat, not to be treated like a piece of one."

She grins and rolls her eyes. "Speaking of meat, have a look and tell me what you think."

I glance down at the new menu, first checking that my regular option is still available before perusing the new section. "It looks good," I tell her. "The noodles sound amazing."

"Want to try it?" she asks, smirking at me.

No.

"Sure," I tell her, sliding the menu back to her.

YOLO.

chapter 19

RILEY

GRINNING TO MYSELF, I hand in his order, then head back to him. I know that he doesn't like changing his section, which actually makes no sense to me. He seems so easygoing, so adaptable and laid-back, I don't know why he doesn't like trying new things.

"How's your morning been?" I ask him.

"Not bad. My client didn't show up, so I had some spare time to catch up on other things," he tells me, reaching out and taking my hand. He turns over my wrist and runs his finger over one of the charms on my old bracelet. "Horseshoe? Are you superstitious?"

"Not really," I explain. "Growing up I used to ride horses in my free time. I used to enter riding competitions and stuff like that. My dad bought me the charm on my sixteenth birthday."

"Do you still ride?" he asks, his thumb now rubbing circles

along the inside of my wrist, sending shivers up my spine. I forget about the hustle and bustle around me, Hunter becoming my only focus. I don't know how he does this, just brings a calm to me.

"I haven't in a long time," I say, smiling sadly. "I should. I'd like to. I don't have much free time anymore. How about you? I don't imagine you have much free time with such a demanding career."

"Not really, to be honest," he tells me. "I work a lot, but I can be flexible if I need to be. I try and spend time with my friends and family when I can. I love what I do, don't get me wrong, but it doesn't define me."

I like that he's family oriented.

"And you obviously go to the gym," I point out, eyes raking over the muscles I can see straining through his white shirt.

"What makes you say that?" he asks, flashing me a cocky look.

I roll my eyes, regretting feeding his ego, but unable to stop myself I reach out and squeeze his rock-hard bicep. "Just an educated guess."

"I try to go after work every other day, just depends what time I finish. How about you?" he asks, glancing over my body. "What do you do that keeps you looking like that?"

"I'm not a gym kind of woman," I tell him with a grin. "I tried going a few times, but I prefer to do hikes, or scenic walks. I like walking or jogging along the beach if the weather is good. If worse comes to worst I jog around the block with Bear before or after work. I don't do anything else other than that, although I probably should."

"Well, whatever you're doing, it's working," he murmurs.

I flash him a smile and then pour him a soda. When his food is ready, I bring him the plate and then move to serve a few other customers who come in while he eats.

"How was it?" I ask him just as he finishes his last bite.

"Really good," he tells me, pushing the finished plate away. "I think you should definitely keep this on the menu."

"Is this going to be your new order?" I ask him, arching my brow. "Or are you going back to the usual?"

He studies me for a second and then replies with "The usual."

I start to laugh. "You have issues."

"Can I take you out this weekend?" he asks me, catching me off guard.

He wants to take me out, like on a proper date? I can't remember the last time I went on a date. I said I didn't want to go there with him, to do this, because I wasn't sure if I was ready. The timing isn't right, but then, is it ever? Wrong timing, right person. My brain is telling me to refuse him, to try to be on my own for a while, to sort out my life, but another organ is telling me to say yes, that I'd love to go on a date with him.

I let my heart lead.

"Okay," I whisper.

"Okay?" he asks, sounding a little shocked.

"Why do you sound so surprised?" I ask him, lip twitching.

"I thought I'd have to do a little more convincing," he admits, studying me.

"Are you calling me difficult?"

"Are you denying it?" he fires back.

"No," I reply, ducking my head to hide my smile. "Where will we be going on this date?"

"It's a surprise," he says, and excitement fills me. This is all so new to me, and it's both thrilling and overwhelming. I don't know what the fuck I'm doing, but maybe it's time I started taking risks. I only have one life, and maybe I should start living it.

"Surprise many women on first dates?" I tease, arching my brow at him and lifting my chin.

"None, actually," he says, scanning my face. "I'd better get back to work." He places money on the table, much more than what is necessary, and says, "I'll pick you up on Friday at four?"

"Sounds good," I reply, making a mental note to ask someone to cover my shift. I haven't taken any time off since I opened the place, and I know I deserve a Friday off. *Without* feeling guilty. "What am I meant to wear to this surprise date?"

His eyes narrow in thought. "Something casual and comfortable. No heels."

"You got it," I tell him. When he leans over and gives me a quick kiss, I don't pull away. I'm not usually one for public displays of affection, and I have no idea why I allow it now, but this whole thing hasn't exactly been in my comfort zone.

"Hope you enjoy the rest of your day, beautiful," he says, smiling.

I don't think anything could now make this day a bad one.

"RILEY'S GOT A DATE," Callie sings, doing a little happy dance. "I can't believe it. I have the morning off and this is what I miss."

"You should have seen them," Preston tells her. "They were all lovey-dovey and shit. In their own world. I dropped a glass and it smashed, and she didn't even realize."

"Really?" Callie murmurs, eyes going wide. "This is long overdue, and we all know it. And I'm happy to hold down the fort on Friday night, because I have nothing better to do, and I think I'd make a great bar manager."

"Why should you be in charge?" Preston asks, scowling. "I

should be the one handling shit while Riley's getting manhandled by Hunter. I'm the backbone of this place."

"Can you stop talking about me like I'm not here?" I growl, looking between the two of them. "No one is manhandling me. And yes, one of you two will be left in charge. I'm thinking of hiring someone too, as well, because as the place gets busier we're going to need a little more help."

"So who are you going to choose?" Callie asks me, hands on her hips. "Your best friend, or this idiot?"

"Your best friend is Kat," I point out in a dry tone. "And he may be an idiot, but he's our idiot, and he makes a mean cocktail."

"But can he handle multitasking and whatever situations may arise?" she continues pushing. "Come on, Riley, I was born to lead. I'm a lawyer."

"Well, you're not," Preston inserts, bending to tie his shoelace. "You left the world of law to serve drinks, remember? And what if a fight breaks out? I can handle that. I'm a man."

"Are you going to allow this sexism?" Callie asks me, stepping toward Preston. "I could handle it if a fight breaks out. We have more security on weekends now anyway. I'm not some delicate flower, so don't even try and play that card, Preston."

"Calm down, you two," I tell them, shaking my head. "I'll decide and let you know."

"Fine," the two of them grumble.

You'd think they were children, and I was their mother telling them off or something. "Callie, can you put a 'help wanted' sign on the door and in the paper or something? The sooner we hire someone, the better."

"No problem," she says, then turns to Preston. "See, she asked me, not you, because I'm more responsible."

"Or because it's a menial task and she has more important things for me to do," Preston replies, smirking.

I throw my hands up in the air and walk out of the staff room.

I don't know how I'm going to put one of them in charge without them killing each other, but I'm going to let Thursday me worry about it.

chapter 20

HUNTER

"CONGRATULATIONS ON OFFICIALLY BEING divorced," I tell my pro bono client, Laurie, who beams as she holds the piece of paper, of freedom, in her hand. Her husband would abuse her but in ways that never showed physical proof. A shove against the wall, a push from behind. He was smart and knew how to intimidate her. But she stayed strong throughout this whole divorce proceeding.

"Thank you for everything, Mr. Brayze," she gushes, a big smile on her face. "I'm so happy this is all done with, you know? Fresh start for me."

"I'm very happy for you, Ms. Karen," I tell her, walking her to her car. "If you need anything else, you know how to get in touch with me."

"Don't think I'll be getting remarried any time soon," she jokes. I can see how relieved she is, in her tone, expression, and body language. I share her relief too. It's always a good feeling when everything reaches a solution and your client is happy with the outcome. You'd thinking working in family law and handling divorces would make me cynical and never want to get married, but for some reason that's not how I feel at all. Maybe it's because my parents still have a happy marriage. Don't get me wrong, it hasn't always been pretty, or easy, but they stuck it out, so I know it can be done no matter how many bitter, hurt, and fed-up people wanting to break their vows come through my office door.

Laurie drives away and I head back to the office, preparing for the rest of the day. Yvonne is sitting at the front desk, her hair in a big bun on her head, looking like a beehive.

"What have I missed?" I ask, stopping in front of her desk to annoy her.

"Callum dropped by with Medusa," she tells me. "Other than that, nothing much. Kat and Tristan are out of the office, and Jaxon is with a client." She points her finger as she remembers something. "And there are doughnuts in the lunchroom."

"What kind?" I ask, perking up. "And I think you should stop calling her Medusa."

"Variety, although I don't know what's left. Are you heading to Riley's for lunch?" she asks me, spinning her chair from left to right.

"I'm not going to have time today. Going to have to have lunch at my desk," I say, glancing at my watch. "And doughnuts, apparently."

"I'll probably go grab some food from there. Although I don't think I'm her favorite person in the world," she says, tapping her pointed blue nails on the table. "I was just looking out for you, Hunter. I know that everyone here thinks you're this player with no feelings, but I know better than that. Yes, you might be a bit of a slut sometimes, but you have a good heart. And I've never seen you like someone so much, so I wanted to see where she stood with you."

I wasn't sure what Yvonne had said to Riley; I'd completely forgotten about it, to be honest, too distracted with Riley herself. "What did you say to her?"

She shrugs, grimacing. "Just asked her a few questions about her intentions."

"Defending my virtue?" I tease, my eyes gentling on her. "I appreciate you looking out for me, Yvonne, but Riley is mine to handle, and you shouldn't say anything to her. I don't want to upset her."

"I know you, Hunter, and that's the problem for me, looking in from the outside. You're looking out for her best interests, considering her feelings, but who is doing the same for you? Because I'm not sure it's her."

Her words hit me, but I know Riley would never intentionally hurt me, or anyone else. Still, putting yourself out there is always a gamble. Riley could decide at any moment to retreat, to go ice queen on me, and to push me out of her life for good, and there's not much I could do besides give her time and hope that she changes her mind.

"Nothing worth it comes easy, sweetie," I tell her, leaning down and kissing the top of her head. "Thank you for worrying about me, but I've got this, all right?"

She nods.

I flash her a smile to lighten the mood and then head to my office.

Some people believe in fate, destiny, and luck, and while I think such things play their part, I believe that if you want something you need to fight for it.

You have to make your own damn fate.

◇

FRIDAY FINALLY COMES AROUND, and I can't wait to see Riley. When she opens her front door dressed in light blue jeans and a white tank top, I can't help but admire her for a few seconds before my manners kick in.

"You look beautiful," I tell her, handing her a bouquet of lilies. Callie told me they're her favorite flowers, and I was more than happy to get some inside information. It's also nice to know that Callie seems to be rooting for me.

"Thank you," she beams, bringing the flowers to her nose and inhaling. "How did you know?"

"I have my sources." I smirk.

She shakes her head, but I can tell she likes them from the twinkle in her eye.

"Come on it, I'll put these in a vase," she says, stepping back for me to enter. I follow her inside and into the kitchen, where she pulls out a clear vase and fills it with water, places the flowers in it. Her apartment is small but extremely tidy, with no clutter anywhere. I wonder if she left most of her possessions with her ex, or if she's just not a woman who needs a lot of stuff. I didn't know one of those existed. I know my sister has a lot of shit; she even drags a giant handbag around with her every time we go somewhere, and I have no idea what she puts in there. Bear is asleep in his bed, a huge fluffy monster taking up most of her living area.

"Are you going to let me know what we're doing yet?" she asks, sounding a little apprehensive, but I can see the excitement in her hazel eyes. She might feel a little out of control not knowing what we're doing, but she's excited about it.

"Nope," I reply, offering her my hand. "You'll just have to come and find out, now, won't you?"

She takes my hand, and I lead her outside to my black four-wheel drive. I open the door for her and wait until she's settled before closing it and walking around to the driver's side. When I slide in, her soft laugh has my head turning, and asking, "What's so funny?"

"Nothing," she murmurs, grinning. "It just still amuses me that you listen to this kind of music."

"Tupac is for everyone," I say, deadly serious, rapping along to the lyrics from the legendary rapper, making her laugh harder.

When she starts to rap along with me, knowing all the words, I think I fall just a little more in love with her.

"Where the hell are you taking me?" she whispers, glancing out the window as we leave the city and head toward the mountains. "Looks like we're going to the middle of nowhere."

"Somewhere I can dispose of your body easily," I reply with a straight face.

She simply rolls her eyes at me. "You can try."

Ten minutes later we arrive at our destination. "Don't move," I tell her, opening my door, and then going around to open hers. "Close your eyes," I say, pulling out a silk blindfold from my pocket.

"Just carrying that around, are you?" she asks, brows raising.

"Yep," I reply, holding out the black silk in front of me. "Are you ready?"

She hesitantly nods, then closes her eyes. I tie the blindfold at the back of her head, then take her hand and lead her away from the car.

"Don't let me fall over something," she tells me, squeezing my hand.

"If you fall, I'll catch you," I say, more meaning to those words than she probably realizes. We walk for a few minutes before we come to a stop, and I face her toward the paddock and then remove the blindfold. I watch as she opens her eyes and glances around, the smile that takes over her face worth bringing her here.

"Pick which one you want to ride," I tell her, nodding toward all the horses in the paddock. "We're going on an adventure."

"We're riding together?" she asks, beaming, eyes alight with happiness. She turns to me and says, "You remembered," while lifting her bracelet up and touching the horseshoe charm.

"I remember everything you say, Riley," I say, smiling in welcome as the man who owns the horse-riding ranch approaches. He lets us choose a horse each. I choose a bigger, black stallion, while Riley chooses a stunning, pure-white mare, her face in awe as she looks upon it.

"It's an Andalusian," she says to me, like I know what that means. "They are really expensive. Look how beautiful she is."

"Very beautiful," I murmur, my eyes still on her as she gives this horse more attention than she's ever given me.

She climbs up on the horse like a pro, while I awkwardly get onto mine. I probably should have mentioned that I've never ridden before. How hard can it be, right?

"Are you okay, Hunter?" she asks me, bringing her horse up next to mine.

"Yes, why do you ask?"

"Because you're holding on to that horse for dear life," she says, tone laced with amusement.

I sigh and decide to go with the truth. "This is my first time on a horse."

She looks surprised, but then a gentle look comes over her. "Just relax, you'll be fine. Pull the reins right or left for which way you want to go, and do this if you want him to move."

She shows me how to click my heels in a way that will make the horse move forward.

"Okay, I've got this."

"Pull the reins like this when you want him to stop," she instructs, and I nod.

I don't want her to go slowly or not enjoy herself because I've never ridden, so I hope that I can get the hang of this thing sooner rather than later. We set off on our trail through the forest, passing trees and beautiful scenery before we make it to the beach. We stop for a moment, side by side, to take in the beauty before us.

"Thank you for bringing me here," she tells me, turning her head toward me. "You have no idea how happy I am right now. I'd forgotten how much I love riding, and this place is just amazing. I've never seen anything like it, and it's been under my nose the entire time I've lived here."

She looks so content and relaxed that I want to buy her the damn horse.

And the way she's looking at me right now, I want to keep that too.

chapter 21

RILEY

*A*FTER AN HOUR RIDE on the beach we follow the trail back. With the wind in my hair, I can't help but smile, feeling freer than I have in a very long time. I've missed this, so much, and now that I've had another taste I know I'm not going to be able to stay away. I had no idea that Hunter had never ridden before, but I've been watching him and he seems more comfortable now. I hope he knows how much this means to me. The fact that he brought me to do something like this when he knew it would be out of his comfort zone says a lot about him. I turn back to check on him, grinning when I see his eyes already on me. Playfully, I wink at him, and then let the beautiful horse gather speed. I glance back to see him catching up, although not looking as excited as me. I laugh to myself as we come to a stop back at the ranch. I slide off the horse and pat her head while I wait for Hunter to do the same.

He pulls me back against his chest when he does, wrapping his arms around me.

"Trying to give me a heart attack, aren't you?" he growls into my ear.

"Did you die though?" I ask, spinning around to face him. "You did well for your first time."

"It was that or fall off and die," he murmurs, being dramatic.

"Thank you for bringing me here," I tell him. "I had such a good time."

He smiles at me and says, "It's not over yet."

There's more?

Do other men put such thought into dates? Because from what I've heard from women at the bar, the best offer they usually get is Netflix and chill. I thought romance and old-school dating were extinct, yet here Hunter is, proving my theories wrong. We return the horses and then we get back in the car.

"What now?" I ask, excitement filling me. I feel so good, like I could do anything or try anything. Like I've been missing out on so much. Work isn't everything, or at least it shouldn't be—I need to get out and live and enjoy my life a little more. He's given me a little taste for adventure.

"Now we're going for another drive," he says, but instead of going back the way we came, he heads the opposite way, toward a four-wheel-drive track. When the ride starts getting really bumpy, he looks over to me, smirking.

I've never been four-wheel driving before, so now it's a first for me.

"Hope you don't get motion sickness," he says, reaching over and squeezing my thigh. "Because we're fucked if you do."

"I'm fine," I assure him. "Can I drive, though? Because this looks fun."

He chuckles to himself and finds a place he can stop so we can swap seats. I didn't actually think he'd let me. It's obviously an expensive vehicle, and I've never done this before, but apparently he trusts me. I put the car into drive and hit the accelerator, laughing at the way the sandy hill makes the four-wheel drive shake.

"Why haven't I ever done this before?" I ask myself out loud.

"You haven't?" he asks, sounding surprised. "Guess today is a day of firsts then."

"I guess so," I whisper. I had no idea a date could be this fun. I was picturing maybe lunch and a drink, or something along those lines, nothing like this. I should have known Hunter would shake things up though; he's not exactly an average man, at least not in my mind.

"Turn left here," he says, pointing. We come up to a mountain, and he gets me to park near one of the big rocks. Before we get out though, he leans over and gently kisses me, smiling against my lips, before deepening the kiss, his tongue tasting mine, teasing me. When he pulls away, he kisses my cheek, and then my nose, before my lips again. "Good thing you wore sneakers."

He chuckles and opens his car door, getting out. I open mine, but then he's there, scowling because I opened my own damn door, which only amuses me.

"I can open my own door," I let him know. I mean, it's a nice gesture, but he doesn't need to do it every time. I appreciate the chivalry, and I know he has some old-school values, but we live in modern times—the world won't end if I open my own door.

"I know," he replies, offering me his hand. "But I like opening it for you."

"Why?"

"Because you deserve to be treated in a certain way, appreciated, and because I'm a fucking gentleman, okay?" he says with a grin.

I can't help the laugh that escapes my lips. "A *fucking* gentleman, huh?"

"Yes," he says, stopping in front of a giant rock. "Now we need to climb up there."

"What would you have done if I hadn't worn sneakers?" I ask him. "You didn't exactly give me the best brief on what we were doing today."

"I'd have carried you up there," he says, stepping up onto the rock and giving me his hand. "Are you ready?"

"I was born ready," I tell him, my competitive side kicking in. I'm going to climb the damn rock, and I'm going to look great while I do it. He lets me go in front of him, and I can feel his gaze on me as I climb to the very top, him close behind. When I make it up there, I turn in a circle, my eyes wide.

The view is breathtaking.

On one side is the ocean, and on the other it's all green from the forest trees. The sky is a clear, deep blue and the sun is about to set. Did he time this just so?

"I don't think I have any words for how beautiful this is," I say, spinning around again, slowly, taking everything in. I smile and move next to him, and he tucks me under his arm, my cheek against the side of his chest as we both watch the sun descend into the horizon. It's kind of romantic, and a moment I don't think I'll forget, as we both stand in the middle of a giant rock, on top of the world. I can't remember the last time I've done something like this, if ever. I smile into his jacket, then look up at him, watching him as he stares at the sky, a peaceful look about him. Once the sun sets we climb back down, and I watch curiously as Hunter opens up the back of his vehicle, pushing the seats forward to make space.

"Climb in," he says, and I do as I'm told.

"Are you hungry?" he asks, starting to set up what looks like a mini picnic. He pulls out different cheeses, dips, crackers, cold meats, and wine. Holy shit, the man came prepared. With the back of the vehicle open, we still get the view down the mountain, and of the water. It's amazing.

"I'm always hungry," I tell him, smiling.

I never knew he could be so thoughtful.

We eat the platter of food, and I can't stop grinning to myself.

"What?" he finally asks.

"You just surprised me, is all," I tell him. "Thank you for taking me out today."

"You're welcome," he says, lying back. He takes my hand in his. Fuck, he's so cute.

Sweet.

I always knew there was more to him than he lets the world see.

Darkness takes over, and we continue to talk, getting lost in each other's minds.

I can't think of a better first date.

chapter 22

HUNTER

"WHERE ARE WE GOING now?" she asks, and I can hear the smile in her voice. She hasn't stopped smiling since we climbed back in the car, and I'm going to take that as a sign that she loved the day.

"To my house," I tell her cheerily. "I thought I could cook you something, and we could have some wine in my Jacuzzi."

"Of course you have a Jacuzzi," she says in a dry tone. "Wait, a Jacuzzi, as in naked in the Jacuzzi together?"

I chuckle at the panic in her voice, because she couldn't mask the excitement mixed in at the idea. "There will be bubbles in the Jacuzzi, and I'll keep my hands to myself, I promise." I pause, adding, "Unless you don't want me to. I can take you home if you like, but I kind of don't want today to end yet."

"Me either," she admits, looking down at her hands. "And a Jacuzzi sounds nice."

She looks a little unsure though, and I don't want her to do anything she doesn't want to, or for her to regret anything. I don't plan on doing anything more than kissing her, and maybe catch a glimpse of that beautiful body in the water. There's no rush.

"It's your call," I say to her, watching indecisiveness pass over her. If she wants to go home, I'll drop her off with a kiss at her door. I've loved spending today with her, and I think, or maybe just hope, that she's changing her mind about me. There's still the chance that she will suddenly decide this isn't a good idea for her, but I'm hoping our connection wins out, and that she's willing to at least explore what's here between us.

"Let's go to yours," she eventually decides. "I'm not ready for tonight to end either."

I nod, not wanting to react too much, but inwardly, I'm jumping for joy.

I COOK HER A steak, with a beet-and-feta salad and roasted potatoes, while she sits at my breakfast bar with a glass of red wine. I also aim to impress her with my mushroom-pepper sauce.

"I didn't know you can cook," she muses, lifting the crystal to her lips.

"I have to feed myself somehow," I tell her, lip twitching in amusement. "My sister will come over now and again and cook for me, but the rest of the time I need to fend for myself."

I want her to know I'm not a boy, I'm a man. I don't expect a woman to look after me or take care of me in any way. I can cook, clean, and I don't expect anyone else to do those things for me.

"I can see that," she murmurs, taking another sip of wine. "I'm impressed, Hunter."

"With what?"

"With everything." She smiles, placing the glass down. "With you. With tonight. I don't think anyone is going to be able to top that date."

"I will," I tell her, grabbing the plates and placing them on the countertop. "Tonight is not the peak of us, Riley; this is just the beginning."

She rolls her eyes and laughs, but she also blushes a little. "We'll see about that," she murmurs. She looks different without a bandanna on her head, her hair down below her shoulders. She looks softer, I think, without the more pinup style she usually chooses for herself. Not that I don't like that look though. I serve the food, and then we sit at the dinner table to eat.

"You never told me who you ended up leaving in charge of the pub," I say, remembering that she wasn't sure what to do about that situation.

"I couldn't decide between them," she says, putting her fork down and scowling. "If I heard either of them say they were the backbone of the place I was going to go to prison for murder. The new guy, Izaac, has some manager experience, so I left him in charge."

I go still, surprised. "So instead of choosing between your two friends you put a random in charge of them? Someone who hasn't even worked for you before?"

She cringes, nodding. "It was that or they were going to kill each other. Now they have some common ground—they both want to kill me, so they're probably best friends now."

I laugh at that. "And planning your mutiny?"

She nods slowly, expelling a deep sigh. "Yeah, it's not going to be pretty when I go in tomorrow. I hope they weren't too mean to Izaac, but Callie thought he was good-looking, so maybe she'll control the sass."

The look we give each other says that we both highly doubt that.

"Do you think he's good-looking?" I ask her, keeping my expression neutral.

She shrugs. "I suppose so. I mean, I was being professional, so it's not like I was checking him out. But yeah, I guess he's a good-looking man. Probably another reason for Preston to be angry at me, but Callie might cut me some slack."

She better not be checking him out.

"Fair enough," I reply, watching as she bites into her steak. "How is it?"

"Delicious," she says, licking the sauce from her lips. "I'm awful at making steaks, I always end up flipping them ten times and cooking them until they're dead."

I glance down at the pinky goodness of my creation. "Well, I guess I'll be making all the steaks from here on out."

She laughs softly, and then says, "I'm good at other things though."

My brows rise. "Like what?" I choke out.

Her eyes narrow, and she puts down her cutlery again. "You know what I mean."

"No, I don't think I do, why don't you explain it to me," I tease, provoking her.

She continues eating, ignoring me, while I watch, entertained by her behavior. "Already giving me the silent treatment?"

"Nope, just not going to take the bait. You like getting a reaction out of me; I'm not going to give it to you," she states, lifting her chin and flashing me a glare.

"Is that right?" I murmur, chuckling. "I'm getting used to that stubborn look of yours."

"I have no idea what you're talking about," she replies, lip twitching. "I'm such a sweet, amicable woman. I don't have a stubborn bone in my body."

"And I'm a virgin," I mutter under my breath.

"I might as well be," she replies, muttering under hers, getting my instant attention.

"What do you mean by that exactly?" I ask, studying her.

She chews slowly, swallows, and then avoids my eyes. "I just haven't had sex in such a long time, I pretty much can't even remember what it feels like."

"How long?" I ask.

She winces, shifting on her seat. "Just over a year."

A year?

She hasn't had sex for *a year*?

Surely that can't be good for her health.

"Wow," I manage to get out. "A year is a pretty long time."

"You're telling me."

Her tone is dry, her expression sarcastic. I can't exactly empathize with her. The longest I've gone without has been now, ever since I decided I was going to fight for a chance to be with Riley.

"Is that why you're so grumpy sometimes?" I blurt out, chuckling. I have to make this into a joke, because right now I'm imagining dragging her to my bed, stripping her down, and kissing her from head to toe, taking my damn time, worshipping her, and then going down on her and eating that pussy until she's come enough times that it makes up for her year of celibacy.

"Probably," she replies, and we both share a laugh. "It's laugh or cry," she admits. "I don't know. Jeremy stopped touching me when things went to hell with us, which was fine with me. But I didn't want to get into anything else, and I don't think one-night stands would be for me."

"You don't need to explain," I tell her gently, reaching over and taking her hand. "You've just made tonight a hell of a lot more difficult on me though."

"Why's that?" she asks, tilting her head to the side.

Fuck, she's cute.

"Because I wasn't going to . . . and now . . . Fuck. I just wanted to kiss you tonight. And now, after that, you have me wanting to show you exactly what you've been missing," I admit, putting my hands up in a surrender movement. "That didn't come out right. Obviously it's up to you what happens or doesn't tonight, but I really just wanted to spoil you and kiss you . . . a little . . . okay a lot, and—"

"I get it, Hunter," she says, tucking her hair behind her ear. "I don't know what's going to happen tonight, but I'm glad you made that awkward speech so I actually have to consider it and decide what I'm ready for."

"That's what I'm here for." I grin. "But yes, just know that I have no expectations whatsoever, and I'm more than happy to just cuddle you in bed if that's all you want to do."

The thought of her in my bed has me feeling really fucking excited, the caveman in me kicking in, and just wanting her in my space. I honestly don't care if she doesn't want to even touch me, I just want her here.

Yeah, I have it real fucking bad.

chapter 23

RILEY

I WANT TO SLEEP WITH him tonight.
Badly.

But that doesn't mean I should, right? Is it fucked-up that the fact he said he only wanted to kiss me makes me want to jump his bones even more? What the hell is wrong with me? We finish up our meal and then get ready to get into the Jacuzzi.

I'm going to be naked.

In a close proximity with him.

And I'm meant to act like everything is normal.

How do I get myself into these situations?

There are going to be bubbles to cover my . . . bits, but what about when I have to slide in? I'm just going to ask him to turn around, and I know he will.

"What are you thinking about so hard?" he asks, coming

up behind me and wrapping me in his arms. "We can skip the Jacuzzi if you like. Or you can go in alone."

"No, it's fine," I tell him, turning to face him, lifting up on my toes to place a kiss on his lips. "But you're going to have to let me get in first."

"Deal," he says.

Once the Jacuzzi is filled, he leaves the bathroom. I jump in the shower and wash my body off before I slide into the warm water, an audible groan leaving me as I instantly feel my muscles relax.

"Are you in?" he calls out.

Pretty sure that's meant to be my line, but anyway . . .

"Yes," I call back to him.

He returns, nothing but a black towel wrapped around his waist. I can't help but stare. His body.

Holy fucking shit.

He has his tattoo sleeves, then more over his chest and down his stomach. His body is built to perfection, toned, his abs so chiseled I want to lick them. He looks like he could be a fitness model, and I'm speechless.

I just stare at him like I've never seen a man before, and I haven't, not one like this anyway.

"Well, since you're not objecting." He grins and lets the towel drop. "Unlike you, I'm not shy."

I open my mouth.

I close my mouth.

He's . . . big.

And hard.

And yeah, he's fucking big.

Thick, and long, and it's looking right at me.

Also, plot twist, there's a piercing going through the head, just under the tip.

Someone has a high pain threshold.

I don't know what to do with this new information.

"Ummm," I murmur, licking my lips. He has no tattoos below his lower stomach, just strong thighs, calves, and a penis that explains his huge ego and confidence. I heard someone once say that lawyers are overcompensating for lacking in a certain area, that's why they want all the power their job gives them, but I can now personally attest that this is not the case.

"Well," I manage to get out. "That explains a few things."

"Like what?" he asks, chuckling. He covers his penis with his hands—well, as much as he can—as he slides into the water. Is that him trying to be respectful so it doesn't fly in my face? Bit late for that, buddy.

"Nothing," I grumble, not wanting to give him an even bigger head. We both sit in the suddenly much warmer water, watching each other. My breasts are covered with bubbles, and I can't help thinking that this moment, right now, isn't exactly first-date material in my books, but then again Hunter and I aren't just meeting each other for the first time. I see his gaze wandering over my face, my neck, my collarbone and shoulders, and then back to my eyes.

"You have such beautiful skin," he tells me, sliding down into the water farther. "So soft and smooth."

I want to say, *You have such a beautiful penis*, but I decide to smile and say "Thanks" instead. It's been such an amazing day, and I know he's not going to make the first move tonight. If I want him, I need to do that, and if I don't, we can spend the rest of the night with this boundary between us. Am I even going to stay here all night? I don't know if that's the best idea. I could always catch a cab home, even though I know Hunter will drive me if I ask him. So much for taking things slow—I'm currently naked in a Jacuzzi with him the first time I let him take me out. I can only imagine how things will escalate from here.

Shit.

I decide to stop overthinking and just enjoy the moment. I'm here now, and even though I'm torn, I'm still here because I want to be. I rest my head back and close my eyes.

"I can't remember the last time I felt so relaxed," I tell him, sighing in contentment.

"You need to take better care of yourself," he murmurs. "You're always on the go, you never take any time off, and you never relax."

"I know," I agree, opening my eyes. The truth is that I put my all into the pub because in some ways, it's all I have. "There's just so much that has to be done to get me where I want to be. And it's not about money, I clearly don't care about money, or I'd have hit Jeremy up for more in the divorce. It's more about proving to myself that I can do this, something of my own to be proud about."

"I get it," he says with a nod.

"You're successful, Hunter," I try to explain. "You have an amazing career, and you're one of the best at what you do. I want to be the best I can be. I want to be proud of my accomplishments and reach the goals I've set for myself."

"And you will," he says, sounding confident. "Just make sure the goals you're setting for yourself are realistic. There's no rush, Riley."

Feeling a little bold, I move closer to him until our shoulders are touching. "That's true. Things take time."

"And they are worth the wait," he adds, eyes on my profile. "I've never seen anyone so beautiful, Riley. I could look at you all day."

Heat rises to my cheeks as I duck my face. Gathering my confidence, I lift my head to look at him.

And then his lips are on mine, my tongue is in his mouth,

his hands in my hair, tangling gently. I move closer, positioning myself in between his legs but not touching anything except his chest where I rest my hands. His skin is warm, smooth, and I find myself wanting to touch every inch of it. It's me who pulls back, and we look into each other's eyes, my breath coming out in pants. He cups my face with his hand, wet from the water, droplets dripping down my neck. He watches them fall, before his tongue touches my neck and trails upward, licking them off me. I shiver, warmth spreading to my lower belly, my nipples pebbling in front of his eyes.

"Riley," he whispers, his gaze lowering to my breasts, his lips soon following. He sucks on them gently, licking and nibbling, cupping them in his hands. It feels so good to have his hands on me, his mouth working magic, my head falling back, my lips parting in a silent gasp.

And then I'm straddling him, his hard cock pressed up against me, my lips on his neck. He runs his hands down my back to land on my ass, squeezing the globes gently, exploring.

"This still counts as just kissing, right?" he asks, voice deep and husky.

"Definitely," I reply, smiling against his neck. I bite down on his skin, enjoying the growling sound he makes when I do, and then kiss along his jawline. When his lips find mine again, the kiss is deep, hungry, and passionate.

We may have planned to take this slow, but I want him so badly right now.

He's all I see, all I want.

And after a year, I think I fucking deserve this.

If Hunter wants to take things slow tonight, he's going to need a lot of willpower, because I'm going to do everything I can to have him.

chapter 24

HUNTER

*W*HEN SHE TAKES MY dick into her hands and
starts stroking, I know she's not fucking around. So
much for only kissing. What the fuck was I thinking that I was
strong enough to sit across from her, naked, without anything
happening? I guess I thought that she'd refrain, that she'd want
to go slow and wait. It's not that I don't want her, because, fuck,
I think I'm harder than I've ever been in my entire fucking life,
but I don't want her to regret it, or to decide she doesn't want to
see me after this.

So right now, I'm stuck between a rock and a hard place.

A really, really hard place.

But as she strokes me, I forget all common sense, all reason.
I just want to please her. It's been so long for her. What if I just
make her come and leave it at that? She gets her release without
us completely crossing the line. I don't know if she'll go for this,

but I can try. I stand up, get out of the Jacuzzi, and then lift her into my arms as she does the same. I grab a towel on my way out of the bathroom, then wrap it around her as I get her to stand in front of my bed. She kisses my neck, and my chest, until I can't take it anymore, so I gently push her back onto my black silk sheets. I run the towel over my body quickly, then throw it on the floor, lowering myself to my knees and spreading her thighs. I kiss her right ankle, and then up her calf, her thigh, then lick and kiss both of her inner thighs, teasing her until I hear her groan in need.

"Hunter," she whispers, lifting her hips up toward me.

I lower my face to her pussy, kissing around before licking her clit gently, then lowering my tongue. Her fingers pull on my hair while she lifts her hips again, grinding her pussy in my face, silently begging for more. I slide my finger inside her, and suck her clit, flicking my tongue out.

"Fuck," she grits out, moaning. "I'm going to come."

I continue at it, until her thighs start to tremble and she starts to moan loudly. I love the sounds she makes, the way she whimpers, how wet she gets as she comes. When I've wrung every last bit of pleasure out of her, she covers her face with her hands, breathing heavily.

"Oh my god," she whispers to herself.

I wipe my mouth with the back of my hand and smile.

She lifts her head and looks at me. "You have no idea how badly I needed that."

"A year's worth?" I tease.

She nods.

"Then I guess we have some catching up to do."

I lower my face again.

◊

SHE SITS THERE, EYES narrowed, arms crossed over her breasts. "So, let me get this straight."

I don't know how someone can be grumpy after four orgasms, but here we are.

"You went down on me. It was fucking amazing. But now you won't fuck me, or at least let me return the favor and give you head?" she asks, her expression a picture of confusion.

"Well, when you put it like that," I murmur, glancing down at my cock, which is hating me right now, still hard, and patiently waiting.

"I don't want you to regret—"

"I'm not going to. I'm not a child, Hunter. I'm in control of my decisions, and what I want. And what I want right now is to fuck you," she states, glancing over my body. "You're being ridiculous."

Maybe she's on to something here.

"Come here," I demand, then watch as she comes to straddle me, her still wet pussy brushing against my cock. "Fuck."

"Don't think so much, Hunter," she says against my lips. "It will be fine. I want this. I'm not going to regret anything, I promise."

She kisses me, working her way down my body. My neck, my chest, my stomach. She lingers over my abs and the V of my hips. When she reaches my dick, she takes it in her hand and then kisses around it, teasing me, before sucking the head into her mouth. She then takes me in, deep, to the back of her throat, a curse leaving my lips. She starts to suck, hollowing her cheeks, putting everything into it. Her gag reflex kicks in a few times, but she simply pauses, and then continues. When she starts to suck powerfully, and slowly, I know I'm about to finish.

"I'm going to come, Riley," I warn her, but she doesn't move her face away. "Riley?"

I'm ignored.

My hips jerk as I come, and she swallows with each squirt, sucking gently, and driving me fucking insane. I'm louder than usual, noises leaving my lips that I don't think I've ever heard myself make before, the orgasm more intense than usual. I fall back onto the bed when I'm done, while she playfully licks my cock again before moving next to me. I wrap her in my arms, kissing her lips and then her forehead.

"That was . . ." I trail off, my mind clearly not working properly. "Fuck, Riley. That was amazing."

She places a kiss on my chest, a small smile on her face. "It's been a while."

"It must be like riding a bicycle," I joke, pulling her closer to me. I've wanted her here, in this very spot, for so long now. I wasn't sure it would ever happen, if I'm to be honest with myself. I exhale, close my eyes, and just enjoy the moment. Eventually we both fall asleep, but it's not long before I wake her up, my mouth between her legs, pleasing her once more.

She's never going to forget this night.

I MAKE HER BREAKFAST—BACON, eggs, and toast— then drive her home. She has to get to work, and although I have the day off, I thought I'd go visit my sister and then hit the gym. I reach over and take her hand in mine, smiling that I can do so now without her feeling too weird about it.

"Well, what a first date," she says into the silent car, making us both break into laughter. "I'm serious though, Hunter. Thank you. I feel so relaxed, and spoiled, and . . ." She trails off, smiling widely.

And loved?

Because that's kind of what I was going for.

I walk her to her front door and give her the lingering kiss I always planned to.

"Can you take another day off next weekend?" I ask, pushing my luck. "How about Saturday or Sunday?"

She nods. "I can make that happen."

"Good."

She gets on her tiptoes and pulls my head down for another kiss. When she pulls away she says, "Message me."

Then closes the door.

I stand there, grinning to myself.

I'm going to take this as a win.

chapter 25

RILEY

"THE BETRAYAL, OH, HOW it still burns," Preston says, hand on his heart. "I can't even look at you, Riley."

"Preston, the guy is pretty good at what he does, admit it," I tell my dramatic friend. "The place is spotless, he handled a fight, and to be honest, I have a lot less work than I usually do."

"He also got the phone number of a chick I was checking out," Preston argues, crossing his arms over his chest. "He's not that good-looking, is he?"

"Um, I can hear you both," Izaac points out, coming to stand next to me. I kind of lied to Hunter, because Izaac is fucking hot, and I noticed it the second he walked in.

"Sorry, Izaac," I say to him. "These two wanted to be left in charge, and I let you be manager instead, and let's say I won't be hearing the end of it until I'm dead."

"I'll write it on your headstone," Callie adds, joining the conversation. "It will read 'Riley McMahon, owner of Riley's pub and a traitor.'"

I flash Izaac an *I told you* look, and he simply chuckles and turns to Preston. "If you want a chick, tell me and I'll back off. And I'll do the same for you. Deal?"

"I didn't realize Riley's sidelined as a brothel," I whisper under my breath, then turn to Callie. "Come on, how long are you going to be mad for? I couldn't choose between the two of you. You are both amazing. But look at it this way, I've made your jobs easier, because if there's any problems and I'm not here, it's now Izaac's problem."

"Thanks," Izaac mutters in a dry tone.

"You're welcome," I tell him, patting him on the shoulder. "And welcome to the family."

Callie slides up next to him and winks. "Don't think *family* is the right word here."

Preston studies me. "So are you going to tell us how your date went or are you going to keep us all in suspense?"

"What do you want to know?" I ask them all warily, leaning back against the counter. "We went horseback riding, had a picnic, and then went back to his place, where he cooked me dinner."

"Whoa, he's good," Preston comments, looking impressed. "Horseback riding? You would have eaten that shit up."

"No shit," Callie adds, sharing a look with Preston. "I knew he'd nail the date. There's no way he'd fuck up the first real chance you gave him."

"Agreed," Preston remarks, clapping his hands together. "So, does this mean you guys are together or what? Is this shit official?"

"Okay, let's not get ahead of ourselves," I tell them, rolling my eyes. "It was one date, and I'm not in any rush, remember?"

"Did you fuck him?" Callie asks, straight-out nosy.

"No," I reply with a straight face, because technically, I didn't. And they don't need to know all my business. No one does. "So that means you lose your stupid little bet."

"Prude," she snickers, but then wraps me in a warm hug. "I'm glad you're opening yourself up to possibilities. I'm proud of you. Even if I'm still angry at you."

I hug her back and say, "Thank you, and I know you are. But you will get over it."

Preston wraps his arm around me as soon as Callie lets go. "I suppose he's not that bad."

"Hunter or Izaac?"

"Both of them," he says, kissing the top of my head. "As long as you're happy, I'm happy."

"Does that mean you're not angry anymore?" I ask, snuggling into him.

"Nope," he replies, letting go of me and walking away.

Tough crowd.

Izaac removes his sweater, his T-shirt riding up with the movement, exposing a pretty decent set of abs.

No regrets.

My phone beeps with a message. It's from Hunter.

How did the mutiny go?

I think I handled it. Although apparently "traitor" will be written on my headstone when I die.

Let me guess. Callie?

I laugh and reply:

You got it. Are you at the gym on your phone?

Maybe.

Are you going to send me a gym pic?

No.

I laugh and type back:

Why not?

Because I'm not a douche.

I laugh to myself and type back furiously:

I guess I'll have to see you flex in the flesh.

Looking forward to it, beautiful.

Warmth fills me. I'm slowly letting him in through the cracks. Let's just hope it's the right decision.

NEXT WEEKEND ARRIVES, AND Hunter and I decide to stay in after both having big weeks. Hunter cooks dinner for us, and we watch movies and cuddle. It's nice, and it feels natural somehow.

"You have really cute feet, they're all small and pretty," he tells me, out of nowhere.

"Ew," I reply, moving my feet when he goes to try and touch them. "Don't touch my feet, or look at them."

"Why not?" he asks, laughing. "They're just feet."

"Feet are yuck," I tell him, glancing down at mine, glad I got a pedicure on my lunch break the other day. "And if you have some foot fetish, you're shit out of luck because if you try to kiss my toes I'm going to kick you in the face."

He throws his head back and laughs, so I tug down on his beard until his face is level with mine.

"That escalated from a simple compliment," he says, scanning my eyes.

"Apparently everything with us will escalate quickly," I reply, kissing his lips.

He cups my face with his hands. "As long as you're not going to change your mind."

"I'm here, aren't I?" I reply, arching my brow. I don't know how else to reply to that, because you never know what can happen. I don't know, and neither does he. Maybe he will realize this isn't what he wants—you never know. This is why no one wants to fall in love or be vulnerable anymore. It's like you're trying to get to know someone, but without fully opening up or giving yourself to them, because then they have the power to hurt you. I don't want to get hurt again. I chose wrong the first time, and I sure as hell don't want to choose wrong again. I don't want to hurt him either. There's a lot going on though, my divorce for one, but I know that if two people want to make it work, they can.

We just need to both want it badly enough, but how do you know if you do so early?

I don't know.

I'm just going with the flow right now, trusting my gut and hoping it doesn't lead me astray.

"Yes, you are," he murmurs, and I decide to change the subject.

"How's work? What cases are you working on right now?" I ask.

"Nothing too interesting," he replies, gripping me by the waist and pulling me closer. "A few straightforward divorces. There's one with an ugly custody battle, so I'm working hard to make sure the father gets equal access to his kids."

"It must be draining sometimes," I tell him. "And a lot of pressure."

"Yeah," he agrees, nodding. "Definitely. I want to help everyone, you know? But it doesn't always work out like that."

I kiss his beard.

"Did you just kiss my beard?" he asks, body shaking as he starts to laugh. "In the middle of a serious conversation?"

I nuzzle his cheek. "I like you, Hunter. I mean, at first I thought you were a womanizer and couldn't take anything seriously." I pause, puffing out a breath. "And well, you kind of are, and you don't, but there's so much more to you. I just like being around you. I like you, I like your beard, and I like spending time with you."

"I like spending time with you too, Riley," he says in a deep tone. "I've been looking forward to seeing you all week. Seeing you at lunch is good, but kind of not cutting it anymore."

"I know what you mean," I reply, sighing. I kiss the lobe of his ear and smile when I feel the shudder that overcomes him. "Let's go to bed."

"Okay," he replies, turning off the TV.

I like that it didn't take much convincing.

I laugh when he picks me up and carries me bride-style to his room, lifting me like I don't weigh a thing.

He kisses me and places me on the bed, pulling off his white

T-shirt so he's standing before me in nothing but gray sweat-pants.

I love those sweatpants.

"You don't wear those out of the house, do you?" I ask, the thought suddenly hitting me as I eye the outline of his cock that is clearly visible.

"Yeah, why?" he asks, glancing down. "I've worn them to the gym before, or just if I'm running into the supermarket or something."

"It's the equivalent of me going out in a thong and white leggings," I tell him, smirking. "And no, I'm not even joking. It's one of the sluttiest things men can wear."

"Do you really want to get into a debate about this right now?" he asks, sliding his thumbs underneath the waistband of his sweats, teasing.

"Not really," I murmur, eyes on his cock. "Remove them."

"You making demands now, Riley?" he asks, unable to hide his amusement. He slides his pants down a little, enough to see the delicious V, not enough to see his cock.

"Keep going," I say, licking my lips. I lose all my inhibitions around him, all my shyness disappearing, too turned on to care. I just want him. We didn't fuck last time, and it's all I've been able to think about since. He wanted to wait, and I waited an extra week. It might not sound like much, but trust me, it was the longest week of my life.

He brings them down a little more, his cock finally making an appearance as he slides the material over it. And then he's naked, and my eyes are having a fucking feast as I take him in from head to toe. I make a sound in the back of my throat, a sound of want.

"Come closer," I plead, wanting him.

He steps forward until his cock is within reach, my fingers

reaching out to stroke him a few times before bringing him to my lips. Opening my mouth, I suck him in as deep as I can, taking him to the back of my throat, his pleasure taking priority over breathing.

"Fuck," he groans, fingers threading in my hair as he watches me. "I want to taste you." He pulls away from me, climbing onto the bed and undressing me quickly. As soon as my red lace panties are off, his mouth is on me, licking, tasting, and sucking, driving me crazy.

"I want you to fuck me, Hunter," I tell him, just needing to feel him. It's been so fucking long, and I'm glad I waited for him, even if I didn't realize that's what I was doing. He ignores me, of course, licking my clit until I can't fight my orgasm anymore, moaning his name as the pleasure consumes me. Before I come back to myself, he slowly slides into me. He's so big, but I'm so wet that it feels good. I pull his lips down on mine, kissing him deeply as he starts to gently thrust in and out of me.

This is what I've been missing.

I won't be making that mistake again.

chapter 26

HUNTER

SHE'S SO WET AND tight there's no way I'm going to last as long as I want to, but I make sure she comes again before I let myself lose control.

Ladies first, always.

I pull out after I've finished, then realize something. "Are you on the pill? Fuck, I should have asked you this before. I'm sorry."

I'm normally much more responsible than this, and I usually use condoms, but I lost fucking control.

"Yeah, I am," she replies, resting her head on my chest as I lay down next to her. "And I'm clean. I got checked after I got separated, since I heard rumors of him cheating."

"I'm good too," I assure her. I got checked out a few weeks back.

"Then we're good," she says, eyes on me. "And I'm going to want to do that again."

I chuckle, and then I give her a soft, slow kiss. "We'll be doing that a few more times tonight, Riley, don't you worry. I'm only just getting started."

I roll on top of her, pinning her arms up above her head with my wrist.

I smile as my lips descend on her neck.

"I'M GOING TO FUCKING kill you" are the words I wake up to.

I open one of my eyes to see a very unhappy Riley sitting on the bed next to me, one leg folded under her. She's wearing my T-shirt and nothing else, her dark hair messily framing her face. Her hand is on her neck.

"You're meant to wake up sated and smiling after all the sex we had last night," I say sleepily, thinking it's only fair to share the rules with her.

She removes her hand and shows me her neck. "Look what you've done, Hunter. Are we back in high school?"

"Shit," I groan, raising my head to inspect the damage. I never meant to intentionally mark her—I agree, it's not a good look—but it's not like I was thinking about it when the two of us were mindlessly, uninhibitedly fucking all night. I didn't think, I just felt, and wanted to please her, my animalistic side taking over. "I didn't mean to."

"I'm going to have to cover it up with makeup." She sighs.

"Well, it was a full moon last night, I guess you just brought out the beast in me," I tell her, grinning, trying to cute my way out of this. "Come here, let me spoon you."

She lays down next to me, still grumpy. "I knew you were sucking too hard, that's why I gently pushed your face away at one point."

I freeze. "Oh, is that why you punched me in the face?"

"What do you mean?" she asks, yawning. "I gently swatted your face aside, because I knew you were going to leave a mark, and I was trying to avoid it."

"Babe, you full on hit me in the face," I tell her, rubbing my cheek. "It hurt. That was not a gentle swat."

"Oh," she murmurs, sounding surprised. "In my mind, it was gentle."

"It wasn't."

She starts to giggle. "So in the middle of you fucking me from behind, I turned around and hit you in the face as you were sucking my neck."

"Pretty much," I agree, remembering the moment.

"Guess I hit you too late though," she points out in a dry, sarcastic tone. "Considering the damage was already done."

"Should have hit me sooner."

She laughs.

I grin.

And then, we spoon.

chapter 27

RILEY

"DO YOU KNOW MANY of my friends try to get me to introduce you to them?" Devon says, cringing. "Seriously. It's fucked."

"It's not my fault," I tell him, lifting my chin. "I don't even talk to any of your friends. Four years younger seems like a lifetime."

"I'm more mature than you," my cousin says, smirking.

"Just because you're growing facial hair doesn't make you more mature," I deadpan.

His lips tighten. "You're a jerk."

"Must run in the family."

We share a grin.

"I'm going riding, do you want to come?" I ask, nodding toward the stables.

He nods, following my line of sight. "I'd love to. As long as you don't get me killed."

I still. "How would I do that?"

He turns to me, eyes bare of all emotion. Empty. Dead.

"You killed me, Riley. Why?"

"Devon?" I whisper, the world changing around me, the pad-dock turning into something else, a memory. "I'm sorry."

I wake up sobbing, tears running down my cheeks, and only then do I remember where I am. At Hunter's, and he has his arms wrapped around me, rocking me back and forth, asking me what is wrong.

"I had a bad dream," I tell him, trying to get myself under control. "I'm sorry."

I don't know if I'm saying it to him, or Devon, maybe both.

"Who is Devon?" he asks me gently, only making me cry harder. I don't want to talk about Devon, or my demons that haunt me whenever I'm weak and let them win. I don't want Hunter to know what happened, because then he'll hate me too and think I'm a bad person. When he repeats the question though, I find myself answering.

"My cousin," I reply, covering my face with my hands. "He was my cousin. My only cousin, actually. We were really close growing up."

"What happened to him?" he asks, kissing my forehead. "If you don't want to talk about it, it's okay."

"He died in a car crash," I tell him.

What I don't tell him is that he was drunk when he crashed.

Or that it was me who bought him the alcohol in the first place.

He was nineteen.

"I'm sorry," he whispers, stroking my back, comforting me.

I haven't spoken about what happened with anyone except my parents, and even they've learned not to bring it up. I told

Jeremy what happened, and he used it against me whenever he could, even calling me a murderer in a fight we had.

I loved Devon like a brother, and when he asked me to buy him and his boyfriend drinks for a party he was going to, I didn't think anything of it. Everyone drinks at that age, or at least that's how I justify it. I was twenty-three—the cool, older cousin, and I did as he asked.

It was the worst mistake of my life.

Everything changed after Devon died. His parents wouldn't talk to me anymore, and I stopped going to their pub. Eventually, they forgave me, but things were never the same. Not only did I lose my cousin, I lost my aunt and uncle too. Things were rough with my parents for a while, but now we are stronger than ever.

If I could go back in time, I'd never buy him that alcohol. I'd go with him to the party and make sure I was there to drive him home. I'd do anything, *anything*, to change the events of that night. I'd make a deal with the devil. I'd take his place. Anything.

But I can't, and now I'm stuck with memories and guilt. And utter sadness. I made a mistake that I will be paying for for the rest of my life.

He always finds me when I'm asleep, because that's when I'm at my weakest.

My baby cousin always was my weakness, and he still is, just in a different way now.

I fall back asleep in Hunter's arms, but even he can't save me from these demons.

They are mine, and only mine, to war with.

chapter 28

HUNTER

*R*ILEY FALLS BACK ASLEEP, but I stay awake, replaying everything that just happened. She was clearly having a bad dream, and saying the words *Devon* and *I'm sorry* over and over again. I also heard her say *I didn't mean to kill you.* I remember when Jeremy said that Riley was a murderer, and I thought he was on drugs or something, because Riley wouldn't harm a fly. There has to be an explanation for this, because I know with everything I am that Riley would not murder someone. I absently stroke her back, wanting to protect her from everything but knowing that I can't. All I can do is be there for her and let her know that no matter what, I'm not going anywhere. Nothing she does can scare me away, I don't frighten easily. I have a good sense of character, and the woman next to me is beautiful inside and out.

That's rare these days.

I close my eyes and fall asleep, her body warmth and scent surrounding me.

Now that I've found her, and had a taste of her, I'm going to do anything I can to keep her.

"WELL, IF IT ISN'T the werewolf of the firm." Tristan smirks, sitting down in my office and making himself comfortable. I should have known Kat would have told him about that.

"It was a love bite, not a claw mark. Let it go," I tell him, shaking my head. "Are you here just to give me shit?"

"Pretty much," he says, flashing his teeth in a grin. "I've got some free time, and the first thing I wanted to do was ask you how you got a time machine to turn back into seventeen-year-old you, when giving hickeys was cool."

"I didn't mark her on purpose," I explain, lips tightening. "Why are we even talking about this?"

"Because you gave your woman a hickey, and my woman saw it, and it's funny," he muses, chuckling to himself.

"I think you joined me in that time machine, Tristan," I tell him in a dry tone.

Jaxon sticks his face in and smirks. "Do you only change at a full moon, or can you shift at will?"

I'm going to kill Kat.

I shuffle all of them out of my office and close the door. It's only then when I look at my schedule on my laptop that I see that Yvonne has marked all the days of the full moon for the rest of the year.

I can't with these people.

◊

MY DAY GOES TO hell quickly when I read the piece of paper in my hand, rage filling me. I start to pace my office as I reread the words, making sure I understood correctly. Jeremy Rodgers is trying to sue me for malpractice, claiming that I breached my fiduciary duty to maintain confidentiality. He's filed a grievance with the state bar. He must have heard about Riley and me being together, and is now accusing me of sharing his personal information with her, and claiming that's why he lost money in the divorce.

The thing that bugs the shit out of me is that his complaint is a valid one. I'm dating my client's ex-wife. And while we didn't start dating until after she was divorced, it looks suspect. I get that. But I have everything to prove that I exercised the utmost care in my representation of him and I never disclosed any confidential information to Riley. This is just a big pain in my ass. I should have known he wouldn't accept the hand he was dealt, but there's no way he can blame me for this loss. I did everything I could to get him to take what Riley was offering before court, but he refused to listen.

I send Jaxon a text telling him to come see me when he's free, and he's in my office a few minutes later.

"Is everything okay?" he asks, closing the door behind him. He warned me about this, and now he gets his *I fucking told you so* moment, but I still wouldn't change everything that's happened. When he sits down I slide him the paperwork, and he quickly reads it, sighing deeply when he's done.

"We knew it could happen" is all he says. "But he's got nothing. He's just pissed that he lost out on some money, and Riley is now happy."

"I know, and I'm sorry," I tell him.

LEADING THE WITNESS ◆ 193

"Hunter, we all love Riley. This isn't on you. If I didn't want you on this case, I would've said so. He's clearly not a smart man, trying to take on our firm," Jaxon continues, game face on. "He just started a war with the most powerful firm in the city; does he actually think he can win?"

"Who knows what the fucker is thinking," I mutter under my breath.

"I guess we will see him in front of the board. I just became your lawyer." Jaxon's smile is all teeth, pure evil. It almost looks like he's looking forward to this.

Good luck to Jeremy, because Jaxon is going to destroy him.

He stands up and takes the piece of paper with him. "I'll get started on the annihilation of your woman's ex-husband."

The way he says it, so casually, is why Jaxon is a man to be feared in the courtroom.

"Thanks," I tell him, meaning it.

"No need to thank me. We're all family here."

He leaves, closing the door behind him.

Fuck.

When will we be rid of this dickhead?

chapter 29

RILEY

"I THINK I'M IN LOVE" by Kat Dahlia fills the pub, and I sing along to it, feeling happier than I've felt in the longest of times. It's been two weeks since I was granted my divorce, and what a fortnight it's been. Having Bear to go home to has brightened my life, and things with Hunter couldn't be any better. My business is starting to thrive, more people coming in every day, and profits rising. For once, everything seems to be going my way. Like the world has given up working against me. How long does this luck usually last? Maybe I should just enjoy it while I can.

"This song is on *your* playlist?" Callie snickers, coming to stand next to me.

"So what if it is?" I playfully huff. "It's a good song."

"You in love, Riley?" she pushes, doing a little happy dance. "Is this the moment where I get to say, 'I told you so?' Because I really love those moments."

I bet she does.

"Just because the lyrics say something doesn't mean that's how I'm feeling right now," I say, flashing her a look that dares her to challenge me. "And yes, you told me to take a chance, and I did. And yes, you were right. I'm happy, Callie. It's kind of a foreign feeling."

One I'm never going to take for granted.

Preston comes to stand on the other side of me. "What are we talking about?"

"This song," Callie says, looking straight ahead.

"You mean how Riley's playlist went from men-hating songs to lovey-dovey ones?" he asks, chuckling. "Oh, Riley, how the mighty have fallen."

"What man-hating songs have I ever played?" I ask him, scowling. "Go on, name one."

"You played 'Come First' by Terror Jr. on repeat," he says in a dry tone. "Not man-hating exactly . . . more 'I don't need a man' songs."

"Another great song," I say in a haughty voice. "What's wrong with it? It's about an independent woman."

Preston and Callie share a look, then both start laughing. "Riley is in love."

"Don't both of you have work to do?" I ask them. "You're both the backbone of this place, remember?"

Izaac walks in, dressed in worn jeans and a black T-shirt. "Sorry I'm late."

I glance at the clock. He's ten minutes late. "No worries, Izaac."

The dinner rush hasn't hit yet, so the place isn't busy for the time being; we just need to prepare for when it hits. I send Hunter a message, telling him I'll come to his place straight after work. I know he doesn't like it when I work late, but he bites his tongue because I'm not going to change my schedule because he thinks it's unsafe. It's my job as the owner to make sure everyone gets home safely. Like a captain on a ship, I have to make sure all my staff members are okay.

Drive safely, babe.

The night goes quickly, and by the time I make it to his house it's 10:30 p.m. He leaves his door unlocked for me, even though he knows I hate it when he does. It's a safe area, but that doesn't mean someone won't try to break in. I open the door and lock it behind me, walking straight to his bedroom. The room is empty, but I hear the shower on, so I place my bag down and decide to strip down and join him. As I step into the bathroom, I see him resting his hand against the tiles, water dripping down his body, head down. He turns when he hears me, smiling and opening the door.

"Well, there's a welcome sight."

I step into the shower, his hands finding my body the second I'm within reach. He pushes me back against the cool tiles, lips slamming down on mine, a hello I'll never tire of. He starts to kiss my ear, down my neck, while his fingers drift down the side of my body from my breast to my hip.

"Did you eat?" he asks, bringing me back to reality.

I nod.

"Good," he murmurs. He always makes sure I've eaten, that I'm taking care of myself. "Now it's my turn to eat."

He lowers himself onto his knees, lifting my right leg up and over his shoulder.

"Fuck," I whisper, closing my eyes as he starts to lick, tease, and suck me. My fingers thread through his thick, dark hair, tugging a little. "Hunter," I beg. I don't even know what I'm pleading for. I want more; I want to touch him; I want my hands on him, too.

He stops to look up at me, eyes half-mast. "What do you want, babe?"

"I want to touch you," I tell him, licking my lips.

"You can wait your turn," he replies, lowering his face back to my pussy. He only stops when he's made me come, my thighs trembling so much I feel like I'm going to fall to the floor. Hunter holds me up, pressing me back against the tiles, keeping me in place. After every wave of pleasure has passed, he lowers my leg, stands up and washes my body, paying attention to my breasts, getting them all soapy, playing with my nipples and driving me crazy. He turns the shower off and dries me off, then himself, before leading me to his bedroom. I sit down in the middle of his huge bed, reaching out to touch his cock as he comes closer.

"How was work?" he asks, glancing over my face and body.

"Do you really want to talk about this right now?" I ask, stroking him from bottom to tip.

His lip twitches before his face transforms into a mask of pleasure as I take him into my mouth, running my tongue along his shaft. He lets me play for a little, then takes control, kissing me deeply. He kisses my breasts, up my neck, and my lips again, his fingers finding my heat, playing with my clit, then rolling me over onto my stomach. I lift my hips up, arching my back as he slides inside of me. He thrusts in and out of me, hand moving to hold on to my nape, squeezing just the right amount. I push back against his cock, moaning, biting down on the pillow in front of me.

"You feel so good," he grits out. "I love watching myself sliding in and out of your little pussy, Riley. It's so fucking hot, I wish you could see it."

The way he's describing it, I wish I could too.

He reaches between us to play with my clit, the slow circles making me so wet I can feel the dampness down my inner thighs. My second orgasm hits me out of nowhere, the tremors taking over my entire body. Fingers digging into the mattress, I hold on for dear life as the pleasure takes over my entire being. Nothing has felt so good. Hunter comes a few strokes later, gripping onto my neck and whispering my name. He kisses down my spine when he's finished, then pulls out and lies next to me, the only sound in the room our breathing.

"Work was good," I say, replying to the question he asked before. "Not as good as now though."

His deep chuckle fills me with warmth. "Good. Now come here and let me cuddle you."

"You didn't tell me how your day was," I point out.

"It was okay. Definitely not as good as now. I've been looking forward to seeing you all day," he tells me, fingers gently playing with my hair.

I can feel his eyes on the side of my face. "How long are you going to stare at me for?"

I hear the smile in his voice when he replies with "At least the next few years."

My lip twitches as I roll over and look him in the eye. "Guess I better get used to it then, huh?"

He nods and kisses my forehead. "You definitely should."

"Hunter?"

"Yeah, babe?" he asks, nuzzling my cheek.

"You better not have left any marks on my neck."

His chuckle leaves me feeling a little skeptical.

chapter 30

HUNTER

"IS EVERYTHING OKAY?" RILEY asks when we're out at dinner the next night.

"Yeah, fine," I tell her, reaching out and taking her hand. "But there's something I need to tell you."

"Is everything okay?" she asks, squeezing my fingers. Our food arrives, giving me a moment to gather my thoughts. I shouldn't be in my head right now; I'll deal with the Jeremy thing when the time comes. I don't want Riley to worry about it, but I know if I don't tell her she's going to be pissed. I want us to work, and that means being honest.

"So, Jeremy is trying to sue me for malpractice," I tell her. She stops tracing the tattoos on my inner forearm with her index finger.

"What?" she asks, glancing up at me through her lashes. "Are you fucking kidding me? *Why?*"

Fuck, she is so beautiful, even when she's angry.

Especially when she's angry.

"Unfortunately not," I tell her, wincing. "He's saying I didn't keep confidentiality and because of that he lost his divorce case. He's not going to win, but I wanted to let you know what was going on."

"This is my fault. I should've just come to you from the beginning. My stupid pride—"

"Stop right there. This is not your fault, you hear me?" I say with emphasis in my voice. She stays silent for a bit, wiping a tear from her eye.

"I'm so sorry you have to deal with this, Hunter," she says, puffing out a breath. "Why does he have to be such an asshole? Just when I thought I'd never have to hear his name again."

"It's fine. I don't want you to stress out about it; Jaxon is handling it," I say, as she lets go of my hand and studies the food in front of her. "Regretting being spontaneous with your order?"

"No," she says, shaking her head. "And trying something new isn't being spontaneous, Hunter. It's what normal people do."

"Normal is overrated." I grin, pulling my plate toward me. "You let me know how your weird ball things taste."

"We have bigger issues than weird balls," she grumbles, looking me in the eye. "Are you sure Jaxon can handle this?"

"Jaxon lives for this shit. Let's not let this ruin our night, okay? It will all be handled."

She sighs and puts one of the balls on her fork and takes a big bite. "Mmmmm, I love big balls."

I almost choke on a fry. "How old are you again?"

"Old enough to get your attention." She winks, finishing the macaroni-and-cheese fried balls she ordered.

"You're a bit cute," I say, eating another fry. "You can show me how much you love big balls after dinner."

She laughs, chewing slowly and watching me. "Do you want a bite? They're actually pretty damn good."

I'm still considering when her arm stretches over the table, offering me a bite. I open my mouth and take a small bite, even though a pet peeve of mine is when someone tries to feed me like this. For her though, I pretend it's fine. It's actually pretty good, not that I want to admit that after all the shit I gave her.

"What do you think?" she probes.

"Not bad," I reply, shrugging. "You going to add them to your menu?"

"I think it's frowned upon to go around stealing people's food ideas."

"But not illegal." I smirk. "And it's not a specialty. They have those at heaps of different places."

"Still," she replies, shrugging. "Besides, you seem happy with the menu as it is."

"It's a winner for me."

"Glad it has the pickiest eater in the world's approval."

"Hey," I say, freezing. "You haven't met a picky eater until you've hung out with my sister. She doesn't drink milk, or eat certain meats like pork, lamb, or duck, but . . . she will eat bacon."

"That makes no sense," Riley comments, shaking her head. "Why bacon but no other pork? It's exactly the same animal."

"I have no idea," I say. "My mom used to cook her pork as a kid and tell her it was chicken, just so she'd eat it."

"How is your sister?" she asks me, an odd look on her face. "I haven't seen her since your birthday night."

"She's good," I tell her. "We had lunch the other day. She asked about you, said she wanted to get to know you a little more."

"Maybe we can all have lunch or dinner one day next week," Riley suggests.

"Sounds good," I tell her.

We finish up our meals, and I pay, which she complains about as usual, and then we head back to her place. Bear jumps on me as we enter, and I pat his head while Riley locks the door. Although I haven't said anything out loud, and Bear is here, I don't like the thought of her alone here, even though I know she's used to it, and that she's more than capable of taking care of herself. Maybe Riley's right—sometimes I need to tame the caveman inside of me.

"Did you miss me, Bear?" Riley coos to her dog, patting him. "Are you hungry? You need to have your dinner."

I follow the two of them into the kitchen and watch while she feeds him some raw chicken and dry biscuits. She turns to me and smiles. "It's so good having him back."

"I can see that," I say, closing the space between us. "You look happy."

"You make me happy," she says, ducking her head. "And having Bear back is the icing on the cake. Got my best friend back and a sexy, tatted, bearded man by my side."

I pull her closer. "Is that all I am to you? A pretty face? Why are you always objectifying me, Riley?" I tease, kissing the spot between her neck and her collarbone. "Will you still want me if I shave off my beard?"

I laugh at the horrified expression on her face before she masks it. "Of course I will. But your beard is so . . . Hunter."

My lip twitches at her response. "Very eloquent."

"I like your beard; is that a crime?" she asks, poking her tongue out at me. "I like everything about you. I like that you have tattoos hidden under your fancy suits. I like your mind, how smart you are, and also how seriously funny you are. I like when you're playful. I like that you always know what to say. I even like that you make inappropriate jokes and rarely take anything seriously."

Everything in me softens at her words, besides my cock, which does the opposite. "I like everything about you too, Riley," I say, kissing her, showing her without words how much her little rant means to me. She sees me. The real me, not the one I usually show to the world. I feel like I can be myself in front of her, and I hope she feels the same way about me. Things start to get a little heated, and I lift her up on the countertop, standing between her legs, kissing her and cupping her face with my hands. She tastes like the strawberry cheesecake she had for dessert, and I can't get enough. When I pull back and lift her in my arms, intending to carry her into her bedroom, I notice Bear staring at me.

"What's wrong?" Riley asks, voice hot and flustered.

"I think I'm getting some dog judgment," I whisper. "Look, he's staring at me with narrowed eyes."

She looks around me to see what her dog is up to. "He's just looking at you, there's no dog judgment. Is that even a thing?"

"Yes!" I say, sure on this topic. "Our dog at my parents' house used to do it too. He'd give me all this dog judgment whenever I was drinking when my parents weren't home. Now Bear is giving it to me because we're about to fuck and he's being weird about it."

"I think it's you being weird about it, Hunter," she deadpans. "Just take me to bed, and close the door."

"Okay," I grumble, carrying her to her bedroom, turning on the light and closing the door. "Now, where were we?"

chapter 31

RILEY

HUNTER CLEARLY LOVES HIS sister, but I keep thinking about the drug situation at his birthday. Was that a one-off? Maybe she just takes recreational drugs when she parties, which isn't uncommon. But what if it's more? I shouldn't really judge someone I don't know, especially when she's the sister of the man I want to be with, and especially when I've been there myself. I send her a message asking when she's free to catch up, feeling a little weird because I don't know her at all. It's time to change that, I guess, and I know she told Hunter she wanted to get to know me more.

"What am I supposed to do if I find someone giving a guy head in the men's bathrooms?" Preston asks me, sounding genuinely curious.

I look up from my phone. "When did this happen?" And I

have no idea what to do. Kick them out? Tell them to hurry up? Awkward.

"Well, it's happening right now," he says, shifting on his feet. "And as a man, I feel like it's really rude to stop whoever is in there before they come. Imagine if it was you! You'd want to come."

"If it was me I wouldn't be having sex in a public restroom, for one," I say, crossing my arms over my chest. "And do you really want to be cleaning up cum in our toilets?"

We have a cleaner who comes in every night, but what if they make a mess? We can't just leave it there. I usually send someone in every hour just to do a check and make sure the place is clean. I do it, too, well, for the female toilets anyway.

"I'd hope she swallows," Preston snickers, and I sigh, praying for strength. Izaac walks past in that moment, and I grab his arm. "We have a situation. In the men's toilets. And the *two* of you are going to deal with it."

"What is it?" he asks, going straight into manager mode.

I look to Preston, who explains the situation.

"Maybe they've finished by now," Izaac says, looking on the verge of laughter. "Should we put up a 'no blow jobs' sign?"

Callie walks over to see what all the commotion is, and I realize she's the one I should have sent to handle this. She has no shame.

"Callie, there's an incident going on in the male toilets," I tell her. "What do we do?"

"This place really is like a brothel." She giggles, grabbing a cleaning spray bottle we use to wipe down the tables. "Don't worry, I've got this."

She storms toward the toilets.

I look to Preston, blinking slowly. "Is she going to spray them with cleaning spray?"

Callie is one crazy chick, and I'm glad she's here. Maybe I should have made her the manager after all.

"I think so," he muses, resting on the bar, palm on his chin. "This ought to be interesting."

We all wait for her to return, curiosity taking over all other priorities. She opens the door and comes straight for us, her cheeks a little pink. A few seconds later, a man and a woman rush out and head straight for the exit.

"Well, I guess it worked. What did they say?" I ask, pulling her close so none of the other customers can hear.

"He asked me to join in, actually," she says, laughing. "And I saw his dick. It was huge."

"Did you consider it?" Preston asks, whispering excitedly. "Holy shit, you did."

"I did not," Callie inserts, rolling her eyes. "I sprayed him on the dick with cleaner instead, and said if his girl wanted to suck him off now, she was going to die from the chemicals. Then I walked out, and they left."

She puts the cleaning spray away, and heads back out to continue working in the restaurant.

Preston, Izaac, and I all share a look, and then burst out laughing.

Callie: 1.

Random horny couple: 0.

"BEAR IS WATCHING US again," Hunter whisper-yells, stopping his kisses. "I can't work under these conditions."

I sigh and look to the door we forgot to close, where Bear is sitting and watching us. "Bear, go to bed."

Bear listens and heads to his bed in the living room.

"Stage fright? Don't like an audience?" I tease, kissing his neck and trying to stop my laughter.

"It's weird," he says, wincing. "I'm going to get up and close the door."

I bury my face in my pillow and laugh, and he does just that, freaked out about my dog watching, even though both of us are still currently clothed. Sure, the clothes won't last long, but it's funny how freaked out he is by this. He rejoins me in bed and pulls me so I'm lying on top of him.

"Hello, beautiful," he murmurs, hands running down my body and landing on my ass.

"Hello, handsome," I whisper, then kiss his lips, then his neck. "You smell so good. What is that?"

"I don't know," he replies. "I don't wear cologne. So I think it's just me. Maybe it's my beard oil."

"You don't? You always smell so good though."

"Soap."

"I'm going to buy you some cologne," I say, sitting up, straddling him and starting to undress myself, giving him a show by trying to be extra sexy.

"Why? You just said I always smell good," he says, then groans when I cup my own breasts and plump them together.

"Good point," I reply, sliding down my bra straps. "I've always tried to pinpoint your scent, but I never could. And it's annoying me."

"Control freak."

"Not in the bedroom," I quip, throwing my bra on the floor. I squeeze my bare breasts, watching his hooded eyes as he enjoys the show.

"No, not in the bedroom," he whispers, sitting up and bringing his lips to one nipple, sucking and licking, and then the other.

208 ◊ CHANTAL FERNANDO

"Mmmmm," I moan, closing my eyes and allowing him to play. My nipples are so sensitive, and I love when he licks them just like that. I can feel how wet I'm getting, and I know it won't be long before he's inside of me. How did I keep my hands off him for all that time? He rolls me onto my back, pulls down my skirt and my white silk panties, and then his mouth is on me. He loves going down on me; he says it turns him on too, which really is a win-win. I don't know how I got so lucky, or why this man chose me, but I'm glad he did.

Maybe all my bad decisions led me here, a little taste of something good.

Maybe I had to be made strong before I was given the man I was meant to be with.

Maybe this is the prize.

Love.

With the right man.

Is there anything else better?

He makes me come, and then fucks me until I come again, feeling sated, adored, and just fucking satisfied.

And then he cuddles me, skin against skin, my body wrapped against his. I feel safe here, his warmth soothing me, not knowing where he ends and I begin. I kiss his chest and close my eyes, and I suddenly realize what he smells like.

Home.

chapter 32

HUNTER

AFTER INVITING MY SISTER over for dinner with me and Riley, I decide I'll cook something for my two favorite women. I also buy a few bottles of wine. They like wine.

"Smells good in here," Riley says. "Do you want some help?"

"No, I've got it," I tell her, but she starts to do the dishes anyway, and tidies up my kitchen counter. "How long do I have until Cleo gets here?"

"An hour," she replies, coming next to me to supervise me making the lasagna.

"Are you going to be a backseat chef?" I ask, arching a brow.

"A what?" she asks, wrinkling her nose.

"It's like a backseat driver, but the chef version. You know, calling out instructions from the backseat, and not letting the driver just drive," I explain.

She studies me for a second, then starts laughing. "Where do you even come up with this shit? Seriously. No, I'm just seeing what you're doing."

"Silently criticizing?"

"Maybe I'm admiring."

"You're a woman. You're always thinking that I'm not doing something right," I grumble, then pause and add, "Except in the bedroom, because you know I have that under control."

"Okay, fine, I was just thinking you should put a little more béchamel sauce on each layer," she admits, smirking. "But I wasn't going to say anything, I was just thinking it."

"I knew it!"

She lifts up on her tiptoes and kisses me. "I'm going to go sit down."

"Please do."

She jumps up on the countertop and opens a bottle of wine. I grab her a glass so she doesn't have to move.

"Do you want a glass?"

"No, I'm good, thanks," I tell her. There's a knock at the door. My sister must be early. "Can you keep an eye on this while I get the door?"

"Sure," she says, jumping off the counter.

I rush to the door and open it to a big, warm hug from Cleo. "Hello, baby sister."

"Mom and Dad aren't happy they didn't get invited to meet your new girlfriend," she says in welcome. "They didn't think you'd ever commit to anything other than your gym membership."

I rub my forehead, feeling a headache coming on. "Nice to see you too, Cleo."

She grins and walks past me to the kitchen. Riley turns, smiling at Cleo. "Hello again."

Cleo, always affectionate, gives Riley a hug, who looks a little awkward at first but eventually gives in to it. "Nice to see you again, Riley." She lets go and spots the bottle of wine. "Oooh, I love this wine."

Luckily I brought some backup with me.

"SO, HOW DID YOU get Hunter to be exclusive with you?" Cleo asks Riley. "Did you have a chat about it and tell him that you don't share?"

Riley flashes me a daring look. "I didn't realize we had to have that chat. Is this a thing, Hunter?"

I shift on my seat. "It's a thing in the dating world, yes, but no, we don't need to have this conversation. I only want you, and I'm not going to fuck that up."

"You must be really good in bed," Cleo whispers to Riley, who almost chokes on her bite of lasagna.

I pour myself some more wine.

"How's work been?" I ask my sister, trying to get off the subject of me usually not being exclusive with one woman and how good Riley is in bed.

"Same old," she says, shrugging. "I've been taking on more shifts, so I haven't had much time for anything else really. I really need to come to your pub, Riley. What nights are the best ones?"

"Friday night is probably the busiest," Riley says. "You should come have a drink. All the staff are really nice; we're more like a bunch of friends than anything else."

"Any hotties?"

"Izaac, the bar manager, is pretty hot," she says, cringing as she looks my way.

"Is he, now?" I quickly insert, not missing a beat. "I thought you didn't notice how attractive he is?"

"Well, I've had time to," she murmurs, clearing her throat. "You know, I see him every day at work. Preston is good-looking too, in a different kind of way."

"Yep, I'll definitely have to come in." She looks to her brother. "Why don't we go together this weekend?"

"Okay, sounds good," I tell her. "But if you're going to hit on guys and shit, then I'm not coming."

"I'll behave," she says, rolling her eyes. She throws Riley a *See what I have to deal with?* look, and Riley just laughs. "How much trouble can I get into while my brother is right there? And his woman owns the place. If I wanted to pick up, I'd go out alone."

"Good," I grumble, sipping on my wine. "Because it would be awkward if I got into a fight at Riley's."

"Riley must get hit on every day; I mean, look at her," Cleo says, leaning back in her chair. "I love the whole red bandanna thing, by the way. Super sexy."

"Oh, thank you," Riley says, lip twitching. "I started wearing those years ago, and it kind of just stuck. It keeps my hair out of my face, and yeah, I guess I like the look of it too."

"It's hot," Cleo announces.

"Well, nice to see the two of you getting on okay," I say, brows rising. "As you can see, Riley, my sister has no filter and will say whatever pops into her head."

"Wonder who I learned that from," Cleo fires back, arching her brow at him. "The shit I've heard you say, Hunter. Riley, I should tell you about all the men Hunter has scared away from me. It goes back to primary school and still hasn't stopped."

"I haven't scared men off you. You do that on your own," I say in a dry, dull tone.

"Last year. Jason Mitchell" is all she says, crossing her arms over her chest and studying me.

"He was a douche."

"You threatened to put him in jail if he came near me again. He was scared," Cleo groans, covering her face with her hands.

"He was scared because he was shady as fuck, and had priors. If you choose someone who isn't a criminal next time, I won't say a thing," I tell her.

"Promise?"

"Promise."

I look at Riley, who is watching our exchange with an amused expression, like one would watch a tennis match. "Izaac have a criminal record?"

She shakes her head. "Not that I know of. If he does, he buried it."

"Smart. I like that." Cleo smirks, patting her stomach. "Did you make dessert, Hunter?"

I scrub my hand down my face. "I didn't make dessert, but there's ice cream in the freezer."

"Cool," she says, smiling warmly at me. "Thanks for having me over and cooking."

"You're welcome," I tell her, gentling. "Riley offered to cook, but I thought I'd show off my skills."

I want to ask her if her money situation is any better, or if she needs more, but I don't want to ask in front of Riley and embarrass Cleo, so I'll wait until I have a moment alone with her.

"Well, the lasagna was pretty great. Tastes just like Mom's," Cleo states, a proud look on her face. She stands and collects her plate and glass. "I'll do the dishes. Does anyone want any ice cream?"

"I do," Riley pipes up, standing and taking her empty plate and mine to the sink. She gets out three bowls and places them on the table, while Cleo gets out the ice cream and serves it. The two of them stop to chat, women shit, something about clothes, and then dogs, and then a joke about me being a pain in the ass.

Still, they are getting along, and that means the world to me.

They're also cleaning up while I get to sit here and enjoy a moment of silence.

Priceless.

chapter 33

RILEY

CLEO DOESN'T ACT WEIRD in the slightest as we get to know each other, so I'm going with the assumption that she has her life under control. If I ignore that whole bathroom situation, Cleo is actually a really cool chick. She's funny, bold, and I can tell how much she loves and adores her brother. I could see myself hanging out with her with or without Hunter, which is saying something.

When she's ready to leave, Hunter walks her to her car while I tidy up the kitchen, wiping everything down. After a quick shower, I slide into Hunter's bed, tired after a long day. When he joins me, there are no words, we let our bodies do the talking, and then I fall into a deep sleep.

With a smile on my face.

◇

WORK IS BUSY THE next day, and I don't even have time to have a lunch break. We've installed two big televisions so that customers can watch sports while they eat, and there's a basketball game on today, so maybe that's why there are so many people here right now. If things stay like this, I'm going to need to hire another staff member, and someone else to help Cheffy in the kitchen.

"Table four is complaining about the wait on their food," Callie tells me, rushing around.

"Let me go check on it," I tell her, gently grabbing her shoulder. She seems a little stressed, trying to get everyone's orders out on time and dealing with the customers. I've got Izaac helping her and Preston at the bar. "Tell them there will be a bottle of wine on the house."

She nods and rushes back to them while I check in with Cheffy, who is a little swamped. Yes, I definitely need another chef, a sous chef, or anyone who can help Cheffy keep up with the new amount of orders and people we are now getting.

"Can I help you back there?" I ask him. I'm no chef, but surely there's something I can do to make it easier for him.

"No," he calls out. "I've got it under control."

He places table four's meals on the table, all looking perfect and delicious.

"Thank you, are you sure? I can chop onions or something," I suggest.

"No," he rumbles, walking away.

Well, okay then.

I personally take out their food, and a bottle of wine, and apologize for the wait. The wine is a cheap bottle but seems to do the trick. People love free shit.

I message Hunter with a picture of how full the venue is

and how his spot is taken if he decides to come in for lunch. He replies with:

> Congratulations. You are incredible. I'll come in for a late
> lunch, hopefully my spot is free by then.

I smile down at my phone. He thinks I'm incredible. I must admit the promotions I've been doing must have helped with bringing in new customers. I slide my phone away and get back to work, adrenaline filling me. This is what I always wanted Riley's to look like. Sure, it's busy on the weekends, but it's never looked like this on a weekday before.

"Do you want to take a break?" I ask Callie as she walks past me with a tray of drinks in her hand. "I'll take over. What table are you up to?"

"Just took table eight's order, and two and nine are waiting," she tells me. "But I don't need a break, I'm fine. I need to get used to this pace."

She heads to the table to give them their drinks, and I approach some new people who just walked in.

I need to get used to the pace too.

MY MISERABLE EX-HUSBAND IS the last man I ever thought would walk into my pub, but here he is, standing at the bar and staring at me. Not wanting to make a scene, I step to him and try to treat him like any other customer. Maybe the bastard is just thirsty.

"Can I get you something to drink?" I ask, keeping my expression blank. I don't know why he's here or what he wants, but I know it can't be good. He never even came in when I first started the business, not caring about a small Irish-style pub, or caring about anything that remotely interests me. The world revolved around him, I was just meant to be there along for his ride.

"A beer," he orders, lip curling. The way he looks at me is pure hate. And I don't even know why. I didn't take anything from him, except what was mine, and yeah, the court ordered him to give me fifty thousand dollars, along with the land my business is on, but I never asked for that, so how can that be my fault? I pour him a beer and slide it over to him. He lays money on the bar top and I'm glad, because I don't want to touch his hand.

"Bet you feel really good about yourself, fucking my lawyer," he starts, and I grit my teeth. "Hope you feel just as good when I get him disbarred."

"That's not going to happen," I say with anger in my voice. "Why are you here, Jeremy?"

What is this asshole up to? He doesn't think he can take on Hunter with his bullshit, does he? Why can't he just let things go? He really doesn't want me to be happy, because even though he's now free and has all the money in the world, he still isn't happy.

If I didn't hate him so much, I'd feel sorry for him.

"Was thirsty and in the neighborhood," he says, and I want to slap that smug look off his face. "Thought I'd see if you knew what was going on. Just how long were you fucking him, Riley? While he was my lawyer? I'm going to bring him down."

"I'm not going to dignify that with an answer. I owe you nothing," I say, pursing my lips together. "I'm free from you, Jeremy, but for some reason you're determined to drag this out. Why don't you just forget about me and move the fuck on? I'm happy, so please, whatever business you have with Hunter, save it for the courtroom and get the fuck out of my life. You don't need to be showing up at my place of work; I have no idea why you'd even want to come here. I don't want to waste any more of my time on you."

Jeremy just stares at me with a strange look in his eye. In a low voice, he says, "I thought we were going to be together forever. We were a team. What happened to us?"

In that minute I see the man I fell in love with. I see the man who picked me up when I was down and helped put me back together. But we aren't those people anymore.

"I don't know, Jeremy. We grew up and went in different directions. Let me go. Find someone who can give you what you want."

The minute those words leave my mouth, the new Jeremy is back. It's like me telling him the truth brought all the anger back. With a sneer on his face and vindictiveness in his words, he says, "I'm going to make your life a living hell, bitch."

I throw the tea towel in my hand on the counter and storm to the back room, bracing myself with my palms on the table, breathing deeply. There's two things passing through my mind: (1) Jeremy is a fucking dickhead, and (2) I really hope this doesn't do anything to tarnish Hunter's reputation.

Callie comes in and rubs my upper back. "Are you okay, Riley? Do you want me to kick that guy out? I can grab the spray."

"No, it's okay," I tell her. "He'll be expecting that. Let him leave when he's ready."

"Is that Jeremy?" she asks softly.

I nod.

"You definitely upgraded," she says, making a tsk-tsk sound. "Hunter is a million times hotter than he is."

Hunter is a million times a better man than he is, which is what counts for me.

"I just don't get why he'd come in here," I say to Callie. "What did he want to get out of it? Just to try and upset me? Why can't he just let go?"

"Because you're happy, and he isn't," she says. "And he resents it. It was supposed to be him who walked away happy— after all, he got the houses and the money, right? Except you made everything out of nothing, Riley. And with everything, he still can't bring himself to be happy and let go. He's miserable. And misery loves company."

"I need a hug," I announce.

She smiles and gives me a big bear hug. "It'll be okay; you know that, right?"

"You're pretty wise for your age," I whisper into her hair. "You'd be a good lawyer."

"I know," she replies, and I can hear the smile in her voice. "And you make a pretty great human being. You're a good person, Riley. Don't let that jerk try to bring you down when you just got rid of him. He's probably just realizing what he lost, and now you've found someone better than him in every way possible. It's a heavy pill for him to swallow."

I nod. "You're right. He's trying to bring me down, and I need to not let him win."

He's trying to bring Hunter down too. The guilt starts to fill me at all the trouble I've been bringing Hunter's way. He prides himself on his professionalism, and his ethics, and now his practice is going to be questioned in court. It's fucked-up and not fair. None of this would have happened if I had gone to Hunter first.

If only I had trusted him.

Shit.

I can't go back and change things now though.

We just have to push forward.

chapter 34

HUNTER

I LEAVE THE DOOR UNLOCKED for her, even though I know she hates it, and hear her steps just as I'm out of the shower.

"Babe?" I call out.

"Hey," she says, stepping into my room, looking as tired as I feel. "Did you have dinner? I brought you some food, just in case you didn't."

"I didn't, I was about to make something for us," I tell her, wrapping the towel around my waist and approaching her. I give her a kiss, then take the bag with a grin. "Thank you. What did you bring?"

"Burger and fries," she says, sitting down on the bed. "The only thing that survives takeout."

"Thank you," I tell her again, putting the bag down on the bed and sitting next to her.

She looks down at the floor and then back up at me. "Jeremy came into work today."

I freeze, gritting my teeth together. "For what? What did he say?"

"He just wanted to tell me he was suing you, and to see if I knew about it. I think he just came in to try to ruin my day, to be honest," she says, jaw clenching.

He actually had the nerve to come into her work? If I was there, I'd probably be in jail right now.

"Can you write down everything he said for me?" I ask, taking her hand, and running my thumb along her knuckles. "I might need that information. If he comes near you again, maybe we should file a restraining order. Jeremy has no proof, he's just sour that you got everything you wanted in the divorce and now wants to claim back his loss, which is the money he had to pay you."

"So he's trying to sue you for the money he had to pay me?" she asks, shaking her head. "The money I didn't even ask for? Fucking hell."

"He's bitter and has to blame someone," I tell her, thumb making circles on her knuckles. "We're going to handle it. This isn't your fault, Riley, this is him being a sore loser and an idiot. He's just going to lose more money in the long run. I didn't do what he's accusing me of—there was no information I passed on, and he didn't even tell me anything that no one else knew. There's nothing you need to worry about."

"I'm annoyed that you have to even deal with this shit in the first place," she says, watching our joined hands. "I'm sorry, Hunter. I hate the fact you have to defend your professionalism, all because I came along and fucked things up by not telling you I needed a lawyer in the first place. If I had let go of my stubbornness and pride, we wouldn't be here right now."

"Nothing is ever smooth sailing, babe. I can handle whatever he throws at me. I don't lose, and he's about to learn that the hard way."

Her ex has no idea what he's dealing with. Jaxon knows people. I know people. And his accusations are laughable. I feel sorry for whoever his lawyer is this time around. Yeah, it's an inconvenience, but that's about it. I'm not scared, nor am I worried. Yes, I hate that my morals and dedication to my position as a man of the law will be questioned before a courtroom, but I can't control that. All I can do is prove the truth.

And that's exactly what I'm going to do.

She buries her face in my neck and brings her arms around my waist. "Why is he such a c-word?"

I grin into her hair. "Did you just call him a c-word?"

She nods. "I feel like we keep getting obstacles thrown at us."

"It's just going to make our relationship stronger."

"Is that what this is? A relationship?" she teases, lips pressing into my neck. "Should I change my social media status?"

"You haven't already?" I joke. "What, no cute pictures or captions—nothing? Are we even together then?"

"Well, we never had the discussion," she says, moving to straddle me. "And you never asked me to be exclusive, remember?"

"Didn't have to, babe," I tell her against her lips. "You were mine the second you kissed me."

I kiss her lips to make a point, showing her what's here between us. There's no denying this shit. She can argue all she wants, but she's mine.

"And are you mine, Hunter?" she asks, eyes hooded.

"Yes," I breathe. "I am."

"Good," she whispers, our lips back on each other, deep, hungry, greedy kisses, her tongue tasting mine, and mine sucking on hers. Kisses that wouldn't be appropriate in public.

She pushes me back on the bed, her body following me down, and everything else is forgotten.

"KAT, WHY ARE YOU sitting on the floor?" I ask as I step into her office. She's sitting cross-legged and reading over some documents.

She looks up at me and shrugs. "Because someone stole my office chair, and I don't have the time to find it."

I scrub my hand down my face. "It's way too early for this shit, I haven't even had my morning coffee."

"Hey, no one made you walk in here, buddy," she replies, seemingly not fazed by the loss of her chair.

"What are you going to do when clients come in?" I decide to ask.

"No clients today," she replies, dusting something off her black pants. "I've got court today. I'll probably leave in about an hour."

I watch her, sitting on the floor like she does it every day, and call out Yvonne's name.

She appears in the doorway, dressed in pink stripper heels and a white pantsuit, delicious coffee in her hand. "What?"

"Can you find her chair? And can I have some coffee? I'm dying and won't be able to function without any."

She sighs and hands me hers. "Here. I haven't had a chance to have any yet. And as for the chair . . . where the hell did yours go, Kat?"

I take the coffee and drink it like my life depends on it. My sanity does anyway. Tristan walks past, and I stop him, pointing at his woman. "I feel like this is your situation to deal with."

He sticks his head in, frowning when he sees her on the floor. "Kat, why are you on the floor?"

"Is she having a nervous breakdown?" I whisper to him, glancing over his shoulder. "Well, she hasn't shaved her head yet, at least."

She glances up at Tristan, something vulnerable in her expression, and I feel like maybe Yvonne and I shouldn't be here to witness whatever she needs to say. I'm about to walk away, when she murmurs, "I'm pregnant."

Tristan stills next to me. "What?"

"I'm pregnant," she says, sniffling. "And I broke my chair. Probably because I'm pregnant and fat, and my chair knew I was about to get fatter, so it committed suicide because it didn't want to have to support my fat ass any longer."

Yvonne and I share a look and then slowly back away. I practically lock myself in my office. Am I meant to congratulate Kat on her pregnancy? Or apologize? I don't know what to do, so I hide. I send Yvonne a message asking her to send Kat some flowers, or something, I don't know. Kat is pregnant. That means she should step away from the firm for some time. Maybe she's overwhelmed, because her career is just starting to take off, but at the same time, she's carrying a baby with the man she loves.

That's a different kind of beautiful.

chapter 35

RILEY

I REACH FOR MY PHONE, the loud ringing waking me from a deep sleep.

"Hello," I rumble down the line, my voice thick with sleep. I sit up quickly when I hear the officer say his name. "Yes, this is Riley McMahon. Is everything okay?"

"We need you to come in to your establishment, ma'am," he says into the line. "There's been an incident here, and the police would like to speak with you."

"I'm on my way," I tell him, hanging up and throwing the phone onto my bed. I quickly get dressed, then I'm out the door, a feeling of dread filling me. I send Hunter a message while I'm stuck at a traffic light, telling him the cops called me and told me to come into work. He replies instantly, saying he's on his way. When I pull up in front of Riley's, my heart stops.

No.

I open the door and stand in front of the building that contains everything I've worked for.

The building that's now half-damaged, the fire department still putting out some of the blaze.

No.

This can't be happening; the place had only just started to do well, and now a fire has broken out?

No.

I wrap my arms around myself, trying not to cry. Tears won't help.

Tears won't put out the fire.

It seems my good luck has run out.

Arms wrap around me, and I'm pulled back against a strong chest. I'm now safe, but Riley's isn't.

And Riley's is me.

I put everything into this place, and now . . . Now I'm going to have to start all over again.

A police officer comes over to speak to us, but I don't even hear what he says, only my own thoughts. I think I'm going into shock.

Suddenly everything turns black.

I WAKE UP IN Hunter's bed, and for a second I think it's all been a dream, but then I see his face. He looks wretched, and no, everything that happened was very real.

"What happened?" I ask, my voice coming out scratchy and broken.

"You passed out," he tells me, handing me a bottle of water. "You went into shock, I think, and there was a lot of smoke from the fire. I told the police that they can interview you another

228 ◇ CHANTAL FERNANDO

time, and I brought you back here. Jaxon and Tristan are at Riley's, handling everything. You have insurance, right?"

I nod. "Yeah."

"Good," he exhales, shaking his head. "I'm so sorry, babe, I know how shitty you must be feeling right now. But we're going to rebuild it, and the place is going to be better than ever. This is not the end for Riley's."

I smile sadly. I know that we can rebuild, it's just such a sad and draining feeling to have everything taken away within a moment. It's hard to handle. "Do they know what happened? Was there an electrical fault or something?"

"They think it was deliberate," Hunter says, wincing. "I know one of the cops who showed up, and he told me. Nothing is for sure yet, but that's their suspicion right now."

"So they think someone deliberately set Riley's on fire? Who the hell would do that?" I ask, but inside I know who would fucking do it. "Surely, he wouldn't? This is low, even for him, and he could go to jail. Does he hate me that much to risk jail time?"

"I don't know, but if it was him, we're going to prove it," Hunter says with conviction. "He's stupider than even I thought if this is his doing, Riley. He's no mastermind—he would've left some sort of evidence behind."

I roll onto my stomach and bury my face in my pillow, and Hunter lies next to me and holds me. I'm going to give myself one day to lick my wounds.

To feel sorry for myself, to be upset and feel the loss of my hard work and time.

One day.

But tomorrow?

Tomorrow I'm going to take the world back. Tomorrow I'm going to fight. I'm going to talk to the cops, I'm going to fill out reports, and I'm going to sort out my insurance.

I'm going to find out who the fuck did this.

And I'm going to make them pay.

I'M SITTING WITH CALLIE, Preston, Izaac, and Cheffy in the pub, which wasn't affected by the fire. The kitchen, however, was another story. I don't know what I'm supposed to do here, because I don't want to lose any of my staff, but it's going to take months before the place is up and running again.

"I can't believe this happened," Callie says, shoulders hunched. "This is fucked."

"I know," I whisper, expelling a deep sigh. "I'm so sorry, guys, I don't know what we can all do for now until the place is up and running. I can afford to give you all two months' wages, so you at least have time to find another job. I'd hate to lose you guys, but I know you all need to work. Hell, so do I. I think you should do what you need to do, and when it's time to reopen, we can see where we all are, and if you want your jobs back, they are always here for you. If you don't, I completely understand too. I love you guys. You have been the best staff I could have ever imagined, and I'm thankful for each and every one of you."

"You've been the best boss I've ever had," Preston tells me, hugging me from the side. "Who else is going to let me hit on all the women? And make up my own drinks, like mother puncher? Who is going to yell at me whenever I'm late but then not yell at Izaac just because he's new?"

I roll my eyes. "Let it go, Preston. That happened once."

"And I'll never forget it," he adds, lifting his chin.

There's a knock at the door, and in walks Kat, Hunter, Tristan, and Jaxon.

"Is everything okay?" I ask them all, wondering what they are doing here.

"Yes and no," Kat says, crossing her arms over her chest and shifting on her feet. "I'm here to offer Callie a job."

"What job?" Callie asks, perking up.

"My job," Kat says, placing her hands on her stomach. "I'm pregnant, and I need someone to cover my spot for at least a year." She glances up at Tristan. "He's been a Neanderthal and doesn't want me working. He wants me to sit on my ass, get fat, break more chairs, and be a domestic goddess."

She smiles though, and I know how much she loves that man, and his fussing over her, and how she will love their baby just as much as she loves Tristan's other two kids from his first wife.

Jaxon speaks next. "And as for the rest of you, I found you all a temporary job until Riley's opens back up. I called in a favor and Knox's Tavern will be happy to have some extra help for a few months."

I step to Jaxon and hug the shit out of him, squeezing him. "Thank you, Jaxon."

I then turn to Kat, place my hands on her belly, and kiss her on the cheek. "Congratulations. This baby is going to be lucky."

Callie runs up to her next and pulls her into a warm hug. "My bestie is knocked up and I find out the same time as everyone else."

"I just handed you my dream job."

"Great tradeoff, I say. They're going to love me so much they aren't going to want you back," Callie teases her, while I smile and shake my head at Hunter.

Hunter, Hunter, Hunter.

How does he manage to solve all my problems and then doesn't even try to take any credit for any of it?

Did a more selfless man ever exist?

"Thank you," I say to him, resting the side of my face against him. "You know you're my hero, right?"

"You don't need a hero, babe, you've got this," he tells me, kissing the top of my head.

And he's right.

I do have this.

But sometimes being strong gets tiring, and it's nice to have someone who you can rely on.

It doesn't make me weak, it makes me human.

And Hunter, Hunter just makes me better.

chapter 36

HUNTER

"WE'VE FOUND A FOOTPRINT at the scene," Officer Bates says on the phone. "So we're going to go from there. If we had a DNA match that would be ideal."

"Thanks for keeping me updated," I tell him, saying 'bye and hanging up. At least they found something. I'm hoping they can link the blaze to Jeremy.

Kat steps into my office and sits down. "Do you have any snacks? I'm hungry."

"What do you feel like?" I ask.

"Sweet and savory," is her unhelpful reply.

I open my drawer and pull out some jalapeño-flavored chips and some taffy. "This will hopefully hold you down until someone does a store run."

"Thanks," she says, opening the packet of chips. "I've been throwing up all morning. It's awful, Hunter. I can't keep anything down. I don't want to live on a diet of water sips and crackers."

"How do you feel about the whole thing?" I ask her. "It wasn't planned, I'm assuming?"

"No, it wasn't. I was upset at the start. I'm right where I want to be, you know? I'm working my way up and becoming an asset to this firm. It's my dream come true. I cried when I found out, Hunter. *Cried*. I don't think that's normal. But then I went to get my scan, and I saw him. Or her. And . . . well, I think I fell in love. There's never a right time for these things. I'm blessed. I'm financially secure, and we already have two beautiful children, and . . ." She takes a deep breath. "And I think . . . I think I'm happy. It's all going to work out, and my kid is going to be beautiful, just like his or her momma."

"Good," I say, smiling at her. "Now, if you need to throw those up, please exit my office."

"Jerk," she mutters, shoving another chip in her mouth. "You're going to miss me when Callie gets here. She would never share her snacks with you. She'll probably lick them so you won't touch them. And the bitch is chatty."

She grins, licks her fingers, and heads back to her own office. Fuck.

Callie can't be that bad, right?

"I COULD GET USED to this," I murmur, as I step into my bedroom after work to see Riley laying there, naked.

"Well, now that I'm unemployed, here is where you'll find me. I can be your sex slave," she says, biting her lower lip, and pushing up on all fours. "I've been waiting for you."

"Oh, have you, and why is that exactly?" I ask, taking off

my jacket and tie. "What have you been doing in my bed while I've been at work?"

"Not eating chips and leaving crumbs everywhere," she snickers, sliding off the bed and coming over to help me undo the buttons on my white shirt. "I cooked us dinner."

I definitely could get used to this.

"What did you make? You're spoiling me, babe," I say, as she removes my shirt, leaving me in black slacks.

"Steak," she replies. "With all the sides. I'm . . . hungry."

I know the look she's giving me. She's not hungry for food. I slowly remove my belt, her eyes widening as I hold it in my hands, arching a brow at her. "Have you been a good girl today?"

"No," she replies instantly, shaking her head. "What are you going to do about it?"

I drop the belt to the floor, spin her around and push her onto the bed on her stomach. I bring my hand down on her ass, one sharp slap, one that makes her jump.

"Ouch."

I grin, spread her legs and start to lick her pussy from behind. She moans and arches her back, giving me more access. I slap her ass again, and this time I get a moan in response. I know she's about to come by the way her thighs start to tremble. I love it when she comes. The sounds she makes, the way she tastes, the fact that I know I've pleased her; I love it all. I get hard just from going down on her.

"Hunter," she moans, and I slide my finger inside of her, throwing her over the edge. Her moans get louder, and louder, and I continue to lick and suck on her clit, letting her ride out the pleasure for as long as she can. She quiets when she's finished, and I stand and remove my slacks and boxer shorts, and then slide into her wet pussy, groaning as the heat surrounds my cock, squeezing the life out of me.

"Fucking hell, Riley," I whisper under my breath, my teeth clenched. I pull out and roll her over onto her side, in the spooning position, lay behind her and slide back in, my lips on her neck, sucking playfully. I slow the pace, going deeper than before, and reach down to play with her clit.

"Hunter," she whispers, turning her face toward me.

"Yeah?"

"I love you," she says, and then kisses me.

When she pulls away, I smile, and say against her lips, "Babe, I think I've loved you from the moment I first laid my eyes on you."

We come together for the first time, finally all of our walls down, showing our true selves to each other.

No boundaries.

Guards down.

Giving ourselves to each other.

Sometimes, rarely, if you're lucky, you will put yourself out there for someone.

You'll take a gamble. A chance. Put your heart on the line.

And it will pay off.

And fuck, that feeling is indescribable.

"WE HAVE ENOUGH EVIDENCE now, don't you think?" Jaxon says to Officer Bates. The police seemed confused about why lawyers were involved, until Jaxon explained that he was a friend of Riley's. I don't know what else he did, but the police seem to be doing their job as quickly and effectively as they can. Jaxon's name carries a lot of weight in this town, and everyone in law enforcement respects him.

"The fingerprint doesn't match, and the footprint is in his

size, but a lot of men could be that size. We need to find the exact pair of shoes to prove he was the one who set the fire."

They'd found fingerprints on a side window someone must have tried to open but wasn't able to, but apparently they aren't Jeremy's. Did he have an accomplice, maybe? If the shoe matches, I think that's enough to make a case against him. I'd love to hear what the asshole's alibi is.

"Let us do our job," he tells us. "I'll let you know as soon as we know something. Right now we have no probable cause to search Mr. Rodgers's house."

We agree and head back to work.

"Are we sure it was him? The fingerprints weren't a match," Jaxon asks, sounding unsure.

"The shoe size did though. And he has the motive," I say, my jaw tight. "Are you thinking otherwise?"

"I don't know; it's just too obvious," Jaxon murmurs, lost in thought. "He had to have known we'd all suspect him first. Maybe he paid someone to do it. He has enough money to do so, and it would explain the fingerprints."

"Maybe," I agree. "I don't know. I guess we will have to see what the police find out. If it's him though, what a clusterfuck. I can't believe he'd do this to Riley, even if he paid someone to do it. She told me he came by and there was a moment where she saw pain. But you don't do this because you are in pain. You do this because you have some serious issues. He's such a selfish fuck."

"You're right, he's clearly got some issues he needs to work out," Jaxon comments, opening the door for me, like a gentleman. "He can sort them out in prison."

"Thanks for opening the door for me, you cutie."

"Any time, honey."

"Do you two need some time alone?" Scarlett asks from

where she sits perched on Yvonne's desk, amusement dancing in her eyes. "I can come back later."

I give her a hug and pull back, arms still around her. "I haven't seen you in so long. Where have you been?"

"Working." She smiles, her floral scent filling the office. "I thought I'd surprise my man by taking him out to dinner, only to catch him flirting with you."

"He's my office husband. You know I'll always be his first love," I tease, stepping back and letting Jaxon approach her. "I can cover for you, Jaxon, if you need to bail."

"Thanks, man," he says, taking Scarlett's hand in his. "I better give her some attention before she leaves me."

I smirk and watch the two lovebirds leave.

"They are such a cute couple," Yvonne comments, heaving a big sigh.

"When are you going to find a man, Yvonne?"

"When hell freezes over," she replies, smirking, her red lips lifting at the corners.

"I'll set you up, if you can't find anyone," I say, poking the beast. "I know a few men. They aren't very fussy."

She throws her notepad at me.

I duck and run to my office to hide.

Who said working in an office all day was boring?

chapter 37

RILEY

*A*FTER TALKING WITH THE insurance company, I start feeling a little better about Riley's. The kitchen needs to be completely redone, as well as the back of the building, but everything else is okay the way it stands. With the insurance money I'll be able to do all this and have the business up and running soon enough.

I'm looking forward to a fresh start, and the fact that I know no one can bring me down, that I will always get back up and fight no matter what, brings a newfound confidence.

Jeremy can't break me.

I take Bear for an hour jog around Hunter's neighborhood, then return to his house to make dinner for us. I've been at his place more than I've been at my own apartment lately, mainly because it's easier for him to come straight home from work, and I have plenty of time on my hands right now too, so I don't mind cooking, cleaning, and playing house. I visited my parents today with Bear, and had lunch with them, something I haven't had the time to do in a while, so it's actually been nice having some extra time on my hands. When Hunter gets home, dinner is cooked, and I've had a relaxing Jacuzzi and am walking around the house in a bathrobe.

"Hello, beautiful," he says, giving me a long, deep kiss. I like that he always kisses me properly, not just a little peck.

"Hello, handsome," I reply, smiling up at him. "How was your day?"

"Not too bad," he says, smelling the air. "Something smells good. Are you sure you want to go back to work? I'm kind of getting used to this treatment."

"Well, don't," I say, smirking. "As soon as those doors are ready to open, I'll be back at Riley's, doing my thing."

"I don't doubt it," he says, brushing my hair back off my cheek. "I like coming home to you though. I don't care if it's me cooking dinner for you every night after work. I just like you being here."

I duck my head, smiling. I can't take it when he's sweet sometimes. It's too much. It makes me want to make stupid decisions, I can't think properly when he's so close to me. "I like being wherever you are, Hunter," I manage, raising my head, our gazes locking. "I don't care what we're doing or where we are."

He kisses my temple. "Fuck, you're cute."

I grin and hug him, breathing in, taking in his scent.

Home.

I don't know how this happened so quickly. Isn't love meant to be a slow burn? Maybe there are no rules for love. I know I wouldn't change anything that's happened between us.

I'm in love with him.

I said it to him while we were making love, and he said

it back. I know I shouldn't have said it then, the timing was wrong, people say stupid shit when they're having sex all the time, it's when we're at our most vulnerable, right before climax, and I meant what I said, but I didn't mean to say it at that time, it just fell from my lips.

"I love you, Hunter," I tell him, feeling bold.

"I love you too, Riley," he replies, smiling widely and shaking his head. "I thought I was dreaming when you said it last time."

"Do you want me to pinch you?" I ask him, lifting my hands to touch his beard.

"I want you to do something else to me," he murmurs, gaze zoning in on my mouth.

"Like what?" I ask, batting my eyelashes at him.

"Well, you can start by kissing me," he says, smirking, his mouth almost touching mine. "And then by dropping that robe. I'm guessing you have nothing on underneath?"

He'd be guessing right.

Not wanting to listen to him fully, but wanting what's going to come after this, I drop my robe first and then flash him a stubborn smile.

He chuckles and reaches down, tracing the curve of my breast with his index finger. "Was that meant to teach me a lesson? Because I'm pretty sure it's still me who wins here."

I laugh under my breath and turn, heading straight to the bedroom. Before I can make it there though, he stops me with his hands around my waist, pulling me back against his body. When he turns me and pushes me back against the wall, his lips slamming down on mine, his fingers sliding between my legs, I'm glad he's holding up my weight, because I'm so turned on I can barely walk.

"Move in with me," he demands. "Bring Bear, and all your belongings, and move in with me."

I still, but he doesn't, his finger now rubbing circles around my clit.

"Hunter," I moan, licking my suddenly dry lips. "Can we talk about this . . . you know. After?"

"No," he states, sliding one finger inside me, and then a second. "No overthinking. What is your gut telling you?"

Damn him.

Of course I'd love to move in with him, but I need to think about it from all angles. It's not overthinking, it's being smart. Yes, I'm at his house a lot, but what if things change?

Shit.

I close my eyes, feeling my orgasm approaching. He's learned how to touch me just right; he knows exactly what to do to make me come quickly.

"Fine," I say, moaning as my orgasm takes over me.

If things change, then they change, and I move on. I'm going to live in the now, enjoy and love the now, and I'll worry about everything else later.

I'm going to be happy, and not be scared of the future.

Anything can happen, but I love my right now. So yes, I'm going to fucking move in with Hunter Brayze. I'm going to take a risk.

He throws me over his shoulder and carries me to his bedroom, to *our* bedroom, where he makes love to me slowly, kissing me everywhere, and telling me without words that I made the right choice.

That he's happy, and that I will be too.

I won't regret this.

And afterward, when we get up to eat dinner, and when my mind is thinking rationally again, I smile.

◊

I LISTEN TO PRESTON, Izaac, and even Cheffy gushing about how cool everyone is at their new job, trying to hide the little sliver of jealousy I have. I'm happy they have good jobs, with fun people, but I have major FOMO. It's normally us getting up to all those shenanigans together, and now they're doing it with some hot chick named Summer, and her even hotter husband, Reid. Cheffy doesn't even like anyone, and he keeps talking about Summer.

Maybe I should apply for a job there too.

We sit in Riley's, pretending the kitchen isn't burned to smithereens, eating some sandwiches I made for everyone, and some other stuff I brought for our mini picnic—chips, dip, homemade guacamole, and cupcakes.

Callie sits next to me, scowling at their description of their new job too. "Maybe I should turn down the law job and work with them," she says to me, frowning. "I was just getting used to a bartender's salary. I can't even remember what a designer bag looks like anymore."

I wrap my arm around her. "No. You're going to take your dream job, and you're going to roll with it. You'll be taking over that firm in no time."

She smiles at me, nodding. "You're right. I need to do this. No more excuses. And I can't sleep with any coworkers this time, because they're all taken and my friends."

"That's the spirit," I snicker, laughing to myself. "Fuck, Callie. I'm going to miss you and your spray bottle."

"We need to have these catch-ups at least once a month until we die."

"Deal," I say, glancing around the room. I hold up my cup of soda. "To Riley's."

We all cheer.

◇

WE'RE AT HUNTER'S WORK Halloween party, and he's dressed as the sexiest Iron Man I've ever seen. I don't know how he talked me into it, but I'm dressed as Wonder Woman. After a few gin and tonics, I'm feeling a little better about that fact.

"Jaxon, looking good," I say, taking in his Batman costume. "Where's Catwoman?"

"In the ladies' room," he tells me. "With Kat, so who knows how long they'll be in there."

"So that's where the party is," I joke, looking toward the bathroom. Hunter's arms wrap around me from behind, pulling me back against his chest.

We've been watching and circling each other all night, and I know both of us can't wait to get home and rip these costumes off each other.

"Diana," he whispers into my ear, using Wonder Woman's real name, making me giggle.

"Yes, Tony?" I reply, tilting my head to the side to see him. "Are you having a good night?"

"Yes, I am," he says, placing a soft kiss on my lips.

We dance to a few songs together, but then Hunter's phone rings, and the rest of the night goes to shit.

"WHAT DID SHE SAY exactly?" I ask as he gets into his car and drives toward Cleo's house.

"That she's gotten in some trouble and she needs me to go to her house, and bring money."

"How much money?" I ask, panic hitting me. Does she have a drug debt? What else could this be?

"Two thousand. I can only pull one thousand out of the

ATM, and I've got a few hundred on me," he says, turning into a shopping center with a bank ATM we can use.

"I'll pull out a thousand too," I tell him, grabbing my purse out of my bag. "I hope she's okay."

He shakes his head. "She didn't sound it. What the fuck is going on? I thought she had all her shit sorted out, but I guess I've been wrong." He turns to me and admits, "Cleo had her wild days, and I know she drank a lot and dabbled in drugs, but she cleaned up her act. At least I thought she was clean. It looks like she's back to her old shit again."

"I think she was on drugs the night of your birthday," I admit. There's probably a lot more I should admit to him too.

"What?" he asks, turning his head to look at me. "How do you know that?"

"Because I know the signs," I tell him, shifting on my seat. Ahh, fuck. "I kind of used to be like your sister."

There, I said it.

Not in a very straightforward way, but I said it nonetheless.

"Drugs?" he asks, sounding surprised.

I nod. "When my cousin died," I try and explain. "It was my fault he died, and I couldn't handle it. So I let drugs handle it for me."

"What do you mean it was your fault he died?" he asks me, sounding confused. "Didn't he die in a car crash? Were you driving?"

"No." I shake my head. "I wasn't. He was drunk and driving, and . . ." I take a deep gulp of air. "And I'm the one who bought him the alcohol. He was underage."

"Riley," he whispers, reaching out and taking my hand. "You were young too. You didn't make him get behind that wheel. You can't blame yourself."

I look out the window.

"When Jeremy met me, I was addicted to cocaine. He kind of saved me in a way, except then he used it against me whenever he felt like it. He'd throw it in my face every time he'd get angry, but that wasn't me anymore. It was so hard being sober and having to deal with the guilt of Devon. I still miss him."

"Thank you for telling me this," he says gently, sounding like he finally understands something. "Jeremy hinted at more to the story of the two of you, but he never said what exactly happened."

I duck my face. Will he look at me differently now? Will my fucked-up past damage my present and my future with him?

He squeezes my hand, and I find the courage to look at him. His eyes—they are the same loving, understanding blue I could never look away from.

"All that matters is who you are *now*, Riley. I don't care who you were."

And just like that, the tightness in my chest releases, and I take a deep breath.

Acceptance.

No judgment.

True love.

This level of understanding is something I've searched for my entire life but never found.

Until now.

We pull the money out, and head to Cleo's to save her, dressed up as superheroes.

HUNTER MAKES ME STAY locked in the car, and I don't like it, but I listen to him. For now, anyway. If there's any sign of trouble, I'm going in. He returns to the car about twenty minutes later, Cleo in his arms. He opens the backseat door, and places her in there.

"We need to drop her off at my parents' house," he explains, sliding back in. I turn back to study her. She's high as a fucking kite and doesn't look very well. "She needs to sober up. Her drug dealer wasn't there; it was just her. So whoever she owes the money to, I'll handle it. But she's going to fucking rehab, because I never want to see her like this ever again."

I nod.

The drive to his parents' is a few hours, and we're all quiet. I check on Cleo every now and again, until she finally falls asleep, twitching a little. Hunter keeps his calm, doing what he needs to do.

And I guess I'll be meeting his parents for the first time while they find out that their baby girl is in trouble.

Dressed as Wonder Woman.

chapter 38

HUNTER

ITH CLEO TUCKED INTO her childhood bed, I talk with my parents while they make us some coffee.

"I'll see what her options are," my mom says, face scrunched in concern. She's a petite woman, with dark hair and brown eyes. She's one of those women who will always be beautiful, or at least she is to me. "Don't worry about anything, Hunter. I will make sure she gets out of this. I just can't believe it; I've never seen her like this before."

My mother is a strong woman, and to be honest, I'm glad she and my dad have this under control, because I'm at a loss. I don't think I could see my sister like that again. My baby fucking sister. It hit me so hard, seeing her sitting on the floor, her head in her hands. There was a bag of white powder next to her, and a mirror. She was a fucking mess, and I was both so angry and so sad.

My mom turns to Riley, her expression softening. "Thank you for coming with Hunter all the way here. I wish it was under better circumstances."

"I'm happy to help any way I can," she replies, smiling as my mom reaches over and touches her hand. Learning about Riley's past was surprising for me, and I didn't really see it coming. I meant what I said though—I only care about who she is now, and knowing the person she is, it gives me hope for Cleo.

"I'll set up Hunter's old bed for you both, there's no way you can drive back home now."

"Thanks, Mom," I say, wrapping an arm around Riley. I notice my mom looking between me and Riley. She's been wanting me to settle down for some time now, always on my case, and she's probably only masking her glee because she's upset about the Cleo situation.

"I'll go check on her," my dad says, leaving the room. My dad is the strong, silent type; he doesn't say much, but he sees everything. He's always been like that. Everyone tells me I look like him, and I like to take that as a compliment, but I think they only say it because I inherited his blue eyes and height.

We drink our coffee and then head to my old bedroom. Riley glances around, taking in my childhood artwork and toys.

"Do you think she'll be okay?" I ask.

I'm out of my element right now. I knew Cleo had tried different drugs before, and experimented in her partying phase, but this is obviously something else. The money she's been borrowing from me must've been for drugs, or because she can't keep up with her own bills because she's spending all of her money on drugs. Either way, she's lost control of her life and needs some help. I can't believe I was complicit in this and helped her further her habit.

Riley nods. "Yes, she will. Especially if your parents are

going to find a rehabilitation center for her, or some kind of program."

I nod once, sharply.

Good.

We will all get through this, and my sister will be okay, just like Riley is.

I close the space between us and take her in my arms.

"I'm here with you, and we will get through this. She will be okay because we will make sure she is, okay?" she whispers to me.

I appreciate her words.

"Okay," I whisper back.

We've got this.

Not even as Diana and Tony, just as Riley and Hunter.

"MR. RODGERS HIRED MR. Brayze for the purpose of getting an advantageous divorce settlement. Instead, Mr. Brayze not only slept with Mr. Rodgers's wife but also disclosed confidential information to Ms. McMahon, which harmed my client." Jeremy's smarmy lawyer says to the state bar review board.

"Ladies and gentlemen. My apologies for having to waste your time because we are here for ridiculous reasons. My client didn't reveal any information, and there is no evidence of this. Mr. Rodgers's case wasn't hindered in any way by Mr. Brayze's actions," Jaxon says to the board. "If you have a look over Mr. Rodgers's case file, there was no information that could have led to what Mr. Rodgers considers a loss. In fact, if I'm being honest, I think Mr. Rodgers got off very easily. As we all know, his ex-wife was entitled to half of everything he accumulated in the marriage since they did not have a prenup. What Mr. Rodgers had to actually pay was mere pennies compared to what the law dictated. There was no malpractice here. This would be a different story if we were in a criminal case and Mr. Brayze was having an affair or leading the witness. But that is not the case."

I watch Jaxon rip apart Jeremy's lawyer.

Jeremy's lawyer interjects, "Leading the witness, huh? That's something I hear you're good at, Mr. Bentley. Maybe the lawyers at your firm may be used to—"

"Okay, I've heard enough," one of the members of the review board says, looking annoyed. "Mr. Rodgers, I don't see how Mr. Brayze hindered your divorce settlement in any way. You kept all of your assets, sans one property, and most of your money. There is no proof of your accusations, besides the fact that your ex-wife has a personal relationship with Mr. Brayze, which he admitted only came about after your case was over. Is it frowned upon that Mr. Brayze is in a relationship with your ex-wife? Yes. But it is not a violation of the ethics code. Please stop wasting our time."

Jaxon and I leave the room and head to his car, waiting until we get inside before we start talking about everything that happened.

"He's a fuckwit," Jaxon murmurs, starting the car. "Did you hear what his lawyer said about 'leading the witness,' as if we're some shady firm? Who says shit like that? Fuck that and fuck him."

After the police questioned Jeremy and got permission to search his house, they didn't find the shoe that matches the print left at the scene or any other evidence that traces him to the crime. A friend of his came forward, stating Jeremy was with him at the time of the crime, giving him an alibi, so it couldn't have been him.

"I don't know what to think. We were so sure it was him,

and really it still could be. His friend could have easily lied for him. I still don't trust him. He's still a loose cannon. I put cameras in my house, just in case. I'm not playing with Riley's safety." I pause. "And my dog's."

Although maybe I should get an actual guard dog, because I don't think the giant fluffy teddy is going to cut it if someone tries to break in. Bear knows Jeremy anyway, so he probably wouldn't even bark.

"Yeah, I agree. Keep an eye out until we find out more information. Who knows what he's planning," Jaxon says, driving us back to the office. "Up your security, and don't let Riley go anywhere alone."

"She's going to love that," I groan, looking out the window. "But yeah, you're right."

We won the battle, but the war won't be over until Jeremy or whoever did this is locked up, and Riley is safe.

Until then, I'm going to have to be a little overprotective, just like I'm going to be with Cleo when she gets out of rehab.

Riley's going to hate it, but she's going to have to deal with it.

"CAMERAS, A NEW ALARM system, and now this?" Riley asks, looking at me like I'm crazy. "Are you sure you're not being paranoid?"

"He set your business on fire, no, I'm not being paranoid," I tell her, watching as our new high fences get installed. "I want you safe, and this will give me peace of mind. Otherwise I'm going to start taking you to work with me."

She shakes her head, laughing. "What? Bring your woman to work day, every day? You've lost your mind, Hunter. I'll be fine, you don't need to worry so much. Sure, we think he burned down Riley's, but I don't think he actually wants me dead."

"Are you willing to gamble your life on that?" I ask her, curling my lip.

She stays silent.

"Exactly. Look, I'm not saying anything is going to happen; in fact, it probably won't, but this is just in case," I tell her, bringing her against my body. "I finally got you, I'm not going to lose you now, Riley, or ever. You'll get used to me being overbearing, I promise. It might even grow on you."

She sighs and glances up at me. "It's cute that you want to keep me safe, Hunter, but I'll be happy once this is all over."

"You and me both," I say, threading her fingers through mine. "Until then, no one is going to get through all our new security."

Riley moved all her stuff in, breaking the lease on her apartment. We had to pay an amount to do so, but it was well worth it. Having her here is . . . it's home. It's like living with your best friend. We're always laughing, joking, or all over each other. We take care of each other. I don't think I've ever been happier in my life. Riley's is being rebuilt, and soon Riley will have her baby back to make her happy again. I told her I'm going to install over-the-top security for her there too. Nothing is going to happen to her business ever again. I kiss her soft cheek as we watch the fences being put in, the sun setting above us.

It's a beautiful view, and reminds me of our first date.

That reminds me.

"There's a surprise coming for you on Monday, so make sure you're home at about ten a.m.," I say, squeezing her hand.

She glances up at me, a curious look in her eyes. "What is it?"

"If I tell you, it won't be a surprise." I grin, leading her back inside. "I just need you to be here to sign for it."

"I'll be here," she says, grabbing the book she's been reading and sitting on the couch. "You know you don't need to spoil me so much. I stay for the penis, not the other stuff."

My body shakes as I laugh. "I know, babe. Trust me, I know. But I think you're going to like this one."

In fact, I know she will. I wish I could be here to see her face, but I have to work, and this was the only time they could deliver it. I sit next to her, and she leans her head on me, getting comfortable. I play with her hair while she reads her erotic novel, knowing that it's only going to be a little time before she jumps me, getting turned on from the words she's reading by a woman named Zada Ryan.

I should thank the woman.

I'm almost asleep when I feel her kissing my neck, and my lips curve with my eyes still shut. "Can I help you, babe?" I whisper.

"I think you can," she replies, mouth on mine, tongue in my mouth.

The day I won Riley over, a day I can't even pinpoint, was the luckiest day of my life.

I'M WITH RILEY WHEN she gets the call.

"What?" she says, sitting up straight and clasping her phone in her hand. "Are you sure?"

Her eyes start to get all teary, and I wonder who is on the other line giving her bad news.

"Yes, I will be there soon. Thank you, Officer."

She hangs up, then brings her eyes to me. "They found who set the fire. Their fingerprints match, and the shoeprint. And it's not Jeremy, Hunter. We were wrong."

I bring her body closer to me, needing to touch her. "Who was it?"

The first tear drops, followed by many more now pouring down her soft cheeks. "A man by the name of Patrick Wakes."

"Why did he do it? Do you know who that is?" I ask her, touching her hair as she buries her face on my chest, wetting my white T-shirt.

"I know who he is," she says, body shaking with sobs. "He was Devon's boyfriend."

I still.

"It's okay," I whisper to her. "What happened wasn't your fault, Riley. No one made him get in that car."

"Now he's going to go to prison. I don't want him to," she admits to me.

I don't share her notions, so I stay quiet.

"We have to go to the police station," she says to me, pulling herself together. She takes a deep breath, inhaling and exhaling. "He knew Devon always wanted his own pub, and he would have had one if he were here."

"But he's not," I tell her gently. "And you are. So you need to live, Riley. Don't let anyone make you feel like you don't deserve to be happy. Because you do."

She stands up and offers me her hand. I stand, cup her cheek and kiss her forehead.

"Are you okay?"

"I will be," she breathes. "With you by my side."

"I'll be your strength when you need it," I tell her. "Which won't be a lot, because you're one of the strongest people I know, Riley."

She smiles sadly. "I wasn't born strong. Life made me this way. And I don't feel like I am right now."

"You are."

Hand in hand, we head to the car, finally getting some closure on the fire.

Looks like we were wrong about Jeremy after all.

He's still scum, just not the arsenic kind.

AS WE SIT OPPOSITE Patrick, I notice he refuses to look Riley in the eye. He's thin, and tall, with red hair and blue eyes, which are currently red from crying.

"Why did you do this, Patrick?" she asks him, voice trembling. "After all these years, you still hate me so much?"

He buries his face in his hands. "The pub was Devon's plan. That's what he always wanted to do, open a few different pubs, make a brand, and eventually open them up all over the world."

"I know," Riley whispers.

Patrick breaks down, slamming his hand on the table and making a wailing type of noise. "I didn't know you opened a pub. I actually managed to forget about you and Devon for a few years. But when I heard about a pub called Riley's, something told me to go. And when I did, I saw you."

"Why didn't you say something?" she says gently.

"When I saw you there . . . so happy. In a pub exactly the way Devon would've wanted one. I just . . . I couldn't . . ." he whispers in between sobs. "I'm the one who told him to come and pick me up that night, it was because of me he'd gotten into that car."

"It's no one's fault what happened that night," Riley says to him. "No one knew how much he had drunk except for himself. He should have told you no."

"You don't understand. I knew he was drunk. But I told him to come get me or else I was breaking up with him. He was supposed to wait for me, but he didn't. I'm the reason he's dead."

Riley starts to cry, and my hand finds her lower back, trying to offer comfort as she comes face-to-face with the man who burned down her business, the same one who also still loves her cousin.

"I'm sorry, Riley," he says to her. "After seeing you I had a few drinks, which turned into a bottle, and I just . . ." He shakes his head rapidly, blinking. "I went back to the pub. Just to see. And it reminded me of him. I don't want to think of him anymore. So I had to destroy it. The guilt—it eats me alive."

"Look at me," she says with authority. Patrick is finally able to look her in her eyes. "You were not responsible for Devon's death, just like I wasn't responsible. Neither one of us could have known what would've happened. You need to let go of the guilt. It's a vicious cycle and look where it's led you." She motions to the room we are in. "I do not forgive you for what you did to Riley's right now, but maybe in time I will. Forgive yourself, Patrick."

Riley hugs him before we leave, showing her strength.

Only the strong can forgive.

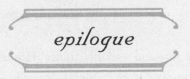

RILEY

TEN ON MONDAY MORNING arrives and there's a knock at the door. Curious as to what Hunter's surprise is, I open the door and am greeted by a man holding a piece of paper and a pen. "Sign here, please."

Hunter left our new fence open this morning but told me to shut it once the deliveryman leaves.

I sign, then follow the man outside, my jaw dropping open at what I see. Right on our front lawn, walking down the ramp of a trailer, is the white Andalusian mare that I rode on my first date with Hunter.

He bought me the horse of my dreams.

A horse.

I cover my face, jumping up and down. Oh my god, I can't believe he did this. I run down toward the animal, slowing as I get closer so not to scare her. The woman leading her smiles and hands me her reins.

"This beauty is yours now," she says, stroking the horse. "Look after her."

"I will," I promise, nodding, tears threatening to leak from my eyes. "I definitely will."

They pack up and leave, and I close the fence behind them, then look at my new horse. "Where am I going to put you, beauty?"

I nuzzle her face and walk her around Hunter's back garden, which is large, but not large enough to exercise a horse. I'll have to look for a stable close by to put her in, with a lot of land where I can ride her. I think I'm in shock, happiness filling me at how thoughtful my man is. How did I get so lucky?

After being miserable all week after finding out the truth about the fire, and the fact that Devon's boyfriend will now most likely be heading to prison after his trial, I didn't think anything could cheer me up. My parents tried, but nothing they said helped. All the pain from losing Devon was hitting me full force, and I was being really hard on myself over the whole situation.

This is the first time I've smiled since I got the phone call.

I pull out my phone to call him, the surprise of such a grand gesture making me forget all of my worries.

If Hunter loves me so much, maybe I'm not such a bad person after all.

"RILEY'S IS OFFICIALLY OPEN!" I cheer as Preston opens the doors. I do a little happy dance. After six months of work, my place is finally back, and I couldn't be happier. I used the fifty thousand dollars and insurance money to help get me here, and since I was given the land in the divorce, I know that this is now all mine. I couldn't be happier with the new setup of the pub.

"Congrats," Preston calls out, grinning. "It feels so good to be back!"

Out of all the staff, Preston and Cheffy are the only ones who came back, but you know what? It's okay. Callie now works at the firm, and Izaac stayed at his new job. We all still get together once a month and remain close friends. I've hired four new staff and can't wait to get back into it, a fresh start.

A second chance.

One I'm not going to take for granted.

Cleo is also a new member to my team. She didn't want to go back to aged care after getting out of rehab, and I told her that she always has a job here, and she took me up on it. I'm so proud of how well she's doing, and I know Hunter is too. Everything is coming together, and after struggling so hard to get it this way, I'm going to enjoy every moment of it.

After my first day, I head to the stables to see Beauty before I head home. Hunter is waiting for me, a candlelit dinner set out on the table. He couldn't make it to my opening today because he was in court, but I know he wanted to be there. He sent a beautiful bouquet of flowers to me, ones I left at work because the sunflowers brighten up the place, and because I smile every time I look at them.

"What's all this?" I ask, leaning in for a kiss.

"A celebration dinner," he says, pouring wine into two glasses. "I'm so proud of you, Riley."

"Thank you." I blush, ducking my head.

"I want to hear everything about opening day," he says, pulling out my chair for me.

I sit down, thank him again, and take a sip of my wine. "Well, the place was packed," I start, then tell him in detail about how it all went, about my new staff members, and about how Preston was letting his new power as manager go to his head.

Hunter listens to every word, hungry for information, laughing at the part about Preston.

"I'm going to come in tomorrow," he tells me. "I don't have too much on my schedule, and I need to experience the new and improved Riley's. Save me my spot."

"I will," I reply, lip twitching. "And don't worry, everything you love on the menu is still there."

"Good," he replies, eyes never leaving my face.

"How long are you going to stare at me for?" I ask, repeating words I've used in the past.

"How does forever sound?" he replies, smiling gently at me. "Fuck, I love you, Riley." He stands up, then lowers himself down on one knee, opening a little black box in his hand. "Will you marry me?"

I look at the pear-shaped diamond ring, my mouth dropping open.

"Yes, of course I will," I say, my fingers shaking as he places the ring on my finger. He stands, and kisses me deeply, and I reach my arms up around him and hold on to him for dear life.

I'm going to be his wife.

Let's hope husband number two goes better than the first.